Banking on Murder

Sir Ray Bims is about to be charged as the principal in a Caribbean bank that's laundering international drug money. Lord Grenwood, octogenarian chairman of Grenwood, Phipps, the London merchant bankers, is appalled. Three years ago he sold the Eel Bridge Rovers Football Club—known as the Eels—to Bims. The club was founded by Grenwood's grandfather and is still associated with the Grenwoods in the public's mind. Now his lordship wants to buy it back to avoid the suggestion of family involvement in Bims's disgrace.

Only hours after refusing Grenwood's offer for the Eels, Bims commits suicide—except that Detective-Inspector Jeckels of the Fulham CID concludes gradually that it was murder. And he discovers a string of people with motive and opportunity to dispose of Bims—among them the husband of Bims's mistress; the Eels' manager who Bims had been about to fire; a well-known concert pianist; a curiously religious pest controller; not to mention several Eels players, and Bims's wife and ex-wife.

But the real motive only becomes apparent when the bank's chief executive Mark Treasure takes a hand in the investigation. This leads to the dramatic capture of the murderer—just in time to prevent another slaying.

DAVID WILLIAMS

Banking on Murder

A Mark Treasure mystery

*For Mila Loxton
who arranged the poison
is this one too.

Gratefully

David Williams

Denmark 1993*

THE CRIME CLUB
An Imprint of HarperCollins *Publishers*

First published in Great Britain in 1993
by The Crime Club, an imprint of
HarperCollins Publishers, 77–85 Fulham Palace Road,
Hammersmith, London W6 8JB

9 8 7 6 5 4 3 2 1

David Williams asserts the moral right to be identified
as the author of this work.

A catalogue record for this book is
available from the British Library.

ISBN 0 00 232446 4

Photoset in Linotron Baskerville by
Rowland Phototypesetting Ltd
Bury St Edmunds, Suffolk
Printed and bound in Great Britain by
HarperCollins Book Manufacturing, Glasgow

This one for
Hannah Charlotte Benson

CHAPTER 1

'Good turn-out. More than I expected. More than George would have expected himself, probably, God rest him. He was younger than I remembered. Did you hear? Only seventy-one.' The octogenarian Lord Grenwood, speaking above the noise of the traffic, was smugly content with the last revelation. He blew his nose vigorously into a capacious white handkerchief, followed this with a tremendous, levitating sniff, then continued in his sharp, penetrating voice: 'Uplifting address, I thought. Bit long, perhaps. Lot of Royal Air Force people there as well as City. Nice church.' The diminutive viscount then pointed suddenly to the right, throwing his arm out in that direction so forcefully he might have been trying to get rid of it. 'That's a statue of Gladstone. Not many would know that these days. Dull fellow, by all accounts. Read Homer for fun. In the original Greek. Winston Churchill said it served him right. Where's Mark gone?'

Because of an arthritic neck, the chairman of Grenwood, Phipps, the merchant bankers, had been addressing his clipped phrases to the air ahead of him, and not directly to the man walking at his side. This was of lesser consequence than it might have been since the man was Harry Karilian, the legendary head of the bank's New Issues Department, and someone well used to coping with his companion's idiosyncrasies. It was true that Berty Grenwood's utterances were just a touch more difficult for the other to catch when the two men were on their feet. It was a question of levels. The slightly built Berty was only five feet four in height while his immense companion was a whole foot taller than that.

'Mark wanted to check something in the church on the

way out. He's catching us up,' Karilian provided in a voice that could not avoid being melodious, even when he dictated amendments to passages of uninspiring prose in company prospectuses. He had briefly earned a living as an operatic baritone before abandoning singing for a banking career—at the timely insistence of a wise and practical Armenian grandfather.

It was 12.30 on a raw Monday in late February. The two had just emerged from the restored St Clement Danes, the elegant Wren church with Gibbs's three-stage spire, set on an island site at the eastern end of London's busy Strand. Berty Grenwood was carrying a bowler hat, and both men were wearing black overcoats—his lordship's fashionably cut and knee length, Harry Karilian's a voluminous creation in cashmere which very nearly reached to his ankles and incorporated a wide astrakhan collar. The coat had originally belonged to a deceased uncle: Karilian was known in the City for his careful employment of written down assets.

The 'George' referred to, whose memorial service had just ended in the church, had been a well-known industrial baron, an important customer of the bank, a personal friend of the directors, and, in his time, a distinguished and much decorated war hero.

'It's the RAF church, of course,' said Berty, reverting to the earlier topic since his companion had shown no interest in Gladstone. 'I'd forgotten George was an intrepid airman. Long time ago that was, of course.' He stopped suddenly to examine the inside of his bowler at very close range, after deciding it might not be his. The effect of this was to have the interior of the hat amplify his voice as he next observed: 'Did you see dear old Humphrey Sprogg tottering in? He'll be the next to fall off the perch. Mark my words.'

It happened that the same Humphrey Sprogg, a retired stockbroker, was hurrying past them at that moment, after successfully—and energetically—waving down a cab.

Though elderly, there was no sign that he was approaching the imminent demise just prophesied—only his hearing was failing a little, which in the immediate circumstance was fortunate. He was younger than Lord Grenwood, though several years older than the recently departed and now formally lamented George had been. Berty Grenwood took undisguised pleasure in outliving his contemporaries, and even more in surviving his juniors.

'You don't think we should take a cab?' Karilian put in, not because of his companion's age, but out of his own distaste for walking anywhere if he could just as easily be conveyed. He had only hesitated in asking Sprogg if they might share his cab for fear the man might have heard Berty's prediction.

'Not at all. It's not raining, and it's only a step to Simpson's,' the other replied, without reference to the chilling east breeze coming up from Fleet Street. He clamped the now legitimized hat on his head firmly enough for it to have withstood involuntary removal by a gale force wind.

'Sorry if I kept you waiting.' Mark Treasure, the urbane, forty-four-year-old chief executive of Grenwood, Phipps had joined them as Berty was leading the way on to a pedestrian crossing—with less notice than the driver now applying the brakes of the approaching No. 9 double-decker bus would have declared reasonable, given a legal option in the matter. 'Why aren't we taking a cab?' Treasure added innocently.

'Needless expense. We're as good as there,' said Berty as they reached the far pavement and he set off westward, his head, neck and trunk in a straight line inclining a little backwards, arms held tight to his body, but bent upwards at the elbows. His legs only ever seemed to move below the knees—but they propelled him with short steps at very great speed.

'Don't know why we didn't keep the car and chauffeur we came in,' Karilian complained to Treasure, who had arrived for the service separately from the others. 'Berty said the church was impossible for parking.'

'Difficult for parking,' Berty corrected to show he had heard. They could see several limousines still crammed into the road space outside the west end of the church, under the stony, disapproving gaze of Gladstone's full-length effigy on its towering plinth. 'Healthier to walk, in any case. Work up an appetite,' the old man added. 'Simpson's was one of my father's favourite restaurants.'

Karilian smoothed down his thick black hair that was being ruffled by the wind. 'Your father invariably lunched at the bank,' he corrected without emotion, as if he were merely keeping the record straight and not getting his own back for having to walk.

'He liked Simpson's for dinner,' his lordship countered with emphasis on the last word.

'I was right about the Reverend William Webb-Ellis,' said Treasure as the three were passing the arched entrance to King's College.

'He was rector at St Clement Danes?' Karilian confirmed rather than questioned.

'Yes. 1843 to 1855. His name's on a panel of incumbents on the gallery stairs.'

'Welshman, was he?' asked Berty.

'Probably. Became famous as the boy at Rugby School who picked up the football and started running with it.'

'So inaugurating that hybrid pastime, Rugby Union Football. And all the other hybrid games spawned by it. Rugby League, American Football, and the rest,' said Karilian with more sorrow than distaste. A soccer man to the core, he was a supporter of Tottenham Hotspurs in North London. 'Pity he couldn't have left well alone,' he added.

'I agree,' said Berty. 'My grandfather was a staunch soccer follower—'

'Your grandfather was a Rugby man who talked himself into founding the Eel Bridge Rovers Football Club, otherwise known as the Eels, in a fit of pique,' Harry Karilian interrupted. 'That was when owning a football team had suddenly become the in thing. His arch enemy had bought the Fulham club. That was the crux of it all. I remember your father telling me. Chelsea wasn't available at any price, but since he lived on the boundaries of Chelsea and Fulham, and owned a lot of land in that part of West London, your grandfather decided to set up his own team.' The speaker made a slapping noise with his lips. 'That was a mistake long term. Should have picked a place with more potential. A football club needs its own clearly defined catchment area.'

'My grandfather thought Chelsea and Fulham were both too big. He was convinced the Eels could carve out a . . . a middle following,' Berty put in with spirit.

Karilian shook his head. 'The area never offered that kind of promise. You were wise to sell when you did, Berty. Pity you'd already paid for that south stand.'

'We had a great party to launch it, though. I was there,' said Treasure with a grin. 'Have those executive boxes ever been a success?'

The opening of the south stand at Hugon Road, the Eel Bridge Rovers' ground in Fulham, had been a big event, matching the size of the investment. There had been few football grandstands to compare with the place at the time, and certainly no other outside the Premier League. Apart from its superior seating, dressing-rooms, spectator bars and restaurants, and management offices, the new building included a conference cum banqueting hall for special events, and thirty glass-fronted private boxes for leasing for corporate entertaining. The boxes had been expected to generate a great deal of income for the club.

'We've never let more than half the boxes in any year. Rather fewer than that this year,' was Berty's doleful answer to Treasure's question. 'That's only part of the problem at the moment, though.' He seemed to rally a little

after this. 'I'm still an Eels director, you know?' he went
on, making token sideways and upward glances to left and
right at his two tall flanking companions. 'Trouble is, the
club's not exactly having a run of success. Makes things
difficult. Over Ray Bims, you see?'

'Doesn't in any way make you responsible for his personal problems,' Treasure responded carefully.

His lordship's lips moved without his saying anything as
he contemplated the people, other than his colleagues, who
were also waiting beyond Somerset House to cross Lan-
caster Place, and with whom he had no intention of sharing
confidences: he now accepted that being in a taxi would
have provided privacy, except he wasn't going to admit it.
'That's what we need to talk about, Mark,' he said eventually, when the lights had changed. He was slightly in the
lead again as they reached the far side of the wide thorough-
fare. 'As a matter of fact,' he completed, 'it's why I suggested lunch this morning.'

In view of the rumours circulating in the City about Ray
Bims since even before the weekend, Treasure had assumed
as much.

'You see, people still think of the Eels as a Grenwood family
responsibility,' Berty announced five minutes later. The
three were seated in one of the wooden booths in Simpson's
ground-floor room with its traditional London chop house
ambience and British trencherman fare. A bottle of claret
had already been opened, and the food ordered.

'No, they don't. Bims has owned it for too—'

'Bims has owned it for rather more than three years,' his
lordship broke in on Harry Karilian who was seated beside
him. Treasure was opposite. 'My family had it for the previous eight decades. Decades,' he repeated heavily. 'I
should never have let it go to that man. If he's disgraced
it'll reflect on the Grenwoods. On the bank too.'

Treasure's unease increased. Berty only ever invoked a

need—usually spurious—to protect the bank's reputation if he knew no other way to enlist its Chief Executive's help on an issue that otherwise wouldn't concern him. 'Oh, come. Bims was respectable enough when he bought the club from you,' he said. 'I remember, it was just after he'd sold his DIY chain to the Americans.'

'He got a good price, too,' said Karilian, leaning his big frame against the back of his chair, and spreading his generously cut, double-breasted suit jacket about him rather in the manner of a monarch in court raiment. 'Bit over thirty-four million. For a chain of twenty-seven do-it-yourself retail outlets in the prosperous South of England.' His recall for such detail was always accurate.

'Which left Bims with no full-time occupation, of course,' Treasure mused.

'You don't think he could have made the chairmanship of the Eels into a full-time occupation?' Karilian questioned, a touch cynically, and as though he knew the answer already.

'He's never wanted to bother with detail,' Berty provided. 'Only with making the big decisions.'

'According to what are described as well-informed sources, he's personally invested in a whole raft of foundered enterprises,' said Treasure. 'Fancied himself as a financial entrepreneur, for which I doubt he has the experience or capacity.'

'Quite right, Mark. He'd been a hands-on, innovative retailer, which is something quite different, of course,' Karilian agreed.

'He's been badly advised, probably,' said Treasure. 'Anyway, the rumour is he'd lost almost everything before he attempted to recoup by going on the board of some dubious new bank he's invested in. In the Cayman Islands.'

'A bank that's turned out to be a front for illicit drug trading. And it's more than a rumour now. I've heard it'll be in the papers tomorrow.' Karilian rubbed his wide upper lip with a thumb and forefinger as he spoke. The grey and black stubble growing there could only broadly be described as an embryo moustache—though it had been kept in that transitory state for as long as the others could remember. 'So are you thinking of buying back the club, Berty?' he asked bluntly.

His lordship moved up and down in his chair twice like a mechanical Jack-in-the-box. 'I'm too old to be chairman again,' he said, staring blankly at Treasure. 'That's part of the reason why I sold before. You know Linkina, the concert pianist, is also a director? He wants me to buy back the club, yes. Thinks the Eels are heading for disaster under Bims. It's Linkina who's put up a new plan for the club, but Bims won't wear it.'

'Andras Linkina is a brilliant Mozartian, but he's no business man surely?' Karilian questioned. He drained his wine glass, drew the bottle towards him, studied the label, nodded to himself, and then refilled the glass.

'What's the plan?' asked Treasure, uncomfortably aware that he might yet be intended to figure in it.

'To sell the Hugon Road stadium for development, and move everything out to the practice ground at Cherton. Lock, stock and barrel,' said Berty, his fingers tapping the stiff white cloth at the table edge as if it were a keyboard.

'Hugon Road is unencumbered? No mortgage? No lease-back? Nothing of that kind?' This was Treasure again.

Berty gave a self-righteous smile—like a favourite nephew whose deceased, impoverished uncle has turned out to be a millionaire after all. 'That's the saving grace,' he exclaimed. 'Hugon Road isn't part of the ordinary fixed assets. My grandfather made it over separately, in trust. And the Cherton ground with it. One ground can be sold if the money it fetches is used to improve the other. Or to improve the club in general.'

Treasure nodded slowly. 'What happens if the club is ever wound up?' he asked.

Berty shrugged as if the question were irrelevant. 'Both

grounds can be sold and the proceeds used to pay off the club's debts,' he said. 'At the discretion of the trustees. Anything left would go to sporting charities.'

'And who are the trustees?'

'At present? Myself, Bims, and young Charles Wigtree of Dottle, Ram and Wigtree, the solicitors. They've always been the club's lawyers. Charles is a director as well as a trustee. Took over from his father.' The speaker straightened in his chair. 'But it hasn't come to liquidation. Not by a long shot.'

'Moving everything out to Cherton might make sense,' said Karilian slowly, bushy brows lowered over calculating eyes. 'The sale of the main ground should fetch a substantial price. Enough to pay for a new set-up at Cherton and still leave a balance. There's no First Division football club in that part of Surrey, so the Eels would stand to recruit support locally. It's not too far for old supporters to travel to matches, either. The really keen ones. Yes, it could work.' The eyebrows rose again as he beamed his cautious approval, and drank some more claret.

'There's a developer interested in Hugon Road?' Treasure questioned.

'Two, as a matter of fact,' said Berty with pride, as if he'd secured them himself, which the others thought unlikely.

'But Bims is against the plan?'

'Dead against it, Mark,' Berty replied, outraged. 'Won't hear of selling the main ground in any circumstances. Says it'd be an admission of failure. Damn fool. He wouldn't even agree to sell the Cherton ground. That's worth nothing in any case. It's on the edge of a green belt.' The speaker made a tutting noise, though whether this was to qualify his view of Bims or his opinion of the countryside protection laws wasn't clear. 'Holding on to the grounds has become a fixation with the fellow,' he continued, which explained the tutting at least. 'The way he talks about it, you'd think he was a member of the family. I mean my family.'

'How many Eels directors are there altogether?' asked Treasure.

'Five,' said Berty. 'The other two are supporting Linkina and me. That's Charles Wigtree, and a chap called Crayborn, accountant with a small practice in Kingston. Firm's not doing very well. Reminds me, I said I'd help him if I could.' Berty scowled, either because of his forgetfulness or because he didn't fancy honouring the promise. 'Trouble is,' he went on, 'even a majority of the directors doesn't out-weigh the fact that Bims owns nearly all the shares.'

'Well, since you feel so strongly about it, I think you probably should buy him out,' Treasure advised. 'You know he's hard up. Offer him a price he can't resist. Might cost you more than he paid you originally, but there it is.'

'And we don't want him staying on the board either,' said Berty firmly.

Treasure shrugged. 'Then make his resignation part of the deal.'

'That's it, Mark,' Berty agreed resolutely, while slapping the table with both hands. 'I'll do it.' He looked from Trea-sure to Karilian and back to Treasure. 'I'll need help, of course,' he added carefully.

'If you really don't want to be chairman yourself,' said Treasure, 'put in someone who understands financial man-agement as well as soccer, who'll see the plan goes through smoothly. It shouldn't be very time-consuming.' He was looking across at the other member of the trio. 'Harry here would be perfect, of course,' he completed quickly.

'Not a chance,' said Karilian just as promptly. 'Apart from my known devotion to Tottenham Hotspurs, I live too far away in North London. And I'm too old as well. The new man you want needs to be a high flyer, Berty, and local for preference. Someone the players and sup-porters can look up to. Identify with. In the right way.' He cleared his throat. 'For traditional reasons, he should ideally be a Grenwood, of course.'

'I agree,' said Treasure, 'but—'

'But since there aren't any Grenwoods handy, the choice is obvious,' Karilian continued expansively, affecting not to have heard Treasure. 'It has to be Mark here, the celebrated chief executive of Grenwood, Phipps. And I don't believe you can ignore the obligation, Mark,' he completed, his pious expression suggesting that he had just fearlessly met a challenge and not cannily ducked one.

'Harry's right, of course. You're the perfect choice, Mark. From every viewpoint,' Berty affirmed.

'I know nothing about soccer.'

'That's of no importance compared to your other qualifications,' insisted Karilian loftily, intent on consolidating his victory.

'I don't have the time to—'

'You said yourself it wouldn't be time-consuming,' Berty put in triumphantly. 'Just turn up for one or two home matches, that's all. There's very little need for formal board meetings. The bank can handle all the work over the deal, and . . . and so on,' he insisted, working his bent arms with vigour, as though he was drying the small of his back with an invisible towel. 'Just you be the rallying figure, Mark. The dynamic focal point for players and supporters. To expunge the memory of Bims. To be the symbol of Grenwood continuity—'

'But, Berty, I'm not a Grenwood.'

'. . . figuratively and morally speaking,' his lordship completed, fervour undiminished.

Treasure exhaled loudly. 'Well, only for as long as it takes to complete—'

'Thank you, my boy. You've lifted a great weight from my mind. I'll make Bims my offer at lunch on Wednesday. One and a half million it is. Covers the one point three million he paid for three new players at the start of this season. The remainder's twice what he paid me for the shares three years ago. He shouldn't be able to resist that.

As you say, it'll all be dependent on his giving us his resignation, too.'

Treasure's eyes narrowed. 'D'you mean you had the
whole thing planned, Berty?'

'In embryo only, dear boy. It needed your clear mind
and personal commitment to resolve it,' Berty offered, now
fingering the gold watch-chain in his waistcoat. 'There's a
directors' meeting and lunch at Hugon Road next Saturday,' he went on hurriedly. 'Before the match in the afternoon. If you could be there, we can vote you on to the board
and into the chair straight away.'

'I think I can probably manage that,' Treasure answered
after consulting his pocket diary.

'Good man,' said Berty, beaming his satisfaction over a
job well done. 'There's a home match on Wednesday night
too. I hesitate to suggest it,' he continued, showing no hesitation at all, 'but if you could show your face at that as
well, it'd be a tactful move. No obligation, of course. None
whatsoever.' He looked about him, evidently prepared to
put down any dissenter. 'There's a party afterwards.
Drinks and buffet. For the team and the officers of the
the official Supporters Club. Happens once a season.
Good opportunity to meet everyone who counts. You
could bring Molly if she's free. Ah, look, the food's
arriving. Good timing, what?' he completed, waving open
his linen napkin like a white flag—except Treasure felt
it was he who had done all the surrendering.

CHAPTER 2

'No, listen to this bit. It says, questioned last night at his
. . . two million pound South Kensington home, Sir Ray
Bims said . . . he would not be going to America. He . . .
refused to comment further . . . except to repeat he was . . .

innocent-of-the-alleged-charges.' Malcolm Dirn, captain of
the Eel Bridge Rovers Football Club, ended his halting
reading from the tabloid newspaper in a rush. He was
seated at the front of the club's stationary private coach.
Dirn looked up, frowned defensively, and gave a vigorous
pull at the crutch of his gold and blue track suit. Reading
aloud made the thirty-two-year-old footballer uncomfortable because he was no good at it—something even his
small daughter would have agreed on. 'What about that,
then?' he demanded bullishly, in a thicker than normal
Wolverhampton accent.

'Nothing else he could say,' commented Jimmy Atler, a
normally taciturn East Londoner. He had also had to raise
his voice above the sound of the piped music played, as it
always was played at this time, because it was alleged to
lift the team's early morning spirits. Atler was pushing an
expensive-looking canvas grip into the overhead rack. Most
things that he owned were expensive—including his winter
tan, and the top-of-the-range BMW 320i he had just left in
the players' car park.

'Is it saying some more, Malc? About Sir Ray?' questioned Stan Bodworski, the Polish mid-fielder whose understanding of English was still a lot better than the way he
spoke it. Like Atler, one of the team's star strikers, Bodworski had been transferred to the Eels in May of the previous
year. He was sitting three rows behind Dirn. 'Is there anything about him being chairman of Eels?' he pressed.

'No. Only what I read out before.'

'I'm not hearing all that.' Bodworski sounded worried,
but he often did.

'It only says he's a director of this Cayman Islands bank.
The American directors are supposed to go before a Grand
Jury. In Miami. So what's a Grand Jury when it's at home?'

Nobody answered Dirn because nobody knew.

'But the bank's not really American or British?' asked
Atler.

'Cayman Islands is British dependency,' Bodworski provided carefully and accurately, aware he wasn't exactly
answering the question. Even so, those about him were
impressed with the information. He folded his brawny arms
across his chest. 'Lot of banks in the Cayman Islands,' he
went on, with more confidence.

'Is that where you keep your loot, Stan?' asked another
player.

'Stop still a minute, everybody,' shouted Jeff Ribarts, the
middle-aged assistant team manager. His was a dogsbody
job, and a lot less important than the title implied, as most
people were aware, including Ribarts. He was standing on
the top step inside the gold and blue painted coach that
was parked close to the players' entrance to the south stand
of the Hugon Road stadium.

'Thirty-one, thirty-two, thirty-three. One missing,' the
asthmatic ex-player completed loudly, glancing up and
down at the clipboard in his hand. He was on tiptoe because
he wasn't tall enough otherwise to see to the back of the
coach.

There should have been thirty-four in the party—Ribarts
himself, eleven players and five substitutes from the Eel
Bridge Rovers first team, eleven members of the reserve
team, five apprentice players and the team coach. They
were due to leave Hugon Road at 7.30 a.m. for the four-hour
Tuesday session at the club's Cherton practice ground.
That was ten miles to the west, in Surrey. Both grounds
had been bought in 1911, in the halcyon days soon after
the Club had been founded. The Hugon Road stadium was
close to the Thames in Fulham.

'Who's missing?' Ribarts questioned, looking at his
watch: it was 7.29.

'Who d'you think, Jeff?'

'Who's always missing?'

'Let's go without him. Those in favour?'

Ribarts ignored the roar of approval that followed the

last proposals, and glanced at Malcolm Dirn. The captain gave a negative half shake of his head. They would wait another few minutes for the absentee. A player who missed the coach was fined.

'Here he comes. Blimey, get an eyeful of that, then. She's another new one, too. Blimey,' repeated an overawed young apprentice player at the back.

There was a lunge by those seated on the right side of the vehicle to see out to the left, in the still dim morning light. A white, open-topped Porsche had ground to a halt next to the coach, throwing up a hail of chippings. The well-developed redhead driving the car threw her arms around the tracksuited Adonis in the passenger seat, pulled him towards her and kissed him long and hard on the mouth, kneading the back of his head with her scarlet-tipped fingers, and applying herself with an ardour that was little short of athletic. Goaded on by appreciative cheers from inside the coach, the woman now opened her hazel eyes wide, to gaze up victoriously over her lover's shoulder at his now scarcely containable team mates. When he left the car, she leaned back and pushed both hands through her windswept hair, flamboyantly adjusted the wide collar of her open fun-fur coat, and made her skirt ride up even higher on her thigh—a performance well visible to most of the interested males peering down on her. It was a bravura finale that the mesmerized audience adored.

''Morning all,' the Adonis offered breezily some moments later as he climbed into the coach to a mixed chorus of jeers and cheers. His name was Gareth Trisall, he was twenty-three, born in the Rhondda Valley, sturdy, medium height, as handsome as his compatriot Richard Burton, unmarried, and another one of the team's three newly acquired star players. Trisall had recently lost his driving licence after pleading guilty to a drink-driving charge. The women who had since been chauffeuring him were as remarkable for their physical attractions as for their sheer numbers.

'What's the charge for the exhibition, Gareth?' called someone.

'Pity he doesn't get it in as often for the Eels. Like last Saturday,' grumbled Dirn, but he was smiling as he threw a mock punch at Trisall's stomach as the other went by.

'You're late, Gareth,' Ribarts had said, and not smiling, as the player had pushed past him at the door.

'Not really. And a pretty good reason if I had been, wouldn't you say, Jeff boy?' Trisall called back from along the aisle.

The white car was now heading out of the car park towards the main road. For all her surface glamour, Ribarts calculated that the driver was easily ten years older than Trisall. All Trisall's women were older, he thought, with money or access to money. They had to pay for the privilege of escorting the idolized Trisall, the highest paid member of the Eels and the one least likely to part with a penny when he didn't need to. Well, Trisall might want all his savings soon if the stories were true, Ribarts thought darkly as he settled himself on the seat in the well, across from the driver, as the streamlined coach moved off.

'Where's the Gaff, then?' asked Trisall, looking about him before he dropped down beside Bodworski. Both these newcomers to the Eels had individually cost more money than the notional transfer price of the rest of the team put together—excluding Atler, the other new player. But even Atler hadn't been in the same price bracket as these two.

Bodworski and Trisall had become friends, at the start largely because they had both been new boys. Although the rest of the players had welcomed them for promising to add sorely needed strength to the ailing team, there had been jealousy over what they had cost and what it was guessed they were being paid. The same could be said of

what the others thought of Jimmy Atler. The difference was
that Atler had made friends with no one.

'The Gaff, he's going in his own car. Got to be back at
ten. Back here, understand? It's for a meeting with Sir Ray,'
said Bodworski, making it sound like bad news.

Gaff was short for Gaffer. It was what the team members
called Felix Harden, the thirty-eight-year-old manager of
Eel Bridge Rovers, the First Division team known univer-
sally as the Eels. Normally Harden would have been on
the coach. It was the rule as well as the tradition that
everyone assembled at Hugon Road first thing, whatever
the day's programme. This made for greater efficiency if
arrangements were altered at the last minute; it dated from
the time, long past, when most players would have lived
close to the stadium and when many would not have had
transport of their own in any case.

Harden had come back as manager three years before
this. He had started his career as an Eels apprentice, then
he had been an Eels player for five years before serving
fourteen seasons with more illustrious teams. But Hugon
Road had always been his spiritual home—his real home
too in a way, since he had been born less than a mile from
the stadium.

Stan Bodworski was often better informed than the others
about the Gaff's movements, and about club news in
general, because Lilian, his Scottish wife, was the Eels'
Marketing Manager. She had got the job independently
after the news of Stan's transfer had broken at the end
of the previous season—and solely on her experience and
abilities, at least that was the official word.

'Chairman Bims is in the news. In the paper this morning,' said Trisall, as the coach waited for an opening in the
traffic before turning on to the main road. He ran a hand
twice across his short dark hair.

'There was talk about that. Before you are coming. He
is risking going to prison. In America.'

'Lot of balls, that is, Stan,' said the Welshman firmly. 'Take it from me.'

'But he's director of a bank where they . . . they wash the money.'

'Launder it.'

'It's drug money. They say that's all it does, this bank.' The speaker's lips pouted to show disgust. 'The American directors are being arrested.'

'No. Being investigated, that's all. Got to find them first, though. That's what the *Telegraph* says.' Trisall took a serious newspaper—or this morning's girlfriend did. 'It's because the bank has a branch in Miami,' he went on, opening and shutting the ashtray in the arm of his seat: the ashtray was pristine clean because officially nobody in the team smoked. 'They don't have anything here. Bet you nothing's proved about the drug money, either. Canny lot of buggers, bankers. Bankers and pit owners, my granda used to say.' He studied his companion more closely. 'The news isn't stopping Sir Ray coming in today to bawl out the Gaff anyway. What does Lilian think about it, then?'

Bodworski shrugged at the reference to his wife. 'Nothing. Says it's not our business.' As the coach moved away he looked back at the lighted club offices where his wife would be hard at work by now. She had driven in with him. The offices were on the top floor at the rear of the south stand, and above the mezzanine floor with its glass-fronted boxes looking on to the pitch.

Trisall sniffed energetically, which is how he did most things. 'Lilian's right, in a way,' he offered, but without real conviction. 'Except I suppose Sir Ray may stand to lose a packet. Could harm the club, that could.'

'The gate money is down. More than expected,' the Pole offered in a lowered voice.

The two men fell silent, looking out of the window, and contemplating the traffic building up on the approaches to Hammersmith Broadway—which was not a lot different from the frightening way it built up on every other weekday morning.

A small boy, half enveloped in a black and white Fulham Football Club scarf, was waiting to cross the road at an intersection. After he had recognized the easily identified coach, he screwed up his face and made rude finger gestures at the passengers with both hands as they passed him.

'Hope your face freezes like that, miserable urchin,' said the Welshman making faces back, sticking out his tongue and wagging his hands behind his ears. 'Probably a solid Eels supporter before we came, boyo,' he added to the Pole.

Both Bodworski and Trisall knew that uninspiring football was the cause of the team's present failure to attract spectators. Of thirty-eight matches played this season, they had lost twenty-three, drawn seven and won only eight. The poorest attendances had been at the last three home matches. The lure of three new players, all bought from Premier League teams, had died early. This was because the star performers had failed to shine, or even to twinkle in their new galaxy. Even the team's place in the First Division was now in jeopardy. It was a classic situation that created all round doubt and insecurity.

The two players were both anxious to know for certain the reason why the club's chairman and its manager were meeting on a Tuesday morning in late February. Top management meetings normally took place on Saturday mornings before home matches. The likeliest guess was that the Gaff was going to be bawled out—but it was just as possible that Bodworski or Trisall or Atler, or even all three of them, were again heading for the transfer list.

After the coach had left, silence descended on the stadium and its flat approach in the still dim morning light. Only the returning pigeons showed movement as they swooped in and pecked about the concreted area for morsels. Groundsmen arrived at 8.30 in winter, and office staff normally came in an hour after that. Apart from the lights in the offices of the south stand, the only others burning were in the Eels Supporters Club which was in an old two-storey building on the street next to the gate.

The stadium was a substantial one, set in seven acres. Three grandstands provided seating for twenty thousand people, but it was rare for spectators in that number to come to Hugon Road nowadays. When the south stand had been rebuilt five summers before this, the Eels had been near the top of the First Division, with the management sure that the club was on its way up into the Premier League.

But the following season had brought disaster. Instead of rising into the higher league, the team had dropped six places in the First Division. It was then that Lord Grenwood had reluctantly sold the club to the keen and confident Sir Ray Bims—recently knighted, wealthy, anxious to become a 'name' in soccer, and certain that the Eels' fortunes were due to change for the better. And his predictions had been right, measured over the following two years, although the team still failed to reach the Premier Division before it hit another bad run at the end of the subsequent season. That run had extended to the present.

So, in the circumstances, when Bims drove his turbocharged Bentley into the stadium at 7.44 it might have been expected that he would have had one of two pressing problems on his mind—either the club's difficulties, or else his personal ones with a Caribbean bank as reported in the morning newspapers. It was surprising then that, to the contrary, his thoughts were on something totally pleasurable as the car purred across the open concourse, its chassis levelling to the undulations in the ground surface as imperturbably as an ocean-going motor yacht responds to helm on placid water. The car scarcely even disturbed the pigeons, except the ones in its immediate path.

After parking in the bay reserved for him in the basement, Bims stepped across briskly to the lift nearby. He was a burly figure, thick-set and muscular, and altogether well preserved for his age, which was fifty-four. His thick, black wavy hair was parted in the centre and still grew well forward on his brow. His nose and mouth were heavily pronounced features, the steel grey eyes small, deeply recessed and seeming seldom to blink under untamed bushy eyebrows. He was dressed in a well tailored, loud, blue pinstripe suit, blue shirt, and the tie of an exclusive club in St James's.

Emerging from the lift on the mezzanine floor, Bims crossed the lobby and let himself into the chairman's suite immediately opposite by punching the key codes at the side of the door. The room he entered was large and square with a full-width sunken gallery on the far side. The gallery was largely out of sight from the door because the bar was set in front of most of it.

The place was expensively furnished in a heavily masculine style, the pine-panelled walls decorated with Eels' trophies and memorabilia. The carpet was as rich to the tread as the leather armchairs and sofas were to the touch. The desk, to the right of the door, was small but unquestionably antique. The bar, recently enlarged, was now prominent enough to put serious drinkers at their ease. There was a television receiver angled in a recess above the bar with a screen of awesome size.

The gallery had twenty-four armchairs in two terraced rows behind a long window. It was reached down steps set against the wall to the far left of the bar. There was a fine view from here of the pitch, or there was when the blinds were open. At present they were closed.

The door in the centre of the wall to Bims's far right as he entered led to a smallish dressing-room and bathroom, both windowless. The dressing-room contained a bed and had been provided originally for Berty Grenwood who had needed to rest after lunch and before the game on afternoon match days.

Bims secured the corridor door electrically after shutting it behind him, then made for the dressing-room. As he entered this, a tall, dark-haired young woman had been emerging from the bathroom. She was entirely naked.

He caught his breath in admiration, not surprise. 'I'm sorry I'm late. The traffic—' he began.

But she had already moved into his embrace and stopped his words, pressing her fingers on his lips and silently shaking her head. Then she kissed him, with a fierce, starved lover's kiss, her body moulding to his, tightening and moving against him.

At length, she drew her lips away with a satisfied murmur. 'You're all right?' she said, the concern in her tone deep and genuine.

'Yeah. I think we'll weather this particular storm.' His voice was deep and gravelly. He began to caress her, his touch firm and possessive.

'I was worried. By the newspapers. Until you called from the car. So are you going to—'

'Talk about it later, huh?' It was a command rather than a request.

'Whatever you say, lover,' she answered. Her concerned expression was replaced by a mischievous smile. 'So aren't I good to be ready like you asked?'

Her firm lissom figure was exquisite rather than generous, matured but not over-ripened. The long straight hair dramatically framed the slim, high-cheekboned face and the deep blue, intelligent eyes. Now she searched his face and neck again with her open mouth, snatching kisses and bites, while her hands were busily involved unknotting his tie, undoing his shirt buttons. She was behaving with nearly the finesse of a well-trained geisha—this Scottish business graduate, the marketing manager of the Eels, and wife of the soccer celebrity Stan Bodworski.

CHAPTER 3

It was an hour later when a troubled Arnold Edingly, President of the Eel Bridge Rovers official Supporters Club, left the club premises. Well wrapped up, he was returning on foot for breakfast at his home, No. 6, Albert Grove, two streets away from Hugon Road. He went regularly to the club early on weekday mornings in the winter to, as he put it, make himself useful.

Edingly was small and dark, with unusually large ears that stuck out a lot from the sides of his head. The ears and the slicked-back hair, small mouth, pointed nose, almost non-existent chin and a disposition to fidget gave him the appearance of a disaffected rabbit. In a way this was appropriate since he was by trade a pest controller, self-employed.

Making himself useful at the Supporters Club included checking the stock of scarves, T-shirts, blazer badges, pennants, souvenir programmes, and all the other merchandise sold in the shop, as well as the beer, cigarettes, and packaged snacks kept in the bar. He spent more of the time, though, in the office updating the membership and subscription ledgers, dealing with the general mail, and the travel arrangements for away matches involving the hire of coaches and occasionally whole trains. The office was upstairs at the back of the club which was housed in two converted small shops fronting on to Hugon Road, next to the stadium entrance. The office window looked across the main concourse towards the south stand. Edingly enjoyed watching the early comings and goings from this vantage-point.

The Supporters Club membership, nine-tenths of it male, currently stood at one thousand, six hundred and eighty-two, and it was falling. There was no paid staff. Volunteers served in the shop or behind the bar on match days. The organizational work was done by members of the committee, all dedicated people, but none so dedicated as fifty-year-old Arnold Edingly. Of course, he was the only one who received an honorarium for his efforts—quite a substantial one.

Eels official supporters were a responsible group with no tearaways among them. The average member was in his mid-forties, with a loyalty to the team that, if it fell short of fanaticism, still bordered on the religious in its depth and fervour. Indeed, Edingly himself was as deeply committed to the Eels during the week as he was on Sundays to the Second Pentecostal Evangelical church where he was a senior elder and a regular lay preacher.

When he reached Albert Grove he went through to the kitchen, stopping on the way to drape his scarf and overcoat over the stand in the narrow hallway. He also briefly rearranged his underclothes while examining his teeth in the hall mirror.

It was a modest house, part of a terrace of Victorian dwellings originally intended for skilled artisans but now mostly owned by upwardly mobile executives. Edingly was not one of these; he had simply been in occupation before the street had been gentrified.

'Messages?' he demanded of his wife, Millie, in a sharp and urgent tone as soon as he entered the kitchen. 'Messages?' he said again before the apprehensive woman had time to answer. Repeating himself was something Edingly did quite often, usually to spur people on. Most people found it irritating—though not Millie, or not so that she had ever mentioned it to anyone else. Her husband settled into his usual chair at the table, opening the copy of the *Daily Express* that she had positioned ready at his right hand.

'Nothing yet, Arnold, no,' Millie whispered urgently, as if this were intelligence of a high order that had at all costs to be kept secret from competitors. She carefully put the plate of eggs, bacon and sausage in front of him.

Millie was a plain woman, and smaller than her husband —if she hadn't been smaller it is doubtful that he would have married her. A bigger wife than Millie would have upset Edingly's curious sense of the proprieties. She worked afternoons serving in a local fruit and vegetable shop: she could have worked there full time but her husband liked to have her at his beck and call during the earlier part of the day. The food had been ready for his return on the dot of nine: he was a creature of habit.

'Well, I got work on hand in any case,' he said assertively, using his knife to ladle dark chutney directly from the jar on to his sausage.

'Yes, Arnold.' She sat at the table and poured his tea. Then she bent to stroke the fluffy grey tomcat that was rubbing against her legs. Millie had breakfasted much earlier—just tea and toast—but she always joined her husband for another cup, to be sociable, except Edingly spent most of the meal engrossed in the newspaper.

Three years before this, Edingly had been one of two pest controllers employed by the local council, before municipal budget reductions had made him redundant. However, his redundancy had not been balanced by any slackening in demand by the local populace for the services he provided —for the elimination of wasps' nests, rodent and cockroach infestations, or the keeping down of the burgeoning urban fox population. It had done a great deal, though, to increase the time it took the single surviving council pest controller to deal with people's complaints. This was why the briefly unemployed Edingly soon discovered that a householder with a hornets' nest of terrifying dimensions in his attic, or a mole pack submarining under his lawn, was ready to pay handsomely to have the scourge removed without delay by a private contractor which is what, *force majeure*, Edingly had become.

In the 'season' Edingly could charge almost whatever he liked for prompt service, especially when dealing with the upwardly mobile, and since the 'season' broadly coincided with the months of the year when club soccer wasn't played, he could eat his cake and have it—working short days in winter, devoting more attention then to the Supporters Club, and still ending up immediately better off than ever he had been before. He even had time throughout the year to develop a sideline in property ownership, a small enough enterprise when he had started it.

'I'll do that cinema this morning. Mice, they told you yesterday? Not rats? Rats?' he asked in a preoccupied tone that Millie knew better than to translate as lack of interest. He refolded the newspaper to a lower part of the same page before propping it once more against the milk jug. He went on studying the contents as carefully as before, lips moving slightly as he read, head shaking in what Millie recognized as silent outrage.

'Mice it was. I'm sure it was, Arnold.' She fingered the cheap blue beads at her throat nervously, hoping like any-thing that she hadn't got the message wrong on the tele-phone. She noticed that he was still on the news section of the paper. He was usually reading the sports pages by now. She was not much of a reader herself. She stroked the cat again which was now lying in her lap.

'More tea in that pot, then?' He always said that at this point, holding out his cup. 'It's a bad day for the Eels, and no mistake,' he added as she poured. He had decided to share his outrage.

'Something in the paper, Arnold?'

'About Sir Ray Bims, the Eels' chairman.'

'Not dead, is he?'

'Not dead, no. No.' He paused significantly as though to infer that death might well have been a happier issue than the one presented. 'Abandoning himself to greed and the fruits of unrighteousness. Living by the profits of drug trad-

ing. That's what it says here. And that's not all, I can tell
you. Since this morning.' He nodded pointedly.

'Go on?' She put down the teapot, and scratched her knee
before clasping her hands around the cat already asleep on
the faded blue pinafore. Millie's expression showed that she
was applying rapt attention to her husband's words. He
liked that.

Edingly gave a long sniff. 'I went over to the main offices
just before eight this morning. In the south stand. To talk
to Mrs Bodworski. About the promotional calendars. We're
running out in the shop. I rang first, but she never
answered. I knew she was in. Saw her arrive through the
window. She came with her husband.' He paused, pulling
on the lobe of his prominent left ear. 'The Chairman was
in too. Came in his car. Bit later, that was. I thought it
was funny, him being so early. Being there at all, really.
On a Tuesday. A Tuesday.'

'You told me ages ago he only comes in on match days,'
she said, to prove she'd been listening that time as well.

'That's right.' He leaned back in his chair, teacup in his
right hand. 'Well, I went up in the lift to Mrs Bodworski's
office. It's on the floor above the Chairman's. The lights
were on, but she wasn't there. And she wasn't in any of
the other offices either. I waited a bit, thinking she was in
the ladies'. But when she didn't come, I left. Went back the
other way, though. On the pitch side. Across the terraces. I
was checking if they'd renumbered some seats in the south
stand, same as they promised. They're part of the club
allocation for the match tomorrow night.'

'And had they?'

'I never looked. Never looked.' He meditated for a
moment, as though this omission might have had important
consequences. 'You see, something else happened. Very
upsetting.' He drank some tea, then put the cup down. 'I
crossed right in front of the Chairman's box. It was the
quickest way. To where I was going. The box is glassed in

like the other fancy ones, you know? Only it's bigger, of
course.'

'Yes, Arnold.'

'Couldn't see in because the blinds were closed. But when
I got to the end, I could hear a noise, like.'

'Like what?'

He pursed his lips. 'Listen and I'll tell you. It came from
a vent in the wall.' This made her brow furrow. 'Ventilation
shaft,' he clarified brusquely. 'At the end. It looked new.
Part of the rebuilding last summer. Goes to the Chairman's
bedroom and bathroom inside. I saw them once. In Lord
Grenwood's day. He showed me over. Now there's a real
gentleman. Real gentleman.' He paused, with a faraway
look in his eyes—or it might have been a calculating one.
'Anyway, you wouldn't have noticed the noise in the ordinary way. Only when everything else was quiet. It was . . .
well, it was groans, whimpers and shrieks.'

'Groans?'

'Whimpers and shrieks,' he repeated, which he would
probably have done in any case if she hadn't responded so
quickly. He began spreading butter on his toast with an
unnatural energy.

'A person in pain.'

'No, two persons . . . making passionate love.' He had
hesitated over the last phrase. He could have used words
less choice and a lot more graphic to describe the sounds
of depraved behaviour he had overheard, but he needed to
spare his wife's blushes—as well as to take into account
her limited understanding of what was involved in love-
making of the more abandoned kind.

Millie's right hand went to her mouth, waking the cat.
'You sure?' Her eyes were eager and he was surprised to
note that her cheeks had failed to turn pink.

'Positive. So would you have been if you'd been standing
where I was. Specially when it came to the end. Real
screams then from the woman. Of ecstasy. Ecstasy.' He

pronounced the last word with a good deal of savour and what could have been a suggestion of jealousy. Now Millie's face flushed a little—but with excitement, not shame, as her husband went on. 'Afterwards, they were talking.'

'Did you hear what they were saying, Arnold?'

'No. Wouldn't have been right, would it? Anyway the voices were low. Very low. Not like before.' Despite the moralizing stricture, there was no disguising the enduring disappointment. 'Know who it was, though. No doubt at all.'

'Was it Sir Ray with someone?' She shuffled in the seat, disturbing the cat again which got to its feet and stretched on her lap before dropping to the floor.

'It was Sir Ray with Lilian Bodworski, all right.' He was spreading strawberry jam on to his toast so liberally now that it dribbled on to his hand.

'On top of what's in the paper about him too.' Millie leaned forward. 'You going to . . . ?' She dropped her voice, again it seemed to foil eavesdroppers although there was only the cat within hearing distance. 'You going to do anything, Arnold?'

He scowled, licking jam off his fingers. 'That's something that needs thinking about. I'm not saying that second wife of Sir Ray's is any different from him. Looks a flighty piece, and hoity-toity with it. But Stan Bodworski deserves better from his wife. Stan's all right. Even if he is foreign.' He ruminated for a moment and gave a low belch. 'Terrible tempers Poles have, of course,' he said.

Felix Harden knocked on the door and entered the Chairman's office after the green light came on and the remote control mechanism released the lock. It was ten o'clock precisely.

The Eels' manager was a freckled, sandy-haired lightweight with a still boyish face who kept himself as fit as any of his players. He was dressed now in a team tracksuit.

''Morning, Sir Ray,' he called cheerfully as he crossed the room, his step a lot lighter than his spirits. His relationship with Bims had always been a formal one and latterly it had become increasingly cool. He was not expecting an easy time today, and the apprehension was worsened by his not knowing exactly why he had been summoned.

Bims was seated behind the desk. ''Morning. Take a seat. Come back from training, have you?' Bims knew this well enough without asking. Harden would not have missed the beginning of the session at Cherton and given Bims the chance to say he was slacking. Even so, the meeting had been called for a time which had made the manager's trip to Cherton hardly worth while.

'I was at Cherton first thing, yes, sir. I'll go back when we're done. That's if there's time.'

'Let's get down to business, then. Because I've made a decision. You've had your coffee, I expect?' Bims hardly waited for the other's nod before he went on. 'Thinking again about last Saturday. It was a bad defeat, you know? Technically very bad. Same as the week before. Replica, I'd say.'

'We drew the week before, Sir Ray. That was against Millwall.'

'I know bloody well who we were playing. I was there, wasn't I? And I'm telling you they were technically bad performances by the Eels. Both times. For that matter, it's applied to the whole season. The lads don't seem to lack keenness, not most of them, but there's still no co-ordination in their game. No cohesion.' The speaker leaned forward, arms on the desk. On occasions like these he wished it was the size of desk that enhanced the power of its user. 'You keep telling me we're going for an attacking game and we end up playing defensive. And to no purpose.' He paused, giving the other a chance to respond and doubting he'd dare now—not before he'd heard the decision.

'You don't need me to tell you there's a lot of dissatisfaction being expressed over your management.'

So this was it, Harden thought. He was being fired. 'I'm doing my best,' he said. 'We had all that sickness through December and January. And there's some this week as well. It's been hard to build the team back. The new players haven't—'

It was a feeble defence and Bims interrupted it. 'Well, maybe it'd be best for all concerned if we let you go,' he said. 'There's not much of your contract left in any case.'

They both knew the manager's second three-year contract had only four months to run, and that he had been pressing to have it renewed since the previous season. 'I was hoping it'd be renewed, Sir Ray. I don't feel I've had a chance this season. It's taken a while to restructure with the new players. But the lads know what I want. It's coming. Really it is.'

'So's Christmas, laddie.' Bims leaned back and clasped his hands behind his head. 'The other directors feel very strongly you've had all the time you should have needed.'

Harden didn't believe that the views of other directors counted for anything—or that they were being accurately reported even if they'd been taken, which he doubted. Bims seldom consulted anyone. Since he paid for everything he didn't need to. Everybody knew that. 'You've got another manager lined up, then?' If there was someone else it had been kept very secret, and that wasn't so easy. If there wasn't anyone, they surely wouldn't want the present manager to leave now, not with a third of the season left. It didn't make sense.

'Depends,' said Bims darkly.

'On what, sir?'

'On you and me, Felix.' The other man smiled for the first time since the interview had begun. It wasn't a warm smile—more cunning than friendly, but it made a change from the sour expression Bims had been wearing so far.

'You see, I've not said I go along with the others. Not totally. Not to the point where I'll deny you the chance to get things right.'

Harden swallowed. There was probably a catch coming, but whatever it was, it was better than being fired. Soccer was his life, and team management his future. He was already too old to be taken on again anywhere as a player. 'I can do it, Sir Ray. I promise you.'

'And I happen to agree with you. To the point where I'd give you another season to prove it anyway.' He rocked forward sharply, picked up a silver paperknife from the desk, and fixed Harden with a steady, piercing gaze.

'A one-year contract, sir?'

'A one-year extension of the old one, Felix. We can think about a new contract when that's up.'

'Fair enough.' It meant his present salary would be underwritten for another sixteen months.

'Yes, you and I together can stand up against criticism from any quarter, Felix. Together we're impregnable. Remember that.' He held the knife like a baton, waving the point at Harden. 'If I support you in the teeth of criticism, I expect the same support from you if people start knocking me. Which I'm telling you they will do if I keep you on for another year.'

'I understand, sir.' But he didn't believe it was as simple as that. He suspected a *quid pro quo* situation. What he had read in the paper had evidently been bad enough to make the all-powerful Bims go looking for allies at Hugon Road on his own account. Maybe people were more anxious to get rid of the Chairman than the team manager.

'But my decision still depends on your facing a few facts, Felix. Admitting you've made mistakes. Accepting you're ready to rectify them.'

'Everybody makes mistakes, Sir Ray,' Harden replied carefully.

'Sure. But you made a big one making me buy Stan Bodworski.'

'But it was you—'

'Not worth a fraction of what he cost me,' Bims cut in harshly. 'I'm not faulting the other new players you bought. Not so much, anyway. But that Bodworski's a bloody dead loss.'

It was a difficult charge for Harden to disprove. Bodworski hadn't exactly justified himself to date, but there had been other circumstances that had contributed. On top of that, it had been Bim's own idea to buy Bodworski, though there seemed to be no purpose in pressing that point now. 'You want me to read him the riot act, Sir Ray?'

'Better than that. I want you to put him on the transfer list.' Bims slapped the knife down on to the desk. 'Stop him from playing in any more games,' he went on. 'Lend him to some other club if you can. We don't need him around Hugon Road any more.'

'But that's—'

'He's bad medicine. Bad for the other players' morale. They don't like him, and they don't respect him as a player. They think we paid too much for him. Half a million too much. And his ten per cent of that's resented. Deeply resented. So's his seventy thousand pound a year playing contract.'

'Nobody knows that's what we're paying him,' Harden put in quickly.

'That's what you believe. They all know. He's let on, no doubt. Bragging. I've got my ear closer to the ground than you think. Closer than you've got yours by the sound of it. So what's it going to be, Felix?' Bims ended, straightening his back and looking at his watch.

It was as bald an ultimatum as anyone could have issued, even Bims. Harden was longing to ask for more time—but for what? To consider his verdict on Stan Bodworski to whom he owed nothing, or very little at least? In any case,

he would only be given Bims pause to reconsider and possibly to withdraw his offer on the future of Felix Harden.
The Eels' team manager knew that his job depended on
his suspending the Pole. It was naïve to think anything
else.

'I expect you're right, Sir Ray. About Stan—' he began,
the words already a dead weight on his conscience.

'Good.' Bims didn't allow the other to continue. 'And
another thing, Felix. There's a crackpot idea about selling
up Hugon Road and moving everything out to Cherton.
I'm deeply opposed to that, and I expect you to be as well.
I'll tell you why . . .'

CHAPTER 4

'OK. So Stan's a lovely fella. The best. But it was him or
us, Felix. You didn't have a choice, love. Not from what
you've said. Keep still, Kevin, will you? How can I dry you
when you're wriggling so? And teddy doesn't need drying,
too. Not at the moment.' Susie Harden was a round, jolly
woman, with a rosy face, and wing-framed, presently
steamed-up spectacles wedged on her blob of a nose. She
leaned further forward on the bathroom stool and went on
towelling the ginger-haired two-year-old. The button-
through dress she was wearing was straining where her
stout knees and short, strong legs were set wide apart.

'But he never really wanted to join the Eels. Except I
persuaded him,' countered her husband, the Eels' manager.
He had been telling Susie what had happened at his meeting with Sir Ray Bims that morning. He was standing in
the bathroom doorway of their home—a detached Victorian villa in Chiswick, with a quite long strip of garden.
It was three miles from Hugon Road, from which he had
just returned. The Hardens had bought the house three

years ago when prices had been sky high. His hundred thousand pound a year contract had seemed to underwrite the price at the time, but the mortgage repayments were hurting, even so.

'Stan got ten per cent of the transfer fee. That's double the usual. And a better contract than he'd ever had in the Premier League. That's what you told me at the time. Seems to me that was quite enough persuasion for him to join the Eels,' said Susie, a realist with two small boys to care for, plus a big one, called a husband, with all three in frequent need of protection from life's seeming injustices. There was no doubt in her mind now that in the present situation her family's well-being deserved to come uppermost. For years she and Felix had put off having children so that she could go on earning as a senior nurse: now with all their savings invested in the house, they relied on his salary alone to support their improved lifestyle—and Felix had just told her how close both salary and lifestyle had come to being terminated.

Felix shook his head. 'That's not the point. If we drop Stan now, it'll look like he's failed altogether with the Eels.'

'Well, hasn't he?' She was buttoning the front of Kevin's Mickey Mouse pyjamas—bought during an expensive family trip to Euro Disney in the previous August.

'No. Not as far as I'm concerned, and I'm the manager. He'll never get back. Not to the Premier League. As it is, we'll have to offer him to other First Division teams for half what we paid for him.'

'Will you have to buy out his contract?'

'Another year of it, yes. Unless we can fix a quick transfer.'

'But that and the transfer fee is Sir Ray's problem, isn't it? Not yours or Stan's. And Sir Ray has so many other problems I'm surprised he goes inventing more for himself. That's judging by the news today.' She looked up. 'I suppose he'll survive, will he?'

Felix looked uncomfortable. 'Outsiders won't think of the Stan Bodworski situation like you've said,' he replied, without answering the last question. 'They'll think I made a mistake buying Stan in the first place.'

'Did you?'

He hesitated. 'No. He's a smashing mid-field player.' But the look on his face showed more resentment than conviction. 'Like Gareth Trisall's a great striker. They were right for the Eels. Still are. And Jimmy Atler.'

'Come on, lovely boy then, on your gee-gee.' Susie picked up the giggling Kevin and put him on her shoulders. She made for the nursery, bouncing him up and down, while his arms clasped her tightly around the neck. Felix picked up the discarded teddy-bear and followed across the landing as Susie remarked: 'Anyway, everybody knows Sir Ray makes you do things you don't want to. Nobody'll blame you for what's happening.'

'Stan will,' he said promptly, with feeling. 'And his wife.'

'Lilian Bodworski can look after herself,' Susie offered abruptly while settling Kevin into his cot. 'He doesn't want her sacked as well, does he?'

'He never said. I expect she'll go if Stan does.'

His wife shrugged to show the extent of her concern— or lack of it—for Mrs Bodworski. 'Can you go and tuck up Nigel, and read him a story, then?' she went on. 'He's had his bath. He's watching TV in bed.' Nigel was their four-year-old.

'Yeah,' he answered automatically, but without making to leave the room. 'I rang Mr Linkina this afternoon.'

'To tell him what you have to do?'

'It seemed best. After what he said in the summer. About ringing him if I had more trouble with Bims.' He moved across to the window and went through the motions of adjusting the closed curtains. 'Him being Polish like Stan, it seemed right,' he continued, looking for more appro-bation, this time from his wife. 'He says not to do anything yet. Not to tell Stan. Not till after the match tomorrow.'

She stopped tidying clothes and toys, and straightened up, turning to face him. 'But you have to tell Stan. Sir Ray won't want him playing tomorrow will he?'

'Mr Linkina says there could be changes soon. Very soon. At top level.'

'Yes, and we know where the first change'll be if you don't get rid of Stan. Sir Ray'll sack you. You know how impulsive he is. When he's angry. Then where would we be? Linkina's a . . . an artiste. A dreamer. He's got no clout. Not where Sir Ray is concerned.'

'He said to hang on. To play Stan tomorrow and tell Bims there wasn't time to make changes.'

She came over to him, her round, normally happy face grave, the eyes reproachful. She rested her hands flat on his shoulders. 'Look, love, you can't afford to play silly bees with Ray Bims.'

'But if I do what he says tomorrow, against my better judgement, and the next day he's out himself, the new chairman's going to think—'

'What new chairman?'

He moved back from her with a sigh, biting his lip. 'I don't know. I'm guessing. From the things Mr Linkina said. Except I'm not supposed to tell anyone. Not even you.'

'Is it to do with Sir Ray and this drug business in America and er . . . and wherever it is? Because if it is, they said on the lunch-time news he can't be touched in England, even if they think he's guilty of something. Not at the moment. He could lose some money, that's all. If this bank of his gets closed down. I forget the details.'

'If I drop Stan, it'll still look as though I'm Bims's stooge. Doing everything he orders when I'm supposed to be team manager, not him. If he's chucked out as chairman, I'll probably be out as well. Just for that.'

'Why?'

'Because I'll have lost respect. From directors and players.'

'What about Mr Linkina?'

His forehead creased. 'Well, like you said, I suppose he's not all that important. Except he'll definitely support me.'

Susie looked thoughtful. A podgy thumb and first finger went to adjust the glasses on her nose. 'You really think you can get away with playing Stan Bodworski tomorrow?' she asked slowly.

'Although the original assets of the Bank of Natural and Manufactured Reserves, the BNMR, came from legitimate investors, the authorities allege that later substantial deposits in the Cayman Islands bank came from known criminal sources, involved with the illegal production and distribution of cocaine and other hard drugs. After ordering the closure of the bank's branches throughout the world, and the seizure of all its assets, the Cayman Islands Central Bank and the United States Federal Bank paid a joint special tribute to the work of the US Drug Enforcement Administration, whose investigations were responsible for uncovering what the joint statement described as "this apparently respectable financial front for a loathsome trade".

'Even though there is no branch of the BNMR in the UK, Sir Ray Bims, the British industrialist, is one of its directors. When questioned by a BBC reporter earlier today at his office in London's Mayfair, Sir Ray strongly denied any knowledge of the bank's involvement in illegal drug trafficking. He said he had been invited to go on the board at the bank's foundation eighteen months ago. At that time, he said, its declared humanitarian purpose was to help Third World countries fund major farm projects and pay for the importation of bargain price manufactured goods that were excess to the needs of developed nations. Although he had invested what he called seed corn money in the bank at the start, he had never accepted any salary or director's fees from the BNMR. He had regarded his personal involvement in the management as one of his many charitable activities. He had no reason to believe even now that the bank's objectives were anything but above board, but because he had been

too busy lately to give enough time to an organization with head-
quarters so far away, he had decided to resign his directorship. His
letter of resignation has already been delivered.

'*Since Sir Ray, a self-made industrialist, sold his Bims DIY*
chain of stores three years ago, he has been involved in a variety of
commercial ventures in the UK. He is also chairman of the struggling
Eel Bridge Rovers Football Club.

'*At Question Time in Parliament today, the Home Secretary—*'

Jimmy Atler switched off the car radio, and breathed
deeply to help his anger cool before he got out of his parked
BMW. Then he locked the car, and moved across the pavement to the front door of the terraced house. It was similar
to all the other red-bricked houses on both sides of the
street, except he noticed its brass knocker was better
polished than next door's, and its stone doorstep so recently
pumiced that you'd think twice before you stood on it.

'Oh, it's you. Better come in,' said the plain young
woman who opened the door. She didn't seem pleased to
see him, which was no more than he had expected.

'How's your mother, Nora?' he asked, keeping the choc-
olates behind his back as though he was ashamed of them.
The question was the one he always asked, but it underlined
the purpose of the visit. Once, on a similar occasion, he had
inquired after Nora's own health and received an offended
'what's it got to do with you?' in reply, as if he'd been prying
for details of some unmentionable gynæcological condition.

'It's been quite a good day today,' Nora answered in that
begrudging way of hers. 'Considering,' she added.

Considering what, he wondered. Of course, a good report
on anything from Nora would have to be qualified. She
probably meant it had been a good day for her mother, but
less so for the person saddled with looking after Mrs
Hawker and to whom a good day was a bit better than a
middling one, but a bloody sight better than a bad one. He
could imagine Nora thinking all that, and was even surprised she hadn't said something of the sort out loud.

'You'd better come through. She's in the middle room,' she offered next.

He followed the thin, sexless figure in the straight sexless, grey woollen dress, and the darned-at-the-elbows fawn cardigan, as they crossed the little hall, past the end of the dark-stained stairs, and along the corridor to the open door on the right. At least, he thought, they don't need to spend the winter in the kitchen any more. At one point Nora glanced behind her and pulled the cardigan down in a self-conscious, protective gesture, probably because she imagined he was looking at her bottom—which he had been, but only because he had to look somewhere, and certainly not for any lewd reason.

Nora would be twenty-seven now. Twenty-eight next month. He knew that because he would always remember the date of Bobby's birthday—his Bobby. Nora and Bobby had been twins. She looked older than twenty-seven, not like Bobby who had always joked about having the secret of perpetual youth. True enough, he'd been the picture of health right up to the end, or almost. He couldn't have gone on dancing otherwise. It was why no one had suspected anything—not even Jimmy Atler himself till it was too late. That was because he'd been away for virtually the whole of the previous winter, playing for a northern football club. They'd seen very little of each other through that time, coming together only for snatched meetings, short enough for Bobby to fake good health, again till quite close to the end.

'Oh . . . Ju . . . Jimmy, it's you. Looking so . . . so brown. Been abroad have you . . . Ju . . . Jimmy? We're . . . we're ever so pleased to see you. Aren't we, Nora? Put . . . put the kettle on. Jimmy'll have a . . . a cup of tea, won't you, love?' The woman sitting crookedly in the armchair lifted her left arm slowly in greeting. Her speech had been slow as well, and disjointed, the words hard for her to form. He had crossed the room and kissed her pale cheek before she had finished. She had spoken through the left side of her twisted mouth. Her right arm was curled upwards in her lap, and when she had made to move her body forward in response to his hug, only the good side had shifted at all.

'No tea, thanks, Mrs Hawker, I'm not stopping. Just passing. Thought I'd drop in to see how you are. You're looking better.' He pulled a chair up and sat beside her. There was no point in waiting for Nora to ask him to sit down. And he wasn't lying to Mrs Hawker, only mouthing the excusing, warming sort of things you said to a sick person. Of course he hadn't just been passing. You couldn't just be passing unless you were on the way to somewhere deeper inside this dead-end section of an unredeemed bit of London's old East End. Even so, living here was better than being in one of the newer and soulless high rise flats, the sort his own parents were in now, for instance. So far as he was concerned, he was glad to be shot of the whole area, childhood memories and all. He was only sorry that Mrs Hawker hadn't been ready to move to a better environment, to the country even. But she'd been adamant about staying: she'd been born in this house.

He looked about him. The room was cheerful enough now with the pretty new paper, and the carpeting. There was even what looked like a coal fire worked by gas. They didn't need it for heat, only Mrs Hawker had said she couldn't do without the look of a nice fire. She had the same in her bedroom, the front room on the ground floor: she couldn't manage the stairs any more. It was why a bath and loo had been installed in the old scullery.

Of course, Mrs Hawker didn't really look any better— only like death warmed up, but not warmed up enough. She was still pretty helpless. Lucky to be alive and sitting up, the doctor had said, after a stroke of that severity. That had been two years ago, soon after Bobby's death. Not the real Bobby, but the secretive, misguided Bobby, the one whose existence Jimmy Atler had tried and failed to wipe from his mind or his conscience.

In truth, Mrs Hawker had made some progress, but not as much as she might have done. It wasn't as if she had been too old to respond to therapy. She was only sixty now, though she looked years older than that, and her attitude to therapy had lacked any will to improve.

'Brought you some of those soft centres you like.' As he put the box awkwardly on the already overcrowded little table beside Mrs Hawker he could feel Nora's eyes on him. The gaze would probably be accusing. Involuntarily he glanced round at her. If anything, her look was more hostile than he had expected—venomous as well as accusing. This would have nothing to do with his failing to bring a gift for Nora too. Once he might have thought it did, but not since the time he had bought her some expensive roses and she had accused him of murdering living plants. She had actually made him feel guilty too, despite himself, and worse even than if he'd nicked the flowers from West Ham Park. He'd done that once too, when he'd been a kid—picked some municipal daffodils there for his mother. There'd been no end of bother over that. He could afford to buy a greenhouse full of flowers for his mother now, but like Nora, she wouldn't want them, not from him.

Nora looked at him the way she did because she wasn't ever going to forgive him for what had happened—to her brother and her mother. There was no point in his going over the argument that he hadn't been responsible in any way. Bobby had been a free agent. And if Mrs Hawker's stroke had been brought on by Bobby's death that was terrible, but it still had nothing to do with Jimmy Atler. Nora just wouldn't accept any of that, of course.

He wished he could come to see Mrs Hawker when her daughter wasn't here, but she was here nearly all the time, despite the fact he had offered to pay for a reliable sitter any time she wanted. Being chained to the house was how she won the moral argument before it was even stated. She was full-time minder to her mother. She had given up her job at an insurance office out of filial duty. Jimmy wasn't to be allowed to forget that—even though he'd never been sure if Nora had actually enjoyed the lousy job, and even though it was he who had paid for the improvements in this house since then, for the additions at the back, the central heating system, the redecorations, the new furniture, even the television set they'd been watching when he arrived. He had provided nearly all the creature comforts they enjoyed—correction, that Mrs Hawker enjoyed. Nora never accepted that she was a direct beneficiary of Jimmy's largesse. She was, though. It wasn't even that he looked for gratitude from her. He'd have settled for human understanding, for just a bit of tolerance from her: sod the bitch.

At least he was content in his own mind that he had done the right thing by Mrs Hawker—what Bobby would have done if he'd been alive and had the money. It was no more than he would have provided for his own parents if they'd allowed him. In a way Mrs Hawker was a salve to his conscience: she was his expiation—not a word Jimmy would have used, or wholly understood, but it covered exactly what he felt.

'How . . . how's your mum and dad, Jimmy?' asked Mrs Hawker.

He saw Nora's lip curl derisively.

'I think they're OK,' he answered, clearing his throat. 'I haven't heard nothing lately. No news is good news, they say, don't they?' There was nothing else he could offer. Mrs Hawker would have forgotten his parents had broken with him, that's if she ever knew. That was when he and Bobby had been together.

His parents now lived near Brentwood, ten miles from here. Once they had been just a few streets away. He wasn't surprised they never took the trouble to visit Mrs Hawker, even though they had been friends years ago, when their children had been growing up. He didn't believe they blamed him over Bobby's death, not like Nora, but he knew they felt bad about Bobby and him living together. It was unnatural, his father had said, and he'd used harder words than that the last time Jimmy had seen him.

'And the . . . the football?' The invalid made a painful movement in her chair. 'That's going all right, is it? With . . . with the new team?'

'We're keeping our end up, yes. Important home match tomorrow night.'

'Fancy!' She paused. 'Pity you're not with West Ham any more. Nora could bring me to . . . to . . . to see you play.' She gave an attempt at a mischievous, lopsided smirk to confirm that they both knew she hadn't meant what she said. Her left hand lifted and dropped as a sort of visible punctuation.

'Haven't been with the Hammers since I was an apprentice, Mrs Hawker,' he replied. 'And that wasn't for very long.'

'Fancy!'

'What's going to happen to Sir Ray Bims, then?' Nora put in suddenly and quite sharply, looking up over the knitting she had restarted. 'Did you hear about him today? On the news? If it's right, he deserves hanging.' She sniffed noisily. 'No, hanging would be too good, and that's a fact.'

Jimmy nodded. 'You're right there, Nora.'

It was about the first time for two years that Jimmy Atler and Nora Hawker had agreed on anything. It was the reason why on this visit he stayed for a bit longer than usual.

CHAPTER 5

'What is it, then, Arnold? More autographed photos urgently requested by my sex-crazed fans?' Gareth Trisall joked—or half joked—as he stepped quickly into the office of the Eels Supporters Club, his bent arms moving like powerful pistons. He had taken the stairs two at a time.

'Well, yes, it's something like that, Gareth,' answered Edingly uneasily, getting up from the desk under the upper-floor window. 'Never had a player whose picture was as much in demand as yours. As yours,' he added in an oily tone.

'Never had a player from the Rhondda Valley before either, so there's your reason,' Trisall offered lightly as he moved about the room, glancing at the framed pictures of past players. He generally found it difficult to stand still.

'We got a fresh batch of prints in this morning. If you could sign three dozen to be going on with? They're over here ready for you.' Edingly stepped across to a table. 'Didn't want to hold you up, but as you said you were having a session with the physio . . .'

'Sign a gross if you want. All good for the image.' The Welshman looked at the time. 'Seriously, I'm OK for ten minutes. Not being picked up till quarter past.' His elbows were now making energetic circular movements as though he was in some way preparing for a take-off, not for writing his signature.

'That's a lovely young lady driving you today, if you don't mind me saying so, Gareth.'

'Ah, Sara, that is. Gorgeous, isn't she?' the Welshman replied as he pulled out the chair and seated himself at the table. 'You could say worth losing your licence for, as well.'

The two had met briefly an hour before this as Trisall

had been getting out of the Porsche at the players' entrance to the south stand. Edingly had made it seem like a chance encounter, but he had checked earlier with the team's physiotherapist and had known that the other man was coming in to the treatment room at five.

'Very nice of you to come over,' said Edingly, still in his most ingratiating tone, even though he deplored Trisall's last sentiment, and the reason for his having lost his driving licence in the first place: Edingly was teetotal.

The older man's fawning was understandable. There was no obligation for the players to help the financially independent Supporters Club in the way that Trisall was doing now. The Football Club had its own official shop open on match days to the general public on the ground floor of the south strand. All the profits from that went to central funds. In a sense the Supporters Club shop was competition, except it carried a much smaller selection of merchandise and only catered for its own members.

'Well, I always believe in helping the official supporters,' the player said condescendingly. 'Not to mention the official supporters' wives and daughters,' he completed with a chuckle. He was well aware that his photograph was mostly requested by women. He continued to inscribe his name with painstaking and deliberate strokes of a ballpoint pen, pausing to admire each print in turn both before and after it had been embellished.

'Must be a problem sometimes, being a football star like you are, Gareth. Idolized by the ladies. Must mean you're subjected to unfair temptations. A lot of them too. Temptations,' Edingly concluded in a pious tone.

Trisall looked up, wondering if he was being ribbed intentionally. It seemed from the expression, though, that the words had been in earnest. Of course, Edingly was known to be a Bible-thumper of the old school. Trisall's grandfather had been the same, which is why the young man stopped himself in time from making a ribald reply.

'Got to be strong-minded, Arnold, of course,' he said self-righteously. It was true too, he mused to himself. It took expert timing and good planning to get the best out of the temptations on offer, especially if you wanted to avoid wasting any of them. Being greedy got you nowhere, except into a muddle.

'Would Stan Bodworski have the same problem, you think?' Edingly thrust both hands into his trouser pockets where they became frenetically active in jangling keys and loose change.

'Stan? Well, he's married for a start,' said Trisall, surprised at the question. 'Good Catholic too. Stays on the strait and narrow, I'd say. Like I will when I stop being a bachelor.' There was no harm in wishful thinking, especially in front of a serious chapelgoer like Edingly.

'That's what I thought. About Stan, I mean. Wouldn't cheat on his wife, would he?'

'Oh no. Not a chance.' The reply was guarded as well as firm because the Welshman wasn't sure what the other was getting at.

'Marriage would be sacred to him? Sacred?' Edingly repeated on a rising note, leaning forward, and balancing on his toes.

'No doubt of that. None at all.' There was no harm in giving a mate a clean bill. Anyway, Stan deserved it. Trisall applied himself to another signature—mouth open, pointed tongue protruding and assiduously matching the upward and downward strokes of the pen tip.

'Would you think Mrs Bodworski is the same?'

Trisall stopped writing and looked up. 'Yes. Don't you then?'

The jangling in Edingly's trouser pockets reached a sort of crescendo. 'There's a problem there, Gareth. Something I thought I ought to mention to you, like. You being Stan's friend. Friend.'

*

Ian Crayborn responded to the first Lady Bims's nervous wave by hurrying across the theatre restaurant to the corner table where she was sitting waiting for him. She was in a blue silk dress, a mink stole, and a state of growing, almost paralytic apprehension.

'Sorry to be late, Joyce. The Guildford traffic's appalling at this time of the evening,' he explained, pressing her hand, hesitating before kissing her chastely on the cheek, then doing the same on the other cheek, but less chastely and even more clumsily. Tonight, he told himself, he really had to stop behaving like a celibate middle-aged clergyman engaged on good works, and be more the debonair widower accountant entertaining an unattached female client.

'Oh, but you're not late. Not really. I was early. There's plenty of time before the play starts.' She tumbled out the words breathlessly, anxious to prevent his feeling he was in the wrong, even though it was nearly half an hour after the time they had arranged to meet here in the ground-floor Harlequin Restaurant.

The last fifteen minutes she had spent in a state of acute uncertainty, concerned that their rendezvous might have been in Figaro's, the theatre's other restaurant upstairs, not knowing whether she should go up the two floors to look for him—and then possibly miss him in the process.

She was confused again now because she hadn't expected him to greet her with kisses, even formal ones, which was why she had appeared to stiffen at the first, and failed to turn her face quickly enough for the second. She was upset with herself still for arriving before him, and ages earlier than she need have done. As it was, she had sat in the car in the car park for ten minutes before coming in, looking at her watch every twenty seconds, frisking the edges of her blonde-tinted hair, and checking the state of her eye shadow.

Of course she should have allowed for him to be late. He had driven fifteen miles in the rush hour, straight down

from his office in Kingston-upon-Thames. She was sure
now that he would have preferred to dine after the performance: it was she who had opted to eat first.

'So long as I haven't kept you waiting too long.' He
smiled, still standing beside her chair. 'What a nice dress
you're wearing.'

'Oh, thank you. Thank you very much.' She overdid the
expressions of gratitude because she simply wasn't used to
compliments. 'I'm so sorry, I really should have insisted
we had dinner afterwards,' she went on, wallowing in her
guilt. 'Then there'd have been time to come to the house
first.' Immediately she wondered if she should have said
that, whether he would take it as a forward sort of suggestion. She had met his wife who had died four years before:
she had been a very proper person. Both sides of Joyce's
mouth twitched twice, involuntarily and in unison. 'Except
you'd be passing the Yvonne Arnaud to get to me, and that
would be silly really . . . with the traffic,' she finished more
flustered than before, and with one hand going to her neck
because there might be red patches gathering at the base
of it. Joyce's neck was rather plump, like the rest of her.

The Yvonne Arnaud was the name of the Guildford
theatre, an angular, concrete building squashed on to a
cramped site beside the River Wey at the bottom of the
town. It was a regular showcase for new plays on pre-
London runs. Joyce Bims, the divorced wife of Sir Ray
Bims, lived in a cottage by herself in a village five miles to
the south-east, along the Horsham road. This was her first
genuine date with a man since her marriage had been dissolved nearly three years ago.

She had known Ian Crayborn since long before he had
become her accountant after the divorce. He had been one
of the accountants her ex-husband had used from the early
days.

The divorce settlement had been a quite generous one.
She had nothing to grumble about really, that's if you didn't

count a continuing sense of utter rejection, and a total loss of confidence because your husband left you after twenty-eight years for a younger, more sophisticated, sexier woman.

Joyce's financial affairs didn't need a lot of professional attention—it was only her income tax return that she really couldn't manage herself. But Ian Crayborn kept an eye on her little investment portfolio as well. All her holdings were in blue chip companies. Ray Bims had made shares over to her as part of the settlement.

She loosened the stole a little, still not sure whether she should have worn it, whether her full-length mink wouldn't have been better. She could keep the stole on, though, and arrange it so that it did more to disguise her fleshy shoulders. She had spent the afternoon in her bedroom trying on other outfits. The stole had gone well with the blue V-necked dress. She didn't have all that many things in what she thought of as her classic collection of good clothes —nor really money that she could justify using to add to it. And there were so few places these days where you could wear real fur, not without risking insults from the animal rights people. The Queen wore furs still, of course, but she was always protected. Within reason, Joyce supported animal rights, only she was bitter about restraints on wearing fur. Her minks were a visible sign of the social status she used to enjoy—of the wealth she and her husband had built through sheer hard work, her hard work just as much as his. She needed all the props available to bolster her painfully diminished and never very strong sense of self-assurance.

'Anyway, you can stop worrying about me, Joyce,' said her companion after he had seated himself opposite her, and breaking in on the private perturbations exercising her mind. 'We're both here safely, and we're going to enjoy ourselves. Have you got a drink? No?' He snapped his fingers in the direction of a dreaming waitress. The woman came over to the table immediately. This pleased Joyce.

She knew that Ian Crayborn wasn't demonstrative by nature, but she did like a man to be quietly assertive—not bull at a gate aggressive like Ray, of course: God forbid.

Watching Ian across the table later, after they had got their drinks and were both studying the menu, she was thinking again that if he had come to the house for her, he'd have had to drive her home afterwards. She had realized that when he had first offered to collect her. She had turned down his suggestion because she had panicked, not knowing how she would handle things when he brought her back—whether she should ask him in for a drink, or a coffee, or even invite him to stay the night, and if that, on what basis. Her stomach gave a little tremble when she considered the last point again.

It was all very well for her twenty-six-year-old daughter Liza, her only child, to say she should be bolder in her relations with men, playing everything by ear. Liza was a physiotherapist who had been living with a bearded vet in Liverpool for the last eighteen months. Joyce failed to understand why they didn't marry, but she understood even less why at forty-nine years of age she herself didn't know how to promote an intimate, enduring relationship with an available, desirable man.

Ian Crayborn, shortish and square, was older than Joyce, but not much older. He wasn't exactly handsome, or athletic, except she knew he played golf. Being a little overweight suited him, and if he had lost most of his hair, his expression was kind, and the heavily framed glasses added to his naturally benign and sage appearance. Of course, she couldn't help comparing him with her ex-husband— much as she tried not to. The two were about the same age, but Ian looked older and perhaps a touch less lively. She was sure though that he was kinder and more cultured than Ray.

If only she knew how he felt about her. It was too easy for her to read more into tonight's invitation than might have been intended. If he cared about her sexually (her stomach gave another little tremble at the thought), why had it taken him so long to do anything about it? Of course, he could have been too shy up to now, or there could have been someone else he was interested in . . . or . . . or tonight could just be a duty airing for a not very important client.

The last and desolating hypothesis prompted her involuntarily to push the stole even further off her half-naked shoulders in a desperate gesture of reckless abandon.

'Really, we should have done this before,' he said suddenly, beaming at her over the top of the menu. 'My fault, of course. I so enjoy your company. But to tell you the truth, I suppose I've been shy about asking you.'

There was a fresh flutter inside her, but of hope this time, not foreboding, and in her breast not her stomach, or somewhere in between. It was what she had wanted him to say. 'Oh, that's silly,' she replied. 'No, not silly . . . I mean, I like you so much, Ian. And we've both . . .' She swallowed without getting out the next word, feeling an uncontrollable blush rising to her cheeks.

'Both been left alone?' he completed for her.

'That's right,' she whispered.

The hopes for expanding the magic moment were very nearly destroyed by the return of the waitress who demanded, through a heavy cold: 'Are you rethy to orther dither?'

'Not yet. Later.' Crayborn waved the girl away without taking his eyes off Joyce. 'I wasn't sure. About your being lonely too, I mean. I've always imagined you must have lots of friends.'

'I have. Most of them married. They only do things in twos. Or multiples of twos,' she continued with feeling, her confidence improving. It was marvellous to find herself talking to a kindred spirit.

He nodded. 'That applies to my friends as well, I'm afraid.'

'But it's so different for a man. I mean, you can, well, take the initiative. With . . . with the opposite . . . sex.'

'I'm not very good at taking the initiative. Not in that way. Well, as you can see.' Both his hands lifted in despair, before coming together again on top of the menu. 'God knows how long it's taken me to ask you out.' He leaned forward, screwing up his face. 'The other thing is, I've always felt you were too used to the high-flying life. With Ray. I'm a bit er . . . low level by comparison.'

'But you're much nicer.' It was a very intimate compliment for her to have paid him, and she was surprised not to feel more embarrassed about it afterwards. 'Have you heard, Ray's in trouble?' she added, in a sterner and concerned tone.

'Yes, I talked to him on the phone yesterday. On business.' He hadn't intended to raise the subject of Ray Bims's trouble himself.

'I didn't think you worked for him any more.'

'I don't. Not very much. He doesn't retain the firm. Not since he sold Bims DIY really. But I look after the accountancy work for the Eels. I'm on the Eels board, of course. Ray arranged that. When he bought the club.'

'So do you think it's true? The terrible things they're saying about him in the paper?'

He shrugged. 'Let's hope not. We'll have to wait and see. I only talked to him about the Eels. I didn't mention anything else, and he didn't either.'

'Well, if he's in a real mess, I hope the second Lady Bims is loyal and supportive. Not just a pretty face. Not just a fair weather wife,' Joyce ended pointedly, her acerbic and quickened delivery leaving no doubt where her own opinion lay.

'I know which of you I'd rather have by me in a storm, Joyce. And your face is prettier too,' he responded gallantly.

'Flatterer,' she said, blushing again and wanting to believe him.

'I mean it.' His hand reached across the table to squeeze hers. 'Have another sherry.'

'I'd love one, but I shouldn't. I'm driving, remember?'

'How silly for both of us to hold back on the booze,' he countered. 'Tell you what, why don't you leave your car here for the night? Isn't there a bus you could get in tomorrow to collect it? Then I could drive you home after the show.' He was still holding her hand, more tightly than before.

'Yes, there is a bus,' she said, putting her other hand over his—rather awkwardly. 'What a good idea. But won't that make it very late for you?'

His eyes held hers. 'I don't care if I don't get home till morning.'

'Oh, well, in that case, why not . . .' her own gaze lowered, 'why not spend the night. I've a spare bedroom,' she added quickly, making herself look up again.

'Wouldn't it be a lot of trouble? Having me?'

Her well-developed cleavage heaved charmingly. 'Oh, no trouble at all. I'd feel so much better if you stayed. Really I would.'

The waitress had reappeared. 'Are you rethy yet?' she asked urgently, and with effort.

'I think so,' said Ian Crayborn, removing his hand gently from across the table.

'Oh yes,' said Joyce with a genuine enthusiasm unrelated to the mere prospect of food. The tip of her tongue ran back and forth across her upper lip. Her eyes were now meeting his unblinkingly. 'I'm ready if you are, Ian,' she said, thinking of her daughter's advice, and consciously playing things by ear.

CHAPTER 6

'And you say there was no one here between six-fifteen last night and six-thirty this morning, Mr Edingly?' said Detective-Inspector Jeckels, serious, pale of face, skinny and with the martyred look of a dedicated jogger—even though Molly Treasure, who met him later, was to observe that the same expression could be induced by chewing cloves or listening to Schoenberg. It happened that the thirty-year-old policeman really was a serious runner who had twice been in the top three hundred finishers in the London Marathon, an achievement most of his less energetic colleagues even so considered more distinguishing than distinguished.

'That's it,' Edingly confirmed. 'This being a midweek match day. Like I told the other two policemen who came earlier. I'm here most mornings by six. Except Sundays and home match days. I come in a bit later on match days because I'm staying all day. All day,' he completed flatly, as if the logic of this was too clear to require further elucidation. He shook his head as he and Jeckels again surveyed the splintered door of the burgled cupboard in the upstairs office at the Eels Supporters Club.

The cupboard was tall and narrow, painted white and attached to the wall in a corner of the room. The door had been secured by an integral lock plus a padlock over a hasp and staple, except that all this protection had been roughly nullified by the insertion of a stout, flat-ended poker in the door closure at two points. The poker had been part of an ornamental set of fire irons normally kept in front of the disused but black-leaded grate on the other side of the room. It had been found on the floor, close to the forced door. This had at least saved the police from having to search further for the vandal's implement, which had now been removed from the scene, labelled, and encased in a plastic evidence bag.

'How much strychnine was taken, sir?'

'Seven ounces. In crystals. Or just under.' Edingly noticed the other's eyebrows lift following the less than precise reassessment. 'Nothing like it for sorting mole colonies. In a glass jar it was. Screw-topped. And the rifle with a box of fifty cartridges. Nothing else. I told the others the same. The same.'

Jeckels wondered why Edingly kept repeating himself, but he wasn't the only one. The policeman had already been given the information collected earlier by the uniformed branch. They had answered Edingly's emergency call at just after six-forty. It was now ten to eight. Normally a detective-constable or at most a detective-sergeant would have been sent to do the follow-up on a robbery of this nature. The detective-inspector was here with a DC because the divisional head of the local CID had a fixation about stolen poisons. The constable was downstairs scrutinizing door locks.

'The rifle was an Enfield two-two?' Jeckels observed, looking at his notes. 'You got a licence for that, sir?' he added, looking up slowly.

'Of course I have. And the rifle was under lock and key. Double lock and key.'

'Yes, sir.' The Inspector's cheerless countenance was unaffected by this hollow confirmation that laws were being seen to be kept. 'Why did you store the weapon here, sir?'

The other shrugged, and dug his hands into his trouser pockets. 'We get more rats in the stadium than anywhere else in this whole borough. You'd be surprised how many I shoot through the season. At first light. Before anyone else gets here. If you've got an eye like me, a rifle's better than a shotgun. Does less damage to property. 'Course, you got to be careful. Lot of pigeons we get, as well. Got to keep them down too or they take over a place. Sitting targets they are, most mornings.' The Inspector was still frowning over the propriety or otherwise of shooting sitting pigeons as the speaker continued. 'So it's better keeping the rifle here, see? Safer as well. Or should be. Should be.'

'Than having it at your house?'

'Well, stands to reason. There's a burglar alarm here. And having a gun at home makes the wife nervous. You know how wives are?'

Jeckels only half nodded. He was a bachelor, but only because no female of his close acquaintance was prepared to alter that status by consenting to marry him. He had proposed to two, but both had found his nearly fanatical commitment to long-distance running and his job too excluding. 'Only the alarm didn't go off last night?' he questioned.

'Switched off, wasn't it?' His legs set well apart, Edingly's hands had begun jangling the things in his pockets.

'You sure you switched it on last night when you left, sir?'

'I'd swear to it. On the Bible. Whoever did this knew the code number for the alarm. And the entry code to the front door. Must have done.'

'The front door works on a code lock? There's no key?'

'That's right. Like they put on the doors in the south stand. Anyway, nothing's been forced downstairs.'

'How many people know the two code numbers, sir?'

Edingly looked defensive. 'I've worked it out since the other police were here. I got a list somewhere. Names and addresses.' He moved across to the desk in the window. 'Yes, here it is.' He picked up a sheet of paper with handwriting on it. After putting on a pair of early NHS glasses, he ran his finger down the page. 'Seventeen. One seven,' he announced, like a Bingo caller, and handed over the sheet.

Jeckels's mouth opened and shut without his saying anything.

'All trusted people, I can tell you,' Edingly offered quickly in a compensating kind of tone, his fingers busier now in his pockets. 'They'll all be at the party tonight. It's for Supporters Club officials. In the stadium. The stadium.'

'Is that so, sir?' Jeckels commented absently. 'So if seventeen people knew the entry and burglar alarm code numbers, we've got to allow they could have passed it on to as many as that again. Perhaps even three or four times as many. That's the way it often comes out, I'm afraid. Anyway, we know who we should be talking to first, don't we, sir?' the policeman continued without enthusiasm, suddenly looking over his shoulder as if he sensed that someone was behind him. There was no one behind him, but the movement disconcerted his listener as Jeckels added, 'Why as many as seventeen, sir?'

'Committee members, and two of the Eels' directors. That's out of courtesy. Because me and my vice president get given the entry code to the Eels' general office over there.' He nodded towards the window. 'Anyway, that's twelve people for a start. And there's other folk who help. Well-wishers. There's no paid staff, you know? Helpers have to be able to drop in when it suits. They have to have access to the premises.'

If the Inspector accepted the logic of this he was slow to show it. 'You say you think the thief must have known the codes, sir?'

'Yes. But it can't be one of the seventeen who's done this. Stands to reason. What's the betting one of them had someone behind him when he's been tapping out the code numbers? They been asked not to allow that to happen, of course.' Edingly's lower jaw moved slowly from side to side making his large ears see-saw in sympathy.

'No one's reported giving the codes to anyone else? By mistake even?'

'No. If they had we'd have changed the numbers, wouldn't we? It's easy enough. Easy enough.'

'And when you left last night at six-fifteen, the place was empty, sir?'

'That's right. Tuesday's not a club opening night unless there's a match.'

'Did you check the rooms before you left the building by any chance, sir?'

Edingly sniffed loudly before he answered. 'No. Wasn't necessary. There was no one here.'

'But you mentioned the front door was unlocked while you were in the building. That was between five-ten and six-fifteen, I think you said, sir?'

'On the latch it was, yes. I wasn't here long. Gareth Trisall was with me. From six o'clock.' There was an uncomfortable expression on the speaker's face as he went on, 'We'd have heard anyone coming in, wouldn't we?'

Jeckels stolidly failed to affirm this highly speculative conjecture by word or look. 'And Mr Trisall left with you.'

'Bit before me.'

'I see, sir. And nothing else has been taken? Not from up here, or from the shop or the bar downstairs?'

'Nothing as I can see.'

'And no one else has a pair of keys to this cupboard, sir?'

'No one. There's only two pair. One in my pocket.' A ring of keys had promptly appeared in his right hand as he spoke. 'And the other pair's locked up at home.'

'Right, sir.' The policeman closed his notebook. 'And you say there's no one that you know of who'd have reason to nick either your rifle or the quantity of strychnine?'

'No one.' Edingly's hands were back in his pockets, working hard again. 'Hope it's not a gink with just rats he wants killed. Who's doing it himself to save my little fee. Dangerous that'd be. And illegal with strychnine. That's for moles only. Killing rodents is a job for a professional. A professional.'

*

The low-ceilinged kitchen of Joyce Bims's cottage was warm, friendly, and prettily furnished in pinewood, with frilly yellow curtains across the two leaded-light windows. The same material had been used on the cushions of the banquette seat set around the little semi-circular table in one corner, next to the electric Aga cooker. It was a cosy place for an intimate breakfast.

Ian Crayborn watched Joyce as she brought the toast-rack and the coffeepot to the table. 'You shouldn't have got up at all, you know,' he said. 'I . . . I meant to steal away quietly without disturbing you.' The look he gave her was nothing short of adoring before his eyes dropped shyly again to make an unconscionably careful study of the half-consumed glass of fresh orange juice on the table in front of him.

They were both suffering from 'morning after' embarrass-ment, he it seemed rather more than she. He had come down some minutes after her.

'You'd have left without any breakfast? That would never have done,' she said, in gentle reproof. 'Sure you won't have an egg?'

'Quite sure, thank you. This and the cornflakes are fine.'

She slid into the seat opposite him holding her middle in tightly to make the movement seem easy, while avoiding looking at him directly. What a lot had happened since they had last sat at a table together, she thought. It was almost too wonderful to credit. She fluffed the side of her hair, hoping that it and her make-up were presentable. She had done her best in the time available since she had got out of bed—the bed he had left in the early hours for no other reason, she was sure, than to save her blushes when daylight came. Except it was so murky outside that daylight hadn't quite come even now. She would infinitely have preferred to have woken with him still lying beside her—repeating the pledges they had made in the night.

This morning she had put on her new green wool suit and polka-dot blouse (both, as it happened, bought for a wedding). The elegant clothes might have been overdoing things, but they gave her confidence. Better that way, and not to look put together as a lot of women would have done this early in the morning. She had not come down in a dressing-gown over her nightdress partly because she wanted to be ready to drive with him back to her car in Guildford, but more because she didn't have a dressing-gown glamorous enough to breakfast in with her lover—and fiancé. She experienced a delicious, weakening abdominal thrill as she inwardly pronounced the words that described both the intimacy and the status of her new relationship with Ian.

'You found everything in the bathroom cupboard, then? The shaving things?'

He stroked his shining chin. 'Yes. You . . . you showed me last night, remember? Before . . .' He coughed lightly, moving his open hand to his mouth in an overly well-bred manner.

'Of course.' She flushed, and busied herself with pouring them both coffee. She remembered well enough. It was when they had met on the landing, some time after they had finished their drinks and said their over-formal good nights without Ian having made even the most tentative amorous advance. She had rather hoped that the drinks would have encouraged him, but they hadn't seemed to do. Perhaps she had not made them strong enough, was what she had thought at the time, though they had certainly had a relaxing, loosening affect on her.

It was when she had been coming out of the cottage's single bathroom, dressed only in her nightdress, thinking he had finished there earlier, that he had reappeared from the guest-room wearing just the white terry-towel gown she kept there for visitors. He had looked almost dashingly youthful without his glasses, with his skin quite pink after the shower he had taken earlier. Affecting confusion, she had started to explain about the shaving tackle her daughter's boyfriend had left the last time he had stayed, turning to show him exactly (and unnecessarily) where it was kept in the bathroom, knowing he was immediately behind her. She had leaned backward a little as she had opened the cupboard, shamelessly hoping he would reach out for her, and thrilling ecstatically when he had done just that. She had turned to face him while his arms had still been around her waist, her eyes closed tightly, her heart pounding so hard when he kissed her that she had thought she might have been about to faint and spoil everything.

She wondered now if it might have been easier if he really had left while she was still asleep, or was assumed to be still asleep. If their next verbal exchange had been on the telephone there would have been more time for them both to come to terms with what had happened. But then on balance she decided it was probably better this way. And the important things that needed saying needed saying soon: she was still a fraction uncertain.

In truth she had been awake for some time before she had got up quietly ahead of him. She knew he wanted to leave well before eight. He had said as much the night before—after they had made love the first time, and not very competently.

'I'm quite used to going without breakfast,' he said as she passed him the coffee cup. 'I mean . . . I often don't make it at home. Just coffee, perhaps. Instant, of course, not the real thing like this. Anything more seems unnecessary when you're alone,' he added, his voice a little sad and toneless.

'Oh, my dear, I know exactly what you mean,' she responded with feeling. Her hand reached out for his involuntarily. At the same moment their knees collided under the table, unintentionally and with no finesse, before separating again as if repelled by electric shock, and coming together

once more, gently this time, as the two moved forward on
the seat to make the contact firm.

Now their eyes met too, their gazes frank and unfaltering,
for the first time in full light since they had lain together
in the blessed and uninhibiting near-darkness of her room.

'I'm sorry . . .'

'I'm sorry . . .'

They blurted out the same phrase in unison, with the
same predictable apologies pending—the regrets of new,
middle-aged lovers for imperfections and appearing
gaucheries that didn't matter a scrap and which certainly
needed neither explaining nor forgiving.

'There's nothing for you to be sorry about, Joyce,' he
came back quickly. 'You were marvellous. Quite wonderful.
I'm not very practised at . . . at that sort of thing. Making
love. Not lately. Not to speak of. Well, not at all, really.'
He drew in a breath sharply through his open mouth, and
leaned forward earnestly. 'And please don't misunderstand.
I know you're the same. I'm sure you are. It's just that
men are more expected to . . . well, as you said at dinner.
But I'm not like that. Since Olivia died there hasn't been
anyone.'

'Nor for me either, not since Ray . . . deserted me,' she
responded quietly.

He smiled down at her hands. He was clasping them
both on the table between his, cornflakes, orange juice and
the rest temporarily abandoned. 'Except in my case, I've
been simply longing for you. Last night I'd wanted so much
to tell you how I felt. All evening. I'd even been practising
all day.' He looked up with a pathetic sort of innocence in
his eyes as he added: 'And the chance seemed to have been
lost. Until—'

'On the landing?' she interrupted.

'Yes.' Their gazes had locked in mutual, unabashed com-
prehension. 'I don't know what gave me the courage even

then. You realize I've adored you from afar for . . . oh, I don't know how long?'

'Oh, Ian, I'd no idea. Was it since Ray and I parted? Or before that, perhaps?' she completed, too keenly, too searchingly, unable to keep a spurned woman's bitter hope out of her voice, and wanting so much an affirmative answer to the last question.

He swallowed. 'I'm afraid so, yes. To me you offered everything a man could want in a wife, and Ray never seemed to appreciate you. You're so lovely. Yes, you are.' He overrode her signalled protests. 'So kind and . . . and intelligent. So good to be with.'

Delighted, Joyce continued to shake her head in a modest disclaimer of all the virtues just listed. 'And if only you'd known how I've felt about you, my dear.' What she really meant was that if only he'd had the common sense to realize why she had been coming so often to his office to discuss trivialities affecting her tax return or her share portfolio— things that could easily have been settled on the telephone or by letter—the two of them could have been enjoying the delights of a conjugal relationship long before this.

Of course, Ian Crayborn had hardly figured at all in Joyce's consciousness before Ray had up and left her. Nor had Ian given her an inkling that he cared for her since then, not until now, not really, or she must have noticed it: she wasn't stupid. She supposed it was all because he was so shy. That much accepted, she was ready, indeed anxious, to believe that he had desired her even while she was still married. And thank God there was still ample time to make up for his backwardness.

'You do want to marry me, Ian?' There, she'd said it. It was what she had to have confirmed in the light of day, or at least in the gentle but adequate illumination from the Heal's double candle-lamp wall bracket above the table. 'You didn't ask me . . . well . . . in the heat of the moment?' Her breasts heaved deeply and effectively in a gesture implying that if he had merely been taking advantage of her she would regretfully if tearfully release him from all obligation. 'Because if it was only that you felt you had to,' she continued, 'after . . . after what happened, I think I'd understand. Even though I love you so much,' she ended, as delicately as she could, and wishing she could be quite certain of his answer.

'Oh, but Joyce, I love you too. And of course I want to marry you. More than anything else in the world. That's if you're sure you want me?'

'Of course I'm sure.'

He half stood up, leaned awkwardly across the table, pulled off his glasses, then, with two fingers in the butter dish, kissed her warmly on the lips. 'That's it then,' he said loudly, sitting down again with a bump, flushed and jubilant.

'So when shall we make the announcement?' she asked. 'Today?' Because the least hint of hesitancy crossed his face she was immediately sorry she had put the question. 'Well, it doesn't have to be so soon, of course,' she added quickly. 'If you want, we—'

'Tonight,' he put in with matching promptness and huge enthusiasm. 'There's a party at Hugon Road. That'll be the perfect place.' Quite perfect, he repeated to himself inwardly with uncommon satisfaction.

CHAPTER 7

'Are you sure now? You don't have to come. Really you don't. It's not too late to change your mind. I'm only going out of duty,' said Mark Treasure to his wife Molly, better known as the actress Margaret Forbes, as they emerged on to the street that evening.

Henry Pink, Treasure's chauffeur, was holding open a

rear door of the Rolls-Royce outside their home in Chelsea's Cheyne Walk. It was crisply cold and cloudless, with a full moon and plenty of stars.

'Of course I'm sure. I told you, going to a match at Hugon Road is something I've always meant to do.' Molly was responding outwardly with enthusiasm, while inwardly feeling stoic and just a touch worthy—like a Member of Parliament who's volunteered to spend a winter's night sleeping in the open in a cardboard box. 'Thank you, Henry,' she said as she got into the car, looking sportive in a sheepskin coat and leather boots, her head enveloped in a colourful silk scarf.

Molly had the first half of the week off. The play she was appearing in at the Royal National Theatre was out of the repertory until the following night. There were other things she would have enjoyed more than going to a football match, but only if her husband could have joined her. They were two busy people with separate professional lives who spent time together whenever they could. This often involved some sacrifice on the part of one of them.

'Do you remember,' Molly went on, as Treasure got in at the other side of the car, 'Berty Grenwood asked us both to the opening of the new grandstand? I couldn't go. I was on tour with something. I promised him I'd make up for it. So this is my chance.'

'They opened that stand four years ago.'

'Well, better late than never,' Molly responded with schoolgirl asperity. 'And it is your debut as chairman elect.'

'Not quite elect. I'm not even on the Eel Bridge Rovers board yet. That'll happen on Saturday.'

Henry Pink started the engine and moved the car off in the direction of nearby Albert Bridge, nosing into the rush-hour traffic which was still heavy on the Embankment.

'So Ray Bims will still be chairman tonight?' Molly asked.

'Unless Berty's persuaded him to resign already. They were having lunch today.'

'You haven't spoken to Berty since?'

'No. He didn't come back to the bank. I should have called him at home, I suppose. Too late now.' Treasure had glanced down at the telephone under the armrest.

Molly unbuttoned her coat before doing up the seat-belt. 'D'you think I'm suitably dressed? Not too glam?' Under the coat she was wearing a red woollen sweater and matching skirt.

'Exactly right, I'd say. We probably shan't need coats. I imagine we'll be watching the match from the chairman's box. It's glassed in.'

'Oh. Pity. I think I'd rather be in the open.' Being cosseted in a heated glass box wasn't Molly's idea of how to be a spectator at an outdoor sports event. She re-tied the scarf under her chin. 'This is what I wore when we went to Twickenham. To the varsity match.'

'That's Rugby, not soccer,' he corrected absently.

'I know that, darling.' The nostrils of her aquiline nose narrowed momentarily before she insisted, 'But one dresses more or less the same for both, doesn't one?'

'These days people don't dress up for either, really. Not in the sense you mean.' He was also wearing a sheepskin coat. 'Maybe soccer followers are an earthier lot. Don't know about the ladies. Anyway, you'll do.' He squeezed her hand.

'We could have been earthier if I'd driven us in my Austin Metro.'

Treasure shook his head. 'Except there'll be quite a lot of irresistible booze involved tonight. And we've a reserved place in the directors' car park.'

'Meaning my Metro's not distinguished enough for a reserved place there?'

'Bit *recherché* perhaps.' He grinned. 'In a way I'm supposed to be putting on a show.'

'Of opulence?'

'Certainly not.' He paused. 'Well, of moderate success, perhaps. They want me to promote all round confidence.' He looked about him a touch covertly, as though undecided whether the car and its leather and walnut interior might be overdoing the objectives. 'Anyway,' he added, with renewed assurance, 'apart from our being free to drink, Henry wants to see the match too, don't you, Henry?'

'That's right, sir,' Pink replied from in front. 'Good little team, the Eels used to be. Not doing so well at the moment, of course. They should beat Hereford in this cup match tonight, though.' Hereford was in the Third Division.

'You're an Eels supporter, Henry?' asked Molly.

'That's what I always tell Lord Grenwood, madam. It's why he gives me free tickets.' The enigmatic reply was accompanied by as near a chuckle as the sober Pink was given to uttering while on duty.

Molly watched a launch on the river that was making faster progress towards Battersea Bridge than they were. 'Ray Bims is a strange man,' she said to her husband reflectively. 'Flamboyant. Quite a lot of women find him attractive.'

'You don't?'

'Don't think so. Too pushy. Too full of himself.'

'Which suggests that's what a lot of women like in a man. Commanding personality.'

Molly sniffed to register disagreement.

'He got his knighthood for outstanding business enterprise, of course,' Treasure went on. 'From a Prime Minister who was fairly keen on rewarding that sort of initiative.'

'Well, I think it was overdone in Bim's case,' said his wife.

'Perhaps. But in fairness you hardly know him.'

'I knew Joyce Bims quite well. His first wife. We were both on the local Save the Children Fund committee. Nice woman. Earnest, rather. Too good for him, probably. I went to their house in . . . somewhere in Chelsea? Off the King's Road?'

'Mulberry Grove,' Treasure supplied. 'He still lives there. With his second wife, Gloria. She comes from a polished background, but her family had fallen on hard times. She's quite a looker and was once a model.'

'Who became a fashion designer.' Molly's eyes had narrowed as she searched her memory. 'You're very well informed about her?'

'Thanks to Berty Grenwood. He rather likes her.'

'Will she be here tonight?'

'Berty thinks it's possible. Laid on by her husband for public relations reasons.'

'I think Joyce Bims went to live near Guildford. That's where their roots were. Where he started his business.' Molly crossed her legs and straightened the coat over her knees. 'Is he really into drug trafficking? As seriously as the papers say?'

Treasure shrugged. 'There's no doubt the BNMR, the bank he's involved in, is crooked. That's according to the American authorities. It's been laundering money from drug operations on a quite massive scale, and doing very little else. The people behind it are drug barons, pure and simple. Of course, Bims is denying all knowledge.'

'Could that be right, though? I mean, could the bank have been up to no good without his knowing?'

'It's hardly possible. Anyhow, he's playing the innocent. It wouldn't surprise me if for that reason he resists giving up the chairmanship of the Eels.'

'Because to resign from anything would look like an admission of guilt? Because it'd damage confidence?'

'Something like that, yes. On the other hand, if he's as strapped for cash as we think, he'll probably need to accept Berty's offer to buy back the club. It's pretty generous.'

Molly fingered a button of her coat. 'They say he can't be put on trial here? For what the bank's been doing?'

'That's because the BNMR's never been registered in this country. Never traded here.'

'BNMR. Sounds like the name of an old-fashioned railway company,' Molly commented, hesitated and then went on: 'But it's a Cayman Islands bank, and the Caymans are a British colony, so surely they could make him—'

'No, it's a British dependency,' Treasure interrupted. 'There's a difference. If it were just a colony they could probably arrange to try one of the bank's directors here in the UK. If they thought they had enough evidence, that is.'

'But not in the case of a dependency?'

Treasure nodded. 'Curiously enough. Because a dependency is actually more independent than a colony. The Caymans run their own show with their own constitution. Their banks report locally to someone called a Regulator, but he doesn't come under the control of the Bank of England. Except the Bank of England has a copy of his latest report on the BNMR. Berty's seen it.'

'And it says they're crooks?'

'Without doubt.'

'*The Times* says there can still be a trial in America.'

'In Florida, yes. The BNMR has a branch in Miami. Trouble is, none of their directors lives in the United States. So there's no one of substance to stand trial there.'

'What about the person in charge of the Miami branch?'

'He was only a salaried employee. He'd have been better than nothing, perhaps, but he was conveniently abroad when the Federal authorities struck this week and froze the assets. They think he was tipped off. He's in Haiti now and likely to stay there, one imagines. The only people in custody so far are even smaller fry.'

'So why don't they arrest the directors who live in the Caymans? Put them on trial there?'

'Same reason as before. Because the authorities can't find any. Only proxy directors. Couple of local retired chaps who were paid pittances to stand in for main board members when needed by local law. To make a quorum at the AGM, that kind of thing. It was a ruse to get by legal regulations. Meant that the proper directors hardly had to be around at all. The trick should have been twigged earlier but wasn't. Chiefly because the bank itself wasn't suspected of doing anything dishonest. Quite the contrary. It's been regarded almost as a super international charity. Even at the United Nations.'

'And what about the other branches? In other countries? Have they all had their assets frozen?'

'The European ones immediately. Same in Pakistan, Indonesia, Chad, and . . . and some other African republics. The Colombian government says it's closed the Bogotá branch. Libya's made the same sort of noises but the branch there is still functioning. Or was earlier today.'

'Shouldn't the freezing have been simultaneous everywhere?'

'It's certainly what the Cayman authorities wanted. But this is a bank that operates in some pretty unsophisticated areas.'

'Because it was dedicated to helping Third World countries?' Molly looked puzzled. 'So have any proper directors of the bank been arrested anywhere?' she questioned.

Treasure drummed his fingers on both armrests. 'Nowhere. And always for the same reason. They're never domiciled in the right countries. Proves how adept the bank has been at secretly breaking laws.'

'So the powerful people haven't been touched?'

'Not so far.'

'But it's known who they are? The names of the directors on the main board were in the paper yesterday.'

'Yes, Bims, and a Swiss, a Saudi Arabian, and an Australian. They're all shareholders too. They'll just need to avoid going to countries where they could risk being arrested.'

'Which could be no more than inconvenient for them,' said Molly hotly.

'Of course, those four may not be the real bosses,' said Treasure. 'They may just be front men. Most of the BNMR shares are in the names of nominees.'

'That's other banks acting for customers?'

'Yes. It hasn't been revealed who the nominees represent, and very possibly it never will be.'

'But surely that—'

'Isn't illegal,' Treasure put in. 'In many cases it'd take a ruling by an international court to make it so, and that's a slow process.'

'Well, if Ray Bims is one of the top dogs I'm glad he's been exposed.'

Treasure puffed out his cheeks. 'I still wonder how he found the money at the time to be even a bit player. The bank was founded eighteen months ago. A lot of his other deals had turned to ashes by then.'

'But if the real money was coming from drug trading, money that needed laundering, why did he need to put up any of his own?'

'Because that would have been the time when the source of funds would have been checked. By the Cayman authorities. It seems Bims managed to put up two and a half million pounds, and it was clean. Traceably so. He may have borrowed it.'

'And that's why they would have wanted him on the board? For his squeaky clean two million?'

'No. His name would have been of equal importance. It added British respectability to the enterprise.'

'His knighthood, you mean?'

'Yes. That would carry confidence in the Caymans.' Treasure nodded towards the window. 'Look, we're nearly there. Welcome to Eel Bridge Stadium.'

Pink had just turned the car right off Wandsworth Bridge Road. Ahead of them the gantry lights of the stadium were illuminating the whole area, silhouetting the ridges of the grandstands against the night sky.

'It's not all that busy,' said Molly in a surprised voice, as the Rolls approached the entrance at reduced speed, avoiding jay-walking pedestrians and darting programme vendors. She had expected huge crowds, not just the trickle of cars and the scattering of intended spectators they could see through the windscreen.

Pink lowered the driver's window and showed their car park pass to a white-coated official. The man waved the car through after volunteering some directions about parking. The concourse was more crowded than the road outside, and enlivened by brightly lit fast food and ice-cream stands near the bank of ticket turnstiles to the far left.

'It's early yet, madam,' said Pink, moving the car more slowly now and making for the underground park in the south stand straight ahead. 'They should get a gate of about three thousand. That's average for a week night, with the visiting team not highly rated.'

'I'd have thought they'd have got that many just to see the newsworthy and notorious Sir Ray Bims,' Molly offered as they progressed over the concourse. 'Good enough numbers for a lynch mob, though,' she added roundly. 'You know, there are probably a lot of respectable people who'd be ready to string him up for what he's done. Drug peddling really is the bottoms.'

CHAPTER 8

'Do get yourselves drinks at the bar. It's over there. The barman will take your coats too. You won't need them,' said Gloria, the second Lady Bims, in a lazy, high-pitched, socialite drawl. Her 'over there', in top register, had emerged as 'owa thah' and 'won't need them' as a slurred and under-consonanted 'woe-nee um'. She smiled from Treasure to his wife, then back again quite quickly. 'So good to meet you both. Sorry, I've no idea where my husband is. Had to get here on my own, of course.' The final syllable had been strained through tightly compressed lips and made to sound like 'hawss'.

'Ray's somewhere in the stadium,' the lady continued, pausing only to take breath. 'Adores wandering about on match nights, seeing things are all right. He's totally devoted to the Eels. But totally.' She inhaled deeply on a cigarette, and gave her frizzy blonde hair a short, irritated shake as if she was ridding it of something undesirable. 'He's like a conscientious head waiter, really. And he gets waylaid.That's why I've been left here alone to cope with all comers.' The thin expressive hands fluttered to indicate how indulgent she was before she added: 'They say he usually ends up with the team in the dressing-room. He gets on so well with the players, you see. It's the common touch, I suppose.' The final comment implied less downright approval than it did a begrudging tolerance.

Aged about thirty, Gloria Bims was tall and willowy, with long shapely legs encased in glittering gold lurex tights. The legs looked even longer and shapelier below the minuscule, dark blue skirt—of a brevity that members of the judiciary have been heard to call intentionally provocative. Above this she was wearing a bejewelled gold blouse —mostly halter neck and divided front, with not much to suggest that it had either sides or a back. While the wearer had no cleavage to speak of, the blouse, split to the waist, exhibited an unconventional amount of bare white flesh when her body was still, and coy glimpses of her underdeveloped breasts when she moved—and she was moving most of the time. The ensemble was completed by dangling golden earrings and a loosely worn serape in shimmering blue and gold. Made from a stiffish material, the serape just might have been intended to provide a decorous wrap for the top of the pliant body, a function it was singularly failing to perform at the moment.

The lady's face, professionally made up, was not beautiful in the classic way. The forehead was a little too wide,
the nose too pronounced, and the mouth a touch too small.
But on first acquaintance, most men would still have been
too engaged by Gloria Bims's challenging blue eyes, by her
figure, and, as now, by the way she dressed for them to be
much aware of minor shortcomings in her facial structure.

This was certainly true in Treasure's case.

'I gather you're expecting three thousand spectators,'
he said with what observant Molly gauged as an over-
ingratiating smile.

'Oh, I'm sure we'll get at least that many,' Lady Bims
declared confidently, sharply altering her profile, smooth-
ing her left thigh, and eyeing herself briefly as though it
might have been her body that the three thousand were all
coming to see.

'With about half of them in here already,' Molly offered
flatly, and still from the depths of her sheepskin coat.

The three were standing just inside the chairman's suite,
where Lady Bims had been waiting to receive guests.
Beyond, the room seemed quite full, though not as full as
Molly was suggesting. Because of the low ceiling, the conversation noise level seemed uncomfortably high.

'It's not quite as awful as it looks or sounds,' Lady Bims
went on. 'People bunch near the door and the bar.' Crossing
her hands, she rearranged the serape. 'Anyway, most of them
will have to leave soon to get to their seats before the kick-*off*.
We'll have a better chance to talk then,' she continued.
'Unless you're going to be riveted by the game.' She seemed
now to be addressing Treasure exclusively. 'I gather Ray
always declares open house in here first. On party nights.
You do know there's a party afterwards? For the official Supporters Club? Bit of a drag, but they're another bunch who
absolutely adore Ray. The party's not in here, thank God. In
the banqueting room on the next floor. Do stay.' She took
another fierce draw on the cigarette. 'And I've just

remembered, Berty Grenwood was asking for you when he came. I think he's on the terrace. That's the glassed-in bit.' The long fingers gave a directional wave.

'See you later, then,' said Treasure, following his wife towards the bar. The hostess turned to greet some new arrivals, but her gaze had lingered on him for an extra moment.

'D'you suppose she's hoping to be booked for a summer carnival? Or a Christmas panto?' asked Molly softly, as they moved through the crush. 'And I hope the game's more riveting than Lady Bims's boobs. If it's not, I suspect we'll both want to go home early,' she added pointedly.

'She's a dress designer, after all,' said Treasure. 'Blue and gold are the Eels' colours.'

Molly looked back in mock surprise. 'You mean she's playing in the team too?'

'Oh, very droll. I'm sure she's dressed like that to show loyalty.'

'Having nothing much else left to show.'

'What she's wearing is no more bizarre than some of the crazy new fashions you see in the papers. By . . . by some of those far out couturiers,' he completed defensively.

'But you wouldn't be so approving if I went out dressed like that. Good evening. Good evening.' The actress had raised her voice and was nodding her head and smiling acknowledgements at the people, mostly men, who had recognized her and were making way for her. 'Anyway, you were dead right when you said some people hardly put anything on for soccer,' she added, again over her shoulder. 'Ah, I can see Berty now. He's got Andras Linkina with him. Over there, by themselves. I'll join them. Be an angel and get me a gin and tonic, will you? Unless there's champagne. And get rid of this coat?' She pulled off the sheepskin and handed it to Treasure.

The two elderly men were seated in the otherwise empty glassed-in gallery, at the end furthest from the bar. They got up and greeted Molly with enthusiasm and a great deal of old-fashioned courtesy. The Polish pianist, who was nearly as short as Berty, had a bull-like figure, a shock of long white hair, and a rugged, weatherbeaten face, save only for his thin-lipped, sensitive mouth. He had kissed Molly's hand before embracing her. Not for the first time she noticed that the fingers on his own hands were quite stubby, not at all the popular conception of what a pianist's fingers ought to be. She was also troubled to see a large piece of fresh sticking plaster on one of his lower knuckles.

'You've hurt your hand, Andras?'

He shrugged. 'Is nothing,' he replied, the voice rich and deep, the words heavily accented.

'It won't affect—'

'My playing?' He interrupted with a guffaw. 'Only maybe that I leave out two more notes in the Mozart I'm playing on Saturday. At my age, I am forgetting more notes than I play anyway. Is good to have an extra excuse.' But he had put his other hand over the plaster.

'And this is where we watch the match?' said Molly, moving to the front of the two-tiered gallery beyond the rows of armchairs. 'Well, it gives a splendid view of the pitch. Dead centre too. But shall we hear anything through the glass?'

'Yes. Through internal speakers. When they're switched on,' Berty Grenwood provided in a half-apologetic tone. 'It's not quite the same as being outside, of course.'

'Not at all the same. Applause by arrangement only? Pah,' commented the pianist loudly, bending his head to one side and turning up both his hands in a gesture of incredulity. 'I am telling Berty it's not going to work when we built the stand. All the other grand boxes are the same. Ray Bims likes it that way. Means he can arrange to hear his own voice when he wants,' the speaker added in a no less strident tone. 'Ah, and here, Molly, is your most distinguished husband.'

Treasure had appeared bearing glasses. He greeted the two men while handing his wife a glass of champagne. 'You saw Bims at lunch?' he asked Berty.

'Yes. And I had Ian Crayborn join us.' Berty sighed as though to imply that the effort involved hadn't been justified.

'There was no deal,' said Linkina. 'Of course, Bims is crazy.'

'He won't sell back the club?' Treasure took a sip of his whisky.

'No, he won't,' said Berty, shaking his head. 'Wants to stay as owner and chairman. And he's still dead against Andras's idea of selling up here and moving the Eels to Cherton. Insists Harden, the manager, is supporting him over that too.' The old man frowned into the glass of mineral water in his hand. 'I doubt that's true, incidentally. You see Bims's wife is here?' He looked up at this, his expression softening. 'Regular bobby-dazzler. Nice woman too. Intelligent. Can't imagine what she sees in him.'

'Berty asked her why she was dressed like Superwoman,' put in Linkina, stretching his arms out to the side and leaning his body forwards to simulate flight.

'She can take a joke,' Berty insisted. There seemed to be no end to his high opinion of the lady.

'She's dressed for the party afterwards,' put in Molly, with more charity than had coloured her earlier comments about Gloria Bims's appearance. 'If I'd known it was that kind of party I'd have worn—'

'Gracious lady, is not really that kind of party,' Linkina interrupted firmly. 'And you are better dressed for it than she is in any case. And now your husband is here I can say you are very much more . . . more fetching too.'

'Andras, if you meant sexier, it's not true, but you're a darling.' Molly leaned forward and kissed him on the cheek.

'I second what Andras said,' said Berty.

'Then you get kissed too,' said Molly, embracing him as

well, 'except I think you're playing the field, Berty. I believe you're secretly in love with Gloria Bims. Tell me, does she normally come here?'

'No.' It was Linkina who replied. 'Tonight we think she's been told to put on a show of solidarity. Bims is usually inviting too many guests to the supporters' party after the match. Some are in here already. Many journalists. He's desperate to earn good opinions from the media. Some hope. Pah!'

'The directors can vote him out of the chair, of course,' said Treasure, reverting to the subject of the earlier discussion.

'But not off the board,' countered Berty. 'And he's no intention of parting with his shares. Nor even of calling in some money he's lent to the club. Not very much money, as it happens, so it may be an empty sort of gesture. Odd, though. I still can't understand why he turned my offer down, out of hand.' He scratched at what looked like an ancient egg stain on the even more ancient sporting club tie he had on.

'We think his selling the Eels would imply guilt over the other business,' said Treasure, repeating Molly's theory. 'Confirming that he's gone bust trying to recoup his fortune illegally. To avoid that, he needs to appear solvent at least. He may even be planning to go to Florida. To go before that Grand Jury.'

'I do not believe he will risk such a thing,' said Linkina.

'Where is he anyway?' asked Molly.

Berty shrugged. 'Nobody knows. Andras and I were looking after the chairman of the visiting club until a moment ago. That's something Bims should have been doing as chairman of the Eels. He'll need to explain his absence when he does turn up.' The speaker looked down sternly at the floor as if he were expecting Bims to appear through it and give an account of himself.

'Where's the visiting chairman now?' asked Treasure.

'Spotted someone he knew over at the bar, just as you came in,' Berty explained. 'He'll be back here to watch the game, I expect. Like Bims, one assumes. Not good enough, though. Ah, here's someone who may know what's happened to him,' he added, his expression brightening.

A worried-looking Felix Harden had emerged through the crush in the main part of the room and was hurrying forward between the rows of empty chairs. He was dressed in his tracksuit. ''Evening, Lord Grenwood. 'Evening, Mr Linkina,' he said, then nodded deferentially to both the Treasures as Berty briefly introduced them. 'Sorry to interrupt,' he went on, 'but have you seen Sir Ray?'

'No. We hoped you might have,' Berty responded. 'So he isn't with the team?'

'No, I've come straight from the dressing-room, sir. No one's seen him since he drove back after lunch. I've got to talk to him before the kick-off. It's important.'

'Are you playing Bodworski?' asked Berty.

The manager's look of concern deepened. 'Did you know Sir Ray's ordered me not to, sir?'

'Mr Linkina told me so, yes.'

'You know they're saying there was also something on the radio this afternoon about Bodworski being dropped?' Linkina himself added.

'Yes, sir. On the sports news,' said Harden. 'Well, I've decided to play him. Because we need him.' He glanced meaningfully at Linkina. 'But I reckoned I had to tell Sir Ray. Not to look underhand about it, see? But I haven't been able to reach him. And now Bodworski hasn't shown up. Not yet anyway, and it's past the squad's reporting time.'

'D'you think Bims could have told him to stay away?' asked Linkina, scowling while pushing a hand through his mane of hair.

'Oh, that's inconceivable,' protested Berty. 'Even Ray Bims wouldn't exceed his authority in that way. Or would he?' He looked around at the others. 'Dammit, Mr Harden here is our manager. He's the one who chooses the team.' The speaker's shoulders moved up and down several times, showing his irritation. 'Look here, Harden,' he continued, after blowing out breath, 'you must play Bodworski, and if you have trouble later with Sir Ray, tell him . . . tell him I approved your action.'

'And that I did too,' put in Linkina. 'And here's another director who'll support us. Good evening, Ian. You are coming at a very good time. And Joyce, I am pleased to see you again,' he added, except he could scarcely disguise his surprise at the presence of the first Lady Bims who was on Crayborn's arm. 'Do you know Mark Treasure and his wife, the famous Margaret Forbes?'

While Crayborn looked inordinately pleased with himself during the following introductions, this was in sharp contrast to the demeanour of his companion, who was distinctly uneasy.

As the result of what for her had inevitably been an agonized decision, Joyce Bims had arrived overdressed in her full-length mink coat, a prized possession she had to this point refused to part with, despite the heat in the room. She feared, in such a mêlée, either that the garment would be damaged or that she would never see it again. Further, while she had actually been looking forward to seeing her ex-husband on the occasion when her engagement to Crayborn was to be announced, she had definitely not expected to be confronted at the door by Gloria Bims, who Crayborn had assured her never came near Hugon Road.

'Joyce, we haven't met since we were both on that charity committee in Chelsea,' said Molly Treasure, who had been quick to notice the other woman's discomfort. 'Come and look at this fabulous view,' she went on, drawing her away towards the front of the box.

'No, I haven't seen Ray since we came back from lunch.' Crayborn was answering Berty Grenwood's question after

Harden had excused himself and left. 'I'd left my car here, and he gave me a lift. I went straight back to my office afterwards. He said he had some work to do up here. I assumed he meant to stay right through till match time. Or, I suppose, till people arrived for this.'

'Was he any more forthcoming than he was at lunch? Over why he's so against my offer?' Berty pressed.

'No,' said the accountant, 'and what I find incredible is the way he virtually ignores the rub-off from this Cayman Island débâcle. It's pretty major, after all.'

'You didn't discuss it at all at lunch?' asked Treasure.

'Not then, nor on the way back here in his car,' Crayborn replied. 'Naturally it was hardly a subject one felt one could easily introduce. It was up to him to do that, and he didn't. Isn't that right, Berty?'

Lord Grenwood nodded glumly as if he regretted not having taken the initiative all the same. 'Nor did he say anything about dropping players,' he grumbled.

'Yes, Ian, did he tell you in the car he'd ordered Harden to put Bodworski on the transfer list? Ordered him,' Linkina put in.

'Certainly not. That's a pretty arrogant thing to do, isn't it, even by Ray's standards?'

'And he's forbidden Harden to let Bodworski play tonight,' Berty added hotly. 'Andras and I have just rescinded that . . . that request. You'll support us, won't you?'

'Sure,' said Crayborn. His hesitation in answering the question had been momentary only, but Treasure at least had marked it. It went through his mind that perhaps the speaker had more reason than the others to stay on the right side of Bims. 'Ray must be mad to want to get rid of Bodworski,' the accountant continued more boldly. 'Apart from anything else, he'll not fetch anything like what we paid for him, will he? Not after such a short stay.'

'Except it was Ray Bims, not us, who did the paying in the first place,' Berty offered.

No one spoke for a moment, then an embarrassed Linkina put in: 'I'm sorry, Mark, to you we must look like a very spineless lot. Dominated by a bully, and by all accounts a criminal bully.' The rugged Pole looked about him defiantly, and not, it seemed, because he feared being overheard but more because he wanted to be.

'Not at all,' Treasure replied. 'I understand your position. You've tried to handle things in a gentlemanly way. To save Bims's feelings. It just hasn't worked.' He shrugged.

'Precisely,' said Linkina. 'So now we take the gloves off. At the directors' meeting on Saturday. Or before that, perhaps. Meantime, Mark, please do not desert us. We all believe you'll be the perfect chairman. To put things right after what may perhaps be—'

'A bloody great bust-up,' Treasure interrupted with a grin. 'If Bims remains as obdurate about vacating the chair as he's been so far. And quite how you get him to give up ownership of the club, I'm not clear yet.'

'Hm, I'm not without the funds to affect that,' said Berty Grenwood, the chairman and principal shareholder of the largest surviving private merchant bank in Britain.

'You think money will do it?' questioned Crayborn. 'That you simply weren't offering the right price today?'

'Sadly, in my long experience, enough money seems to do most things in the end,' Berty replied dolefully, as if the truth he was expounding was cause for regret rather than solace in someone whose resources were, to say the least, formidable.

'Yes, but in this case there are other avenues we should explore too,' cautioned Treasure, who was used latterly to protecting his aged employer against an increasing inclination to solve problems by hurling money at them.

'Is there a loo in here?' Molly demanded from behind

Crayborn. She was rejoining the others with Joyce Bims in
tow, fur coat now draped over one arm.

'Through the only door in the far wall. Leads to a dressing-room and bathroom beyond,' said Berty. 'Bit of a battle
to get to it at the moment, I'm afraid.'

'No, that's no good. It's locked,' said Joyce. 'I . . . I tried
it when we came in,' she went on, somewhat abashed at
having to own that her need had been of such long standing.

'Ah, that was probably to protect it from the mob,' Berty
offered knowingly, tapping the side of his nose with his
index finger. 'Used to lock it myself on occasions like this.
When I was chairman, that is. No doubt Ray Bims will . . .
no, he won't, he's not here.' Then the old man's perplexed
expression changed to one of sudden enlightenment. 'D'you
know, I believe I still have the key on me. Always keep
useful keys. Well, you never know, do you?' He produced
a keyring from his pocket, held it up a foot or so from his
face, and fingered through its contents carefully. 'Yes,
here's the fellah. The gold-coloured one. Remember it well.
Take it, dear ladies,' he completed, trying now without
success to detach the key from the ring. 'Oh, take the whole
thing.'

'Thank you, Berty,' said Molly, promptly, accepting the
offer and heading into the assembled mass, with Joyce
anxiously moving close behind her.

The two women reached the dressing-room door more
easily than might have been expected, once more because
her celebrity and determination combined to make Molly
a formidable crowd parter.

She had just put the key in the lock when a male voice
erupted joyfully close by: 'Molly, how marvellous to see
you. And looking so absolutely ravishing.'

'Timothy.' She turned about and responded with genuine
pleasure to the personable author friend who had broken
away from a group of other men and was now embracing
her warmly. 'I enjoyed your new book. The biography,'

she went on. 'You must tell me how it's doing. Have you met . . . ?' she turned again to introduce Joyce, except that the lady had already disappeared through the dressing-room door with an unstoppable sense of purpose that, it seemed, would have remained so even if it had been the Prince of Wales who had been waiting to make her acquaintance. Molly lifted her eyebrows, smiled and continued: 'Your reviews in the Sundays were splendid. And I heard the Radio 4 interview. Was there anything on television because—'

The high-pitched cry that stopped the actress in mid-sentence was muffled but still highly audible. It had evidently emanated from beyond the door that her erstwhile companion had just closed behind her. As Molly turned, the door reopened and a somehow crushed-looking Joyce Bims staggered backwards through it, one hand feeling the way behind her, the other dragging her precious mink coat along the floor. Her eyes were bulging, her expression frightened and incredulous.

'Joyce, whatever's happened?' Molly took the other's shoulders firmly from behind and drew her back into the room.

'It's Ray. In there. He's . . . he's . . . Oh dear, it's awful . . . terrible.'

At a questioning nod from Molly, her author friend hurried past the stricken woman and into the dressing-room, closing the door behind him.

'Has Ray had an accident? Should we get a doctor?' Molly asked Joyce gently.

The other woman shook her head from side to side. 'I don't think it'd be any . . . He's so cold.' She began to cry. 'I mean, I think he's dead. His shape,' she uttered between sobs. 'You can't believe his shape.'

CHAPTER 9

Eel Bridge Rovers has one of the fanciest dressing-room complexes in British football, on the ground floor under the south stand. The main door opens on to a large lounge area. Beyond this there are two facing rows of double-fronted lockers set well apart with padded benches running between. Further along are the showers and loos, and on the other side of those the exercise and treatment areas. A side door opens off this far end into the corridor leading to the pitch.

Now, shortly before match-time, most players were changed ready for play. Some were getting injury bandages or elastic supports checked or renewed, others were loosening up on exercise machines, and a few were watching a soap opera on the television set in the lounge. There were not many left who were still changing.

'You were very nearly late again, Gareth,' said Jeff Ribarts, coming up to Trisall who was standing on the carpet in front of his dressing-room locker.

'Well, "very nearly" is still good enough, isn't it? You're not going to frigging fine me for a frigging "very nearly", are you, boyo? Or are you?' the Welshman responded belligerently. He had been undressing, and was wearing only underpants. Now he pulled those off as well, turning his back on the Eels' assistant manager in a movement intended to show contempt—and succeeding in that.

Naked, Trisall looked like a Greek god, as virile and physically dynamic as Ribarts had once been himself, before asthma and other afflictions overtook him—though he would have denied that he had ever been arrogant like Trisall.

'I didn't say anything about fining, Gareth. Only if I tell the Gaff you never get here before—'

'Stuff it, Jeff.' The rugged Welshman turned about, closing some of the three-foot space that separated them. 'Nobody's moaning about the way I'm playing, are they? Not the Gaff, not you, not Malc Dirn, not anybody?'

'No, they're not. Except—'

'Right, then,' the player interrupted again, stabbing a finger towards Ribarts's breastbone. 'When they do, you'll be entitled to complain about something that matters, won't you? But not till then. OK?'

Trisall stepped back again and for a few seconds limbered up on the spot, like a boxer—flexing limbs and rippling muscles, shadow sparring towards the other man's head with open palms, but smiling with it. Ribarts's resentful eyes were nearly as good as a mirror to someone with a narcissistic streak.

'Been drinking, have you, Gareth?' Ribarts inquired, stony-faced. 'Is that why you're so bolshie?'

Trisall stopped the sparring and looked momentarily abashed before rallying with: ''Course I haven't been drinking. What you bloody take me for, a frigging idiot?'

Taking alcohol before a match was strictly against club rules, and transgressors could be fined heavily or even suspended. Ribarts's question had been prompted by annoyance and hunch, not genuine suspicion—except Trisall really had been drinking. The player realized he might have got close enough to the other man for him to have smelt his breath.

'Lay off him, Jeff. I can vouch he hasn't been boozing,' called Jimmy Atler, who was changed already under his tracksuit, but who had gone back to his own locker opposite Trisall's. He was looking at the other player as he added: 'Gareth's been with me at my flat ever since we left here this afternoon.'

'That's right.' The Welshman took up the point quickly.

'Sorry, Jeff. I'm a bit tense, that's all. We all are,' he said, hurrying now to get into his playing gear. 'With Stan Bodworski gone missing, well . . . Hereford aren't going to be a pushover tonight, are they?'

Ribarts's attitude visibly softened. 'Don't you believe it. We'll murder 'em.' He smiled. 'OK, Gareth. But better get a move on. The Gaff'll be back in a sec for the game briefing.' He was looking at the Welshman's face as he spoke. 'Do you want a plaster for that cut on your cheek?'

'No, thanks. It's nothing. Healed up already.' Trisall touched his cheek and gave as bashful a look as he was capable of producing. 'Cat was a bit frisky last night, that's all.'

'Doesn't anyone know where Stan is?' asked another player, an Irishman called Lanigan. He had been sitting on the bench further along, easing the laces in a boot and taking in the last few exchanges.

'No, nobody does,' Ribarts answered, annoyance showing again in his voice. Knowing the general whereabouts of all the players was one of his responsibilities—though, as he'd said to Felix Harden earlier, he could hardly be blamed when one of them went over the hill on a match day. Harden hadn't appeared to agree, which Ribarts had found hard, except he allowed that the Gaff had enough problems already.

'So why would he be letting the team down on a match day?' Lanigan continued to question. 'That's a bastard trick, that is.'

'Don't be so bloody sure of yourself. Stan's OK. Maybe he's been let down himself,' said Trisall ominously.

'You know why he's not here, then?' asked Ribarts promptly.

When the Welshman refused to be drawn further, it was Atler who asked: 'Is it about Stan the Gaff's gone to see the bosses upstairs?' Knowing why the team manager did that, whenever he did it, was regularly a subject of burning interest to all players, and most especially to one of the so-called stars who, like Atler, had been falling short of his best performance.

'I don't know. It's not my business,' the assistant manager replied pointedly, implying it wasn't the questioners' business either.

'But did you hear what they were saying on the radio after lunch? On the LBC sports news?' Lanigan put in. 'They said there's a rumour Stan's been suspended. That the Gaff's put him on the transfer list.'

'I heard. You don't believe everything they say on the media, do you?' said Ribarts.

'You mean it isn't true, Jeff? The rumour about Stan?' Atler asked, pressing the point.

'Ah, here's the Gaff now,' said Ribarts, pointing towards the door and relieved to have an excuse not to answer the last question—for the reason that he didn't have an answer. 'In the lounge, all of you, then. For the briefing. I'll see about the others.' He moved off in the direction of the exercise area.

Lanigan got up and went through to the lounge where most of the players were assembled already. Trisall, now changed, closed his locker and stepped over the bench to join Atler. 'Thanks for backing me up, Jimmy. Saying I was with you,' he offered quietly as they both made towards the lounge. 'Shan't forget that.' He looked around, then lowered his voice even more. 'I'd had a drink, see? Only a social one, like. But you know how frigging particular they are? Worse than any Premier League team. Ribarts is like a frigging nanny.'

'That's OK,' said Atler. 'I'd had a drink myself, as a matter of fact. So we're sort of covering for each other.'

'Everybody sitting comfortably? Then I'll start the good news,' announced Felix Harden, standing in front of the blackboard that was set up in the lounge. It was his standard opening at match briefings, with no hint in his manner that he was personally upset about anything—on the contrary, he was making a huge effort to seem confident.

'Right, lads,' he went on. 'Hereford. Great team. Doing a comeback. Up three places in the Third Division this season. Not to be underestimated. Just like the Eels, eh? Because we're going to win tonight, no question.' He paused and grinned. 'Like us, Hereford are short in the mid field. One of their star players is sick.'

'Is Bodworski sick then, Gaff?' one of the players interrupted.

'Short in the mid field,' Harden repeated, raising his voice, stolidly ignoring the question, and wishing he hadn't mentioned illness. 'So they'll most likely be playing a four-two-four formation . . .'

The so-called tactics briefing that followed was really more of a pep talk—a morale booster for the team. The members were all familiar enough with the game strategy that had been worked out in practice on the field that morning. At that time Harden had been vacillating over whether to play Bodworski, so the player's likely absence had been taken into account. Now the manager was intending simply to recall key points and to send the players on to the field with their tails up. He was nearly finished when the telephone started ringing. He stopped talking and waited for it to be answered.

Ribarts was nearest to an instrument—the one at the lounge end of the locker area. He picked it up, meaning to get rid of the caller whoever it was, except that the worried expression on his face and his several muffled responses signalled to the roomful of people watching that he wasn't treating with just an ebullient fan or a well-wishing girlfriend—the usual type of last-minute good-luck caller. When he did put the phone down, he nodded to Harden and remembered to smile. 'No problem, Gaff,' he called. 'Hereford supporter wanting to put big money on the Eels.'

'Great,' Harden responded over the thin laughter. 'So

like I said, a big win tonight, lads, and another on Saturday, and the Eels will be back on the road to promotion.' He looked at his watch. 'We're on the field in two minutes. Good luck, everybody. And let's have a great win.'

As the others got up and filtered in the direction of the door, Ribarts hurried over to Harden. 'That was Mr Linkina, Gaff. From the chairman's suite. He wants to speak to you. Something about Sir Ray. He's coming down. I tried to say it was too late before the game. I don't think he heard.'

'Yeah,' Harden answered sharply. 'Much too late.'

Staff Nurse Hilda Brax, and Student Nurse Jacky Gilroy had the ambulance doors open even before the vehicle had properly stopped outside the Casualty Entrance to Fulham Cross Hospital.

'Name's Bodworski, is it?' jolly Nurse Brax, who was from Trinidad, asked the yellow-clad paramedic from the ambulance as they slid the laden stretcher out on to the trolley.

'That's her.'

She took the report sheet and scanned it quickly but methodically. 'Like the footballer?'

'The same. It's his missus.' The man formed a quick, silent O with his lips, to signal 'That surprised you,' before he went on, 'She's a bit sedated, but very much with us.' Then he raised his voice so that the patient could hear. 'You're going to be OK, love, don't worry.'

Lilian Bodworski mustered a wan smile. Her dark eyes were glazed, her breathing slow. There was an emergency dressing over the left side of her forehead, and the cheek below that was red and raw. The rest of the face was deathly white, while the long black hair was blood-encrusted at the front, and roughly fastened away from the dressing, splaying out in an incongruously glamorous fashion over one side of the pillow. There was no telling from the blue-blanketed outline, below the woman's neck, that hidden beneath was a body of exquisite shape—or, in the circumstances, a body that had certainly been exquisite until a very short time before this.

A male orderly and the paramedic hurried the trolley through the hospital automatic doorway and down the wide corridor to Casualty reception, the nurses keeping pace on either side.

'You radioed there were internal injuries.' This was Nurse Brax to the paramedic again as they came to the second set of doors.

'Most likely, yes,' he replied. 'Looked like she'd been properly roughed up. She won't say, but she hadn't moved from the phone when we got there. On the floor, collapsed she was. Could have taken her a long time to get that far, too. To the phone. We had to get the caretaker to let us in. Control have told the police.'

With practised movements that still produced some painful reaction in Lilian Bodworski's face, they lifted her from the stretcher on to the bed in one of the screened cubicles. The move had been supervised by the Casualty Ward Sister who, like the other nurses, had not long been on duty. Seven of the ten cubicles were unoccupied: it was still early in the evening. With equal care the nurses next removed the patient's clothing—a chunky-knit sweater and a thick woollen skirt, with skimpy underclothes beneath. The top garments were replaced with a white paper hospital robe.

'Hello, Mrs Bodworski,' said the young Indian doctor. He had come from the next cubicle around the end of the screen. The worn-out-looking stethoscope in his hand was somehow as unexpected as his plummy British accent. 'Been in the wars, have we?' he questioned spiritedly, high-noting the last syllable like a Camberley Field Marshal. He handed back the report sheet to Nurse Brax. 'Let's look at this bump first, then.' He lifted the head dressing, nodded at the wound as if it were an old friend, and replaced the dressing. 'Few stitches'll fix that. Won't know it happened in a week or two. Promise you that.' He smiled at the patient. 'Hit the corner of something, did we?'

She half nodded and whispered some words that the doctor didn't catch.

'The arm of a chair, she said, doctor,' Student Nurse Gilroy vouchsafed earnestly. It was her big line. It made her feel good, even indispensable, to be the channel of vital information like that. She needed to develop an easy familiarity with doctors since it was her firm ambition to marry one.

'I see.' The houseman smiled his approval at Student Nurse Gilroy, making her legs go wobbly. 'Wooden chair arm, was it?'

The patient looked confused, then half nodded again.

'Good. Fewer bugs than you get in uncut moquette, what? Could also mean a few splinters, of course. Well, you can't have everything.' He delighted the student nurse again by beaming at her. Nor was she to know that he was thinking she'd be quite beddable if she lost a bit of weight. 'Anyway,' he went on, 'we'll find out the worst when we clean you up in a minute. So, let's have this blanket off in stages, shall we, ladies? Just shout if you feel the cold, won't you, Mrs Bodworski?'

'Could you excuse me a tic, doctor? Telephone,' said the Sister, disappearing towards her office.

While the other nurses shifted the blanket about, the doctor pulled the paper robe down from the top and began gently examining the patient's bare neck and shoulders, then her chest and ribcage. 'That hurt, did it?' he asked, as he pressed her lower left ribs again, exerting a little more pressure than he had used the first time, and, because he was only human, just failing to take a wholly composed and professional view of Mrs Bodworski's divertingly well shaped breasts. As he fingered the skin above and below the painful area, the patient winced again. 'It wasn't a chair arm that did that, though, was it?' the doctor observed seriously. 'Few fractured ribs, I should think. X-ray will tell us. Nothing that won't mend, of course. Hello, what's this?' As he had moved to examine the patient's abdomen his eyes had lighted on an ugly swollen bruise on her upper left thigh. 'Looks vicious, that,' he said. 'You were punched in the ribs, then kicked down here? That right?' It was the kind of diagnosis housemen on casualty duty were more used to making late on Saturday nights, after the pubs had closed, than this early on a Wednesday evening.

There was no audible response from Lilian Bodworski, only her eyes gave what could have been confirmation.

'Thought so,' said the doctor. He was examining the lower limbs when the Staff Sister appeared again with a uniformed woman police constable holding a notebook at the ready.

'Can I ask Mrs Bodworski some questions, doctor?' asked the WPC who was blonde, trim, and toothy, and wore glasses with serious frames.

'Only in the time it'll take to get her on a trolley. She's going to X-ray.'

'Right, Mrs Bodworski. My name's Celia. Can you please tell me who attacked you?'

There was no response from the patient.

'Was it your husband who attacked you?'

The second question had been more tentative than the first, and produced the same reaction, or lack of one.

'If it wasn't your husband, was it someone else you knew?'

This time the patient's eyes showed confusion. She moved her head slightly, then directed a frightened, appealing look at the doctor.

'So was it a stranger? A burglar? Someone who broke in?'

It was the Sister who intervened. 'I think that's enough

for now, dear,' she said to the WPC. 'You can see, she's very upset.'

'But we don't want whoever it was to get away. Not if we can help it, do we . . . Lilian.' The woman officer hung on stoically, doing her job.

'Did you hear that, Mrs Bodworski?' said the doctor. 'Don't you want your attacker caught? So he can't do it again, what?'

The patient closed her eyes.

'Right. On the trolley,' the doctor directed with military firmness, then he turned to the WPC, adding: 'Better luck next time, miss.'

The woman shrugged and closed her notebook. 'It's missis, actually, doctor, but constable will do,' she said, moving to one side to let the trolley through.

CHAPTER 10

'I still think Gloria Bims took it all incredibly well,' said Berty Grenwood. 'Damned plucky woman. Must have been a terrible shock, but she seemed hardly ruffled. Well, outwardly at least.' He was clutching a long glass of iced Malvern water in front of him with both hands, like a votive offering. 'Same goes for Bims's first wife, of course. Awful thing for her, finding him like that.' He shook his head so energetically that the ice in his glass rattled.

Berty was sitting on a stool behind the bar counter in the chairman's suite where he was dispensing the drinks. He had taken over as barman since the regular one had gone home. Mark Treasure, Andras Linkina and Dr Gordon Fitzmount, an Irishman and the team's doctor, were standing on the other side of the counter, not far from where Treasure had first joined Berty and Linkina nearly two hours earlier. There was now no view of the football

pitch through the glassed-in gallery on the other side of the
bar. The blinds had been lowered shortly after the match
had begun, and had remained closed ever since.

The previously crowded room was empty save for the
four men at the bar, and Arnold Edingly and Detective-
Inspector Jeckels who were seated in a far corner at the
desk.

The discovery of Ray Bims's fully clothed body, gro-
tesquely arched on the dressing-room bed, had abruptly
terminated the pre-match gathering in the suite. As soon
as word of the death had got around the room, the remaining guests had left quickly, out of deference to the widow.
The after-match party for the Supporters Club officials in
the banqueting room had been postponed for the same
reason.

But the match itself had been played. The Eels had won,
three goals to nil.

Meantime, Ian Crayborn had taken Joyce Bims home
shortly after she had given a brief statement to a uniformed
police sergeant. A police presence on the scene had been
evident soon enough, since a contingent from the local force
had been on duty as usual for the match. The second Lady
Bims had left some time later, after accepting Molly Treasure's slightly impulsive offer to see her home to Chelsea
in the Rolls. Henry Pink, long since hardened to disappointment, had been duly summoned on his portable telephone
from his seat in the stand. Molly had been glad of an excuse
to leave since, temporarily at least, she had lost the taste
for football.

Because a number of journalists had been about when
the body had been discovered, Grenwood, Linkina and
Crayborn, advised by Treasure, had issued an immediate
press statement on behalf of the football club, and which
had been approved by Gloria Bims. This deeply regretted
Sir Ray's untimely death, but gave no details of the cause
beyond saying that an autopsy would be taking place.

While this had been sufficient to imply that death might not have been through natural causes, it didn't actually say as much. For the time being, at least, the announcement diverted media attention from Hugon Road and the second Lady Bims, which is what it was intended to do.

In view of the current unsavoury news stories about Bims, Treasure was certainly aware that this respite would be short lived, but it gave the Eels' directors till morning to decide how to cope with the development publicly from the club's viewpoint. The second Lady Bims, the statement had said, would not be available for comment until after her husband's funeral, all inquiries before that were to be handled through Sir Ray's office in Mayfair, address and telephone number provided.

'Have you come across strychnine poisoning before, doctor?' Treasure inquired of the fortyish, jovial, oversized and overweight Fitzmount who was holding a half-empty pint tankard. The pewter tankard had been refilled several times already.

'Yes, but not since I was a hospital intern in Belfast,' the doctor replied. 'The stuff's more difficult for punters to come by these days, thank God. Did you see his face? Yes, of course you did. You were in there with him when I arrived.' It was Fitzmount, fetched from the Eels' bench, and dressed, as now, in his team tracksuit, who had officially pronounced Bims as dead. He finished his pint before adding in the same penetrating Ulster brogue: 'Must be a horrible bloody death for the pain of it to be etched in the face like that.'

'You diagnosed the cause of death straight away,' said the banker.

'Oh, sure. The signs were classical. He expired in spasm. In a titanic, arching convulsion. Head trying to reach his heels. There was also that pot beside him labelled strychnine, of course.' The doctor chuckled. 'Anyone who could read would have made the same diagnosis. No, it happens there hasn't been a case in my bit of West London for some time. In this area, we keep off the strychnine and stick to the booze, isn't that the truth of it, Lord Grenwood?' he completed, planting the empty tankard noisily on the bar, then absently shifting it about.

'Quite right, my boy,' said Berty. 'He's a very good doctor, you know,' he told the others. 'Keeps my wife and me up to scratch as well as the Eels.' Then his face showed that a message had registered. 'Let me get you another beer, Gordon,' he said, reaching behind him for a bottle.

'If you insist, thank you.' Fitzmount beamed, then went on, 'Candler, the police doctor who was here just now, he says he sees quite a few victims of strychnine poisoning. Nearly all suicides. Wouldn't be my choice for the quick trip to oblivion.'

'What would Candler's other cases have been, I wonder?' Treasure asked. 'Accidents or murders?'

'Some of each, I should think,' the Irishman replied. 'In time past, a lot of careless gardeners ingested strychnine by mistake. It was a favourite, as well, with people wanting to do away with wives or husbands excess to requirements. It's soluble in alcohol, of course.' He glanced involuntarily at his beer. 'And that way the taste's disguised. Or made a touch more palatable, which is what applied in Bims's case, I expect. We're assuming that's how he took it, of course, pending the analysis of what had been in that glass besides brandy.'

A used balloon brandy glass had been found on the dressing-room table, along with the strychnine. It seemed, thus, that Sims had been fastidious about choosing the appropriate vessel for his final if tainted drink. Treasure speculated idly on whether this made Bims the kind of man who used the butter-dish knife when breakfasting alone—and decided it probably did.

Linkina's thin mouth tightened. 'Strychnine or a bullet was what Bims had at hand. This is so, yes?' he asked

slowly, the accent again emphasizing the end consonants.
'Ever since he has stolen the poison and the rifle last night?
So he planned to kill himself. It was not something he did
on impulse. If it had been, would he not have done it
earlier? As soon as he had the means? Even in Edingly's
office?' He looked across towards the two men at the desk
as he continued: 'Probably he was thinking of nothing else
all day, poor fellow.'

'Vacillating over whether to do it, you mean?' Treasure
questioned, but doubtfully.

'I hope it was nothing I said at lunch that . . . that tipped
the scales. Oh dear,' mourned Berty, absently twisting at
the hairs protruding from his right ear. 'Can you tell us
exactly when it happened, Gordon?'

'Not really. He was pretty cold, so he'd probably been
dead three hours or more. The autopsy should give a better
time fix.' Fitzmount glanced at his watch. 'I expect they'll
do a preliminary dissection of the body tonight.'

The last melancholy prediction precipitated an uncomfortable pause. Treasure ended this by breaking in confidently with: 'Well, I'm sure it was nothing you said, Berty.
The Eels were just a sideshow in Bims's life. His big concern
was obviously the Cayman business. He was taking that
more seriously than he let anyone imagine. Much more
seriously. Could even be he got more bad news from
America this afternoon. Possibly the situation had suddenly
become hopeless for him. It's certainly been heading in that
direction.'

Linkina frowned. 'But he's the last man one would have
guessed would take his own life. In any circumstances,' he
said, his hands, palms upwards, making a kind of weighing
gesture. 'He was too brash and confident. And a bully, too.'

'People of that type often react more dramatically than
others in real adversity,' supplied the doctor after swallow-
ing some beer. 'I'm only curious that he chose the poison,
not the gun. It was the more painful of the options.'

'Ah, a rifle's a damned cumbersome thing when you point it at yourself,' said Berty, with the assurance of someone who did it regularly.

'Not necessarily accurate, you mean?' Treasure asked. 'Not a two-two calibre rifle, held backwards?'

'A higher calibre wouldn't be any better,' said the doctor, in a more considered tone than before. 'A shotgun would be more . . . more reliable for the purpose, I suppose, though just as cumbersome.'

'Well, he had a pair of shotguns at home,' Berty put in promptly. 'Purdeys,' he added, as though their provenance was relevant, then shook his head again after deciding it probably wasn't. 'But we don't know what else was going through his mind, of course,' he completed lamely.

'Nor why he didn't leave a note. Strange, that,' said Treasure, who made as though he was about to pursue the point, but then shrugged his shoulders and asked instead: 'I also wonder what he did with the rifle.' He was preparing to enlarge on that when, like the others, he saw Arnold Edingly shuffling across the room in their direction. At the same time he noticed Jeckels get up from the desk and go back into the dressing-room after unlocking the door.

The Detective-Inspector had arrived only fifteen minutes before this, looking for Edingly, and had found him talking to Grenwood and Linkina here in the chairman's suite. Jeckels had been following up information from the uniformed branch that the missing strychnine had been found and in what circumstances.

The President of the Eels Supporters Club now gave an obsequious cough. 'Unless there's anything you need me for, Lord Grenwood, I'll be getting along then,' he said, from where he was now standing just outside the group at the bar. 'The police are done with me. Done with me.' The repetition of the last phrase had the effect of implying an ill-considered if not unjust abandonment on the part of the forces of law and order.

'Oh, we don't need you for anything, Mr Edingly,' said Berty, compounding the shortcoming. 'I'm only sorry about the party being cancelled. We'll set it up again, no fear. Yes, you pop along by all means. Unless you'd care for a drink?'

'No, thank you, my lord.'

'No, of course, you're teetotal. I'd forgotten. So am I at the moment. Touch of gall bladder trouble since lunch.' The elderly viscount broadcast the last intelligence like a weather report that was pertinent to the interest of all his hearers.

'It's not that, my lord,' Edingly replied. 'I'm not feeling very sociable, as you might say. What with my strychnine probably being at the root of things.' This was followed by an unexpected sigh of relief. 'Of course, we know now who stole it. And who must have stolen the rifle as well,' he completed, the expression on his face suggesting that the last deduction was a source of even greater consolation than the other.

'We were just wondering if the rifle has been found, Mr Edingly?' said Linkina.

'Not yet, sir. It'll be in Sir Ray's house, I expect. It wasn't in here. Or in his Bentley downstairs. They looked. The police. It's a relief to know it wasn't taken by . . .' He paused, looked down at his feet, then up again as he added: 'Not by Stan Bodworski who's gone missing. And let's hope it wasn't him that beat up his wife like that either.' The last sentence came out at speed and in one breath.

'Who says it was Bodworski who assaulted his wife?' Linkina demanded in an outraged tone. He and the others had only a sketchy, third-hand report on the assault so far from Fitzmount. The doctor, in turn, had got his information on the telephone from the hospital. Like Bodworski's own disappearance, his wife's plight had not ranked as the most shocking feature of the evening.

The lower part of Edingly's face had stiffened at the

pianist's question, while the eyes narrowed in a despairing way. 'It's what the players are thinking,' he said, without volunteering who might have put such a thought in their minds in the first place. He gave another sigh. 'We'll just have to pray some good'll come out of all the bad things that have happened tonight,' he ended with apparent piety, and the silent wish that he hadn't mentioned what he'd known about Sir Ray Bims and Lilian Bodworski to anyone.

'Well, the Eels have beaten Hereford for a start,' said Berty with gusto, he being only one of those present who confidently looked for some early fulfilment of Edingly's prayerful entreaty.

'That's right, sir,' the pest controller replied as though the news was fresh. 'Well, good night then.'

'I'd better be off too,' said Fitzmount. 'I need to drop by the hospital and have a look at Lilian Bodworski.' He had not been able to see her earlier because of his responsibilities at Hugon Road. Now he finished his drink, also said his good nights, and left behind Edingly.

Berty drank some of his mineral water and smacked his lips. 'Bad form to mention it earlier,' he said, 'but now Bims is . . . er . . . no longer with us, we can fire ahead putting those board changes in motion. And with my buying back the club. I'll alert the lawyers in the morning. Public announcements will need to wait till after the funeral, perhaps. What d'you think, Mark?'

'Depends a bit on how much the media make of Bims's suicide. I imagine they'll go to town on it. Saying he took his life to avoid being arrested over the Caymans' scandal. The best way to distance the Eels from that is to distance them from Bims and everything to do with him.'

'So we should make all the changes quickly. Tomorrow?' questioned Linkina.

'I think it'd be as well to be prepared for that,' said the banker.

'Hm. Pity Ian Crayborn had to leave, but there it is,'

Berty mused. 'We can talk to him first thing in the morning, though,' he added brightly. His shoulders lifted and lowered in a gesture of positive anticipation.

'And the move to Cherton can be on the agenda for the end of this season,' Linkina offered in an equally satisfied voice while rubbing together his heavily insured fingers.

'Certainly there shouldn't be any more problems over your buying back the club, Berty,' said Treasure.

'None at all. Gloria Bims has to sell her husband's shares to other directors within three months,' Berty declared. 'That's laid down in the club's articles. Won't take three months, of course. Not if she needs the money. I shall offer her the same terms as I offered Ray at lunch today.'

'She's bound to accept,' said Linkina confidently. 'Probably make her better off than she'd have been if her husband was still alive.' His face clouded. 'But of course I didn't mean . . .' He left the sentence and its import begging.

'She'll have to accept the price or agree to go to arbitration on it. That's what the articles stipulate. Applies to the heirs of all shareholders,' said Treasure who had been glancing through the articles that morning. 'I agree Berty's existing offer is more than generous, but you never . . .' He stopped what he was saying and turned to greet Detective-Inspector Jeckels who had emerged quietly from the chairman's dressing-room and who was now approaching the three at the bar. 'Got everything you needed, Mr Jeckels?' the banker inquired.

'I think so, sir, thank you. I'm just on my way to the players' dressing-room,' the policeman replied in a cheerless tone, as though the prospect didn't please him.

'Can I get you a drink, Inspector?' asked Berty.

'No, thank you, sir.' The reply was so firm that the others expected him to add righteously that he was still on duty, but he didn't. He paused, scratched his nose, glanced suddenly over his shoulder and back again and then said: 'So, I'll be on my way,' which, considering the build-up, was a less stirring piece of intelligence than Berty Grenwood for one had expected. Then the speaker cleared his throat, ignored the anticipatory farewell nods of his listeners, and asked: 'You all knew Sir Ray Bims well, of course?'

'Lord Grenwood and Mr Linkina did. I'd met him a few times,' said Treasure.

'I see. Would any of you say he was the suicide type?'

'Probably not,' Linkina answered. 'We were discussing the point earlier.'

'Seems to be the general opinion, that does,' Jeckels observed, starting to rub the sides of his trousers vigorously with open palms, possibly as some kind of further limbering up action prior to his actually moving off.

'We also came to the conclusion that Sir Ray had been going through a very difficult time. Perhaps intolerably difficult,' said Treasure. 'You must know about that?'

'About him and that bank of his? Yes, we know all about that, sir.'

'Is there any doubt in your mind that he did commit suicide?' the banker pressed.

Jeckels, still massaging his thighs, considered the question carefully before he replied. 'That's not for me to say, sir. It's other people's opinions I'm interested in for now.' He turned his gaze back to Linkina. 'You've heard nothing more as to the whereabouts of Mr Bodworski, I suppose, sir?'

CHAPTER 11

Five minutes later Detective-Inspector Jeckels had proved his intention. He was sitting opposite Gareth Trisall in an isolated corner of the lounge in the Eels' dressing-room. The whole place was nearly empty, but smelling of embrocation, damp hair, and after-shave lotion. It was also very untidy, particularly the locker and shower areas which were strewn with wet towels and soiled playing gear. Jeff Ribarts was near the lockers, collecting discarded items and depositing them in a wicker laundry basket—something the players were supposed to do for themselves. Ribarts was affirming the last point by issuing a discontented grunt every time he dropped anything into the basket.

With the Supporters Club party cancelled, there had been no reason for players to have remained at Hugon Road following the match, and, after Bims's death and the continued presence of nosey police and pressmen, every reason for them to have left. Only Trisall and Atler were still in the dressing-room—Atler out of sight in the exercise and treatment section, topping up his tan on one of the sun beds, something he did at every available opportunity.

Originally, Trisall had arranged to be picked up by Sara in the Porsche at ten, half an hour or so after the party had been timed to begin. She hadn't been at the match, and neither of them cared for parties that involved the whole team—in contrast to parties where Trisall alone would be lionized. He had intended just to make a token appearance at this one.

The Welshman had been trying to reach Sara ever since the end of the match, at nine-fifteen, to get her to come for him straight away, but there had been no response from her home or her mobile telephone. This was why he had still been around when Jeckels had sent someone to look for him.

'So after Mr Edingly told you what he thought was going on between Sir Ray and Mrs Bodworski—'

'I didn't believe him, did I?' Trisall interrupted, but keeping his voice down. They were both doing that. 'I thought he was just stirring things up, like.' As Edingly must have been doing when he'd told the coppers the same thing, he thought. He just wished Edingly had kept him out of it.

'But you believed him later, sir?'

'That Bims might be having it off with somebody? Yes. Not Lilian, though. OK, I've always felt she's a bit . . . a bit unsettling, if you know what I mean?' He cracked his clenched knuckles over the front of his chequered cashmere sweater.

'She's very sexy, sir?' said Jeckels, thinking that was what Trisall really meant.

'Oh, she's sexy all right. No doubt about that. But it's more than that. Like . . . even though she's gone on Stan, that . . . er . . . that people might think she could be open to different offers.'

'Fancied her yourself ever, did you, sir?'

The Inspector's attempt at a confidential expression to go with the off-the-record question presented itself to Trisall more as an offensive leer. 'No, I frigging didn't fancy her myself,' he responded stoutly, if not entirely truthfully, and loud enough for Ribarts to have heard if he was listening hard enough. 'And even if I did, Stan's my best mate. Where I come from, boyo, you don't mess with the wife of your best mate,' he completed, with as wholesome a tribute to the quality of Tonypandy manhood as anyone could have offered since Tommy Farr went fifteen rounds with Joe Louis in 1937.

Jeckels shifted uncomfortably after the snub. 'But you thought Sir Ray Bims might have believed Mrs Bodworski would consider a . . . a different offer from him, like you said, sir?'

'I reckoned he might have been trying it on, yes. Anyway, it needed sorting. With Lilian. In case she was being harassed by Bims and didn't know what to do about it. Like she couldn't very well tell her husband, see? Not without the balloon going up. You got to remember Bims was her employer, and Stan's as well. Very awkward. Tricky.' He gave a meaningful nod and sat back in the black imitation leather arm chair. 'So after I left Arnold Edingly,' he added, 'I went straight over to Lilian's office.'

'But she wasn't there?'

'That's right.'

'We know she was supposed to be in Birmingham last night, at the Sports Trade Fair. Coming back this after-noon.'

'That's what the girl in the general office told me as well.'

'But you told my uniformed colleagues you did see Sir Ray?'

'That's right. As Sara—that's my girlfriend—as she was driving us away from here, his Bentley came out of the car park in front of us. He was by himself.'

'And you followed him, sir?'

'Yeah. Along the King's Road. All the way to Sloane Square. We couldn't help it.' He gave an energetic roll of the athletic shoulders. 'Well, we could have helped it if we'd wanted to, I suppose, but seeing what Arnold had just told me, we decided to keep on his tail. To see where he was going. Especially when we saw he wasn't going home.'

'You knew where he lived, sir?'

'Sure. Mulberry Grove. That's this end of King's Road. He finished up at the Hans Tower Hotel. We were going there too. Coincidence, that was. And we parked in the basement like him. Sara and me, we were meeting some friends in the bar. We thought Bims was doing the same. She went up in the lift with him. From the basement.'

'You didn't?'

Trisall shook his head. 'No. He hadn't seen me, and I didn't want to run into him. I took the stairs. He didn't know Sara,' he added.

'Did he go into the bar?'

'No. Up to the fifth floor. So did Sara. Curious, she was, see? She's a real caution, that one. There were plenty of people in the lift, so he didn't tumble what she was up to, even when she followed him out. To see where he was going. Room 529, if you're interested.'

Jeckels made a note. 'What do you think he was doing there, sir?'

'What a lot of men do in hotel rooms close to home. He was meeting a bird. Must have been. Sara saw him press the room buzzer.'

'He didn't have a room key?'

Trisall shook his head. 'Plastic cards they use there. But he didn't have one, no. Sara didn't see who opened the door, but it couldn't have been Lilian Bodworski. She was in Birmingham, wasn't she?'

The Welshman was spelling out the reason why he had decided to cooperate with Jeckels. He knew Lilian was in hospital, that she'd been beaten up, and that her husband had disappeared. The police were probably going to think that Stan had attacked his wife after he had been told she had been unfaithful to him with Ray Bims. Trisall was doing his best to lead them away from that conclusion, for his own peace of mind as well as his friend's. He was fairly sure that Edingly, a known gossip, had told others what he had found out about Lilian and Bims—or said he had found out—and that one of those he'd told had passed on the bad news to Bodworski. Trisall had very nearly told Bodworski himself, but only because he believed that Edingly was wrong about his suspicions—and dead wrong to spread them.

'And did you see Sir Ray again last night, sir?' asked Jeckels.

'No. But his car was still in the basement when we left at midnight.'

'You had dinner at the hotel, sir?'

'No. Round the corner in Sloane Street. But we left the car there all evening. Safer than in the street.'

'But you didn't see Sir Ray again?'

Involuntarily, Trisall pressed the healed-up cut on his cheek. 'No. Not ever again. Poor bugger.'

The Bims's large, detached, red brick villa in Mulberry Grove had been built in a pseudo-classical style in the mid-'twenties, along with all the other matching red brick villas lining both sides of the street. It had lyrical Dutch gables, pretty Venetian windows, and a front door in the centre, under an ornate pedimented portico. The door was approached by six splayed stone steps flanked by iron railings. There was a small paved forecourt on to the street and an impressive sized walled garden at the back.

Gloria Sims and Molly Treasure were in the drawing-room which, in the daytime, offered a view on to the garden.

'We were putting on a show. That's all. By arrangement,' Gloria was saying, the energy behind her penetrating tone unaffected by the evening's devitalizing events. 'I promised to support him publicly till he'd sorted out the Cayman bank business. Let me freshen that drink.' She got up, took Molly's glass and carried it with her own to the drinks trolley. She was still wearing what she had just disparagingly described to Molly as her drum majorette outfit.

'Very little gin. Heavy on the Slimline, please,' the actress said with a smile, tucking her stockinged feet under her on the sofa.

Molly had been in the room before, when the previous Lady Bims had been in occupation. She remembered it then as being less evidently designer influenced, but also a lot less pleasing—which added a further credit to the several that Gloria Bims had collected since the two had been alone together.

Hand-blocked wallpaper, velvet drapes, and a magnificent oriental rug provided a warm setting for prettily covered, deep armchairs and a long sofa. The antique side tables and wall cabinets had been carefully chosen, but it was the bold modern art and bits of sculpture around the room, along with some exquisite porcelain items that underwrote the æsthetic overall balance, while each of the individual pieces offered a focus of its own. From the comments Gloria had made to Molly when they had first entered it was clear that this unusually successful room was very much her own creation, including the Adamesque fireplace where pine logs were presently burning in an almost dutifully picturesque manner.

When Henry Pink had delivered his passengers to Mulberry Grove, Molly had sent him back with the car to wait for her husband at Hugon Road: she, in turn, had accepted an invitation to stay for a drink. In the course of the drive she had been concerned that the house might be under siege by reporters and photographers, but there had been none visible when the women arrived. Presumably it was still too soon after the news of Sir Ray's death, or else the wording of the press communiqué really had diverted media attention elsewhere.

Gloria had seemed as unmoved about the still imminent threat to her privacy as she had been earlier about the shock demise of her husband. Her single concession to keeping the world at bay had been to leave the telephone answering machine switched on to intercept calls.

'The marriage was a mistake in the first place,' she enlarged as she returned with the drinks, then settled again into an armchair. 'The trouble started when we tired of each other physically. After that the other parts of the relationship weren't enough to compensate. Not for either of us. For different reasons. We're both very fickle people.'

'The other parts being?' Molly asked.

'For me, his loot, my *deah*,' the other woman affected with resignation. 'That's if I'm totally honest. He was loaded when I met him, but loaded—and crazy about being involved with a fashion house. I was fed up with running my business on small change. So we . . . melded nicely. I believed I had the talent to make it to the top. Given the financial backing.

'Sounds more like a business deal than a marriage,' said Molly, emboldened by the other's disarming openness.

Gloria picked up a cigarette from the box on the table beside her. 'I did offer to settle for the business deal. And to throw in conjugal rights without benefit of ceremony.' She fingered the silver lighter beside the box before picking it up. 'But that wasn't Ray's style. Not at the time anyway. He may have learned better since. After getting a knighthood, I really think he was secretly aiming for a life peerage and figured our just living together might spoil his record. That divorcing boring old Joyce was enough of a good thing.' She lit the cigarette and blew the smoke out sharply. 'Anyway, he lost too much of the loot. And my inspiration faltered at the most critical time. And my judgement, perhaps. It was his idea to do a . . . a popular version of my spring collection. Designed for the purpose, of course.'

Molly gave a quizzical look. 'Is that something that's known in the trade as a line of better dresses?'

'Yes, exactly. Definitely not mass produced, and fairly pricey. That was the year before last.' She sighed. 'In the end the whole thing was *very* pricey because the collection was a flop. My fault, not Ray's. Except, as I say, it was his idea.'

'But surely that wasn't what ruined him financially?'

'Oh, certainly not. It was a flop but not a crippling one. It was the disappointment more than the cost. And much more for him than for me, in a way. The stuff wasn't bad, either. I'll show you some of it in a minute.'

'But there were recriminations between the two of you?'

'Right. Then sexually, as I said, we just didn't seem to have it going any more. The difference in ages was suddenly an issue which it never had been earlier. And he got more and more difficult to live with when his other deals turned sour.'

'Some of those being disastrous, I believe?'

'You believe right.' Gloria drew in hard on the cigarette. 'He was like a compulsive gambler. Backing anyone who came to him with a hare-brained project. So long as it cost.' She shook her head.

'And the Cayman bank project?'

'That was different. Quite different. Even I believed it'd be profitable. And worthy with it, by the way. Very much so.'

'Legitimate, you mean?' Molly questioned carefully.

'Better than legitimate. When Ray first talked to me about it he made it sound like a moral crusade. It was going to bring unheard-of benefits to backward countries.'

'As well as profits to its backers,' said Molly with a rueful smile.

'That too. He hoped to have tripled his investment by now. But don't misunderstand me. He had the morality of that worked out as well.' Gloria leaned forward slightly, her brow creasing, her expression earnest. 'He said giving things away to underdeveloped communities didn't help them. It just prolonged the backwardness, because it didn't offer an incentive. To work for a change to something better.'

'It's a reasonable argument, I suppose,' Molly offered carefully.

'Well, it's the one Ray believed in,' Gloria insisted. 'Perhaps I'm over-simplifying, but he was totally convinced the BNMR was a force for good. As well as the one to put him back in the money. But he admitted it could be misunderstood. Purposely so by the cynical. It's why he needed to keep his image clean. Why he needed to wind up all the old, freak projects. To get them out of the way. It cost a bit to do that in some cases.'

Molly looked thoughtful. 'And it put them back in the news, perhaps?' she said.

'Yes. Pity, of course. To trot out the lame ducks again.

But it couldn't be helped. That was why Ray was mad keen to be seen backing the Eels, and inconsolable when they lost a match.' Momentarily her face for the first time showed the grief that might have been expected in a widow of two hours. 'And the other thing was our marriage,' she continued. 'It had to look solid, he said. I agreed to that, long before the BNMR got into the headlines this week. Otherwise we'd have divorced a year ago.'

'And all this for an organization that seems to have been a front for drug pushers after all?' Molly commented.

The other woman stubbed out her cigarette. 'I'm still positive Ray never knew it was that. If it was,' she said, the fingertips of one hand circling her forehead delicately, then making a trace down her cheek till they reached her earring. 'You know he was planning to go to Florida at the end of this week?'

'To appear before the Grand Jury?' There was surprise in Molly's voice.

'That's right. I mean, he wouldn't have done that . . . couldn't have, not if he hadn't believed the bank was above board. And that he could prove it.' Gloria's hand stopped caressing the earring and dropped sharply to her lap before she added: 'So how could he have done this crazy thing tonight?'

'The suicide? You don't believe it makes any sense?'

'No way.' Gloria breathed in and out sharply. 'I don't even believe it was suicide.'

'Was he depressed earlier today?'

'I don't know. I last saw him alive at breakfast yesterday. He was driving to Birmingham for a dinner last evening. To do with some dreary sports exhibition. He was staying the night in Birmingham, then driving back early for a breakfast meeting with his lawyer.'

'Here at home?'

'No. At the Hans Tower, I expect. That's where he usually has breakfast meetings.' Frowning, she pushed the serape off her shoulders and added: 'D'you find it hellishly warm in this room, or is it just me?'

'No, it is warm,' Molly agreed. 'They predicted a change in the weather tonight. There's rain on the way.'

Gloria got up and moved towards the long curtains at the back of the room. 'I'll open the doors to the terrace for a moment. Oh, you were asking about the garden earlier. Come and look. I'll put the outside lights on.' She drew aside the curtains and unlocked a pair of glazed doors, pushing them open. At the same time she flicked on a light switch on the right near the doors, then stepped outside.

A split second later there was a brief stifled scream from outside, the sound of a scuffle, then of metal furniture being pushed aside, scraping on paving and toppling on to it.

Molly put her shoes on quickly and was moving towards the open doors. Before she could get there, Gloria was being bundled back into the room by a dark, thickset man, who Molly had never seen before. His darting eyes looked more fearful than crazed.

The man was dressed in an Eels' tracksuit—in the same two colours as the outfit Gloria was wearing, except her serape had gone, and the front pieces of her blouse had separated from the top of the narrow skirt, leaving her nearly half naked and looking especially vulnerable. Her powerful captor had one arm held tightly around her bare waist, and the other hand clamped over her mouth. She wasn't struggling, only her eyes indicated the terror she was enduring.

'Shay . . . shay still and I won't hurt her. Where . . . where's Bims? Where's he? Upstairs?' The intruder's words were heavily accented. His voice was slurred and as he rearranged his stance he very nearly fell forwards.

Molly stopped moving. 'Sir Ray died this afternoon,' she said in a rock steady tone, and with perfect articulation. Early in her career she had played in countless country house dramas where characters entered unexpectedly through French windows, centre stage. The experience was working to make the present situation bizarrely familiar. Determined to carry off what might be the most important ad lib of her career, and ignoring her wildly beating heart, the actress swallowed hard and demanded: 'You're Mr Bodworski, aren't you?'

Stanley had greeted Livingstone with the same measure of insouciance.

Gloria's captor didn't answer, only his grip on her seemed to harden.

'Since I'm sure you are Mr Bodworski, I can tell you your wife is injured in hospital, and the police are looking for you,' Molly went on, outwardly more confident, standing tall and aloof, and continuing to address him reprovingly, as if he were the butler caught watering the brandy in the second act. 'I advise you to release Lady Bims immediately,' she added. 'Immediately, I said. You can telephone the police from here. Or we'll do it for you. If we tell them where you are, I'm sure . . .'

But Bodworski didn't allow her to finish.

CHAPTER 12

Detective-Inspector Jeckels didn't much care for hospitals, not even one as celebrated as the Fulham Cross. It was the smell of the places that upset him, of cigarette smoke in the loos and dead flowers in the corridors. He still associated smells with his first and last visit to a hospital as a patient. As a small boy, in acute pain, he had been rushed to a country infirmary in the middle of the night where his appendix had been removed promptly by an over-eager junior surgeon, all because the patient had not dared to admit to anyone simply that he had been eating unripe and, even more pertinently, *stolen* cherries. Though the

experience had later helped to make Jeckels a better policeman—and in particular a patient, careful interrogator of
frightened subjects—it had done nothing to minimize his
dread of hospitals.

He had reached the third floor of the Fulham Cross by
the stairways, taking the steps two at a time. This had not
only demonstrated his marathon-standard fitness, but had
also saved his having to suffer the inevitable whiff of hot
dinners in the lift. The Night Sister had made him wait for
five minutes before allowing him to go to Lilian Bodworski's
bedside. He had used the interval first to review the all too
brief comments passed on by WPC Celia Coates after her
own earlier and truncated confrontation with Mrs Bodworski. With time still in hand, he had next gone over his own
notes on the evening's interviews so far, in preparation for
typing them out later.

Jeckels may have lacked colour, as well as the fire and
sociability that could have improved his chances of further
promotion. But he made up for these things, in part at
least, with his much to be commended sense of application.
As an example, the careful reappraisal of his own notes
made at this point so affected the line of questioning he later
followed with Mrs Bodworski that it completely altered the
police perception of how Ray Bims had come to die.

It was only unfortunate that that perception was in-
accurate.

'Feeling better, are you, Mrs Bodworski?' the Inspector
asked, pulling the plastic and metal chair closer to the bed
in the interests of security—although the patient in the next
bed appeared to him to be dead, and the one on the other
side was wearing earphones. The six-bed side ward had
been the first door to the right after he had left the landing
and lift area. The nursing station, where Jeckels had been
made to wait, was several paces further along the wide
central ward corridor.

The side ward had two rows of three beds facing each

other. Mrs Bodworski was in a centre bed. The bed across from hers was the only one unoccupied. The walls were painted apple green: Jeckels could have guessed they would be. 'You look fine,' he next assured her, and not going strictly by present appearances, except the undamaged parts of her had made him conscious of her attractions— the eyes, the Garboesque face, the perfection of the bare arms, the promise in the outline of her breasts, under the hospital nightgown. He shifted the chair even closer, and caught his breath when he drove his knee against the metal underside of the bed.

'Let's hope I'll be back in one piece soon,' the patient answered, half smiling, optimism coming through in the tone as strongly as the soft Highland accent. 'Is there any news of my husband?' Her hand went to touch the adhesive bandage on her forehead, the palm briefly but purposely shading her eyes. She supposed he could see she had been crying. 'It wasn't Stan, you know. Who did this.' It was why she had consented to see him. She was anxious to put her husband in the clear. She owed him that. She was sure now it couldn't have been Stan, even if he had found out about Ray Bims. At first, in her confusion, she had thought it could have been him, which is why she had earlier tried to disguise from the doctor how her injuries had been caused.

Less than an hour ago, Dr Fitzmount had told Mrs Bodworski about Bims's death. It had felt like another blow to her body, as bad as the one that had fractured two of her ribs. That she and Ray had been making passionate love so recently had been the first and illogical reason why she had not been able to credit that he was dead. Later, when she had come to terms with what had happened, it had been just as hard for her to accept that he had taken his own life. Indeed, she felt she knew for certain that it couldn't have been suicide, even though she had no way of proving it—or had no reason to think that she had.

'No, I'm afraid there's nothing yet on Mr Bodworski.

But he'll turn up all right, you'll see,' said the Inspector
with forced conviction. 'Most likely he just misunderstood
about being in the team tonight. Anyway, we're doing our
best to locate him.' He noted the dissatisfaction in her face,
but before she could express it verbally he continued: 'Now
then, can you tell us who did this to you?'

'No. No, I can't. It was dark most of the time. And he
. . . he was wearing a stocking over his face.'

'And you didn't recognize him? By his voice? His shape?
The way he moved?'

She shook her head.

'I see. So how did he get in? There's no sign of a break-in
at the flat. Did you open the door to him?'

'Yes.'

He waited for her to elaborate, but she didn't. 'Both
doors?' he questioned, spacing out the two words, while
surreptitiously massaging his bruised knee under the bed.
'Your flat's on the second floor, and there's an entryphone
on the street door, isn't there?' He knew there was. He'd
checked again on his way back here, following his call at
the Hans Tower Hotel. The flat was in a large block, close
to South Kensington tube station.

'I didn't hear the voice on the entryphone. Only the
buzzer. I . . . I thought he was someone else. My husband.
He's always losing his keys.' In truth she had thought it
was Ray Bims. He seldom came to the flat, but he could
have done this evening. She had been waiting for him to
phone, but in the circumstances he might have decided to
come in person. If Stan had been playing in the match,
he'd have been at Hugon Road by six. He had treatment
on his leg from the physiotherapist before every game. Ray
knew that.

'And you opened the door to the flat to him also because
you thought it was your husband?'

She nodded, remembering well enough how she hadn't
wanted to keep Ray waiting in the corridor.

'So what happened next? No rush, Mrs Bodworski.' He was pleased at the way the interview was going. The woman police constable had put her failure to elicit information down to the victim's state of shock. Jeckels accepted that, to an extent, except he had read somewhere that a woman in distress was more likely to unburden to a male than to a female police officer.

'The . . . oh!' Mrs Bodworski winced. She had tried to take a deep breath after she started speaking, but the pain to her ribs had prevented her. 'The . . . the corridor was nearly dark,' she began again, then paused for a second, her hand holding her ribcage. 'He must have taken a bulb out. There's . . . there's usually a light just outside the door. A wall bracket.' She was breathing more deeply now, but slower. 'When I opened the door he rushed me. Slammed the door, and pulled me towards him. He held my face to his chest. To stop me screaming, I suppose. And . . . and I couldn't see anything after that.'

Jeckels showed surprise. 'You mean he kept you like that? Close to him?'

'No. Not after he'd put the hall lights out. The switch is next to the door. Then it was pitch dark. He still had hold of me. I was scared stiff. I didn't know whether he was going to . . .' She stopped again and swallowed. 'What he was going to do. Then he hit me on the forehead. He was wearing gloves.'

'Were they wool or—?'

'Leather with thick ribbing, I think. I'm not sure, though.'

'What else was he wearing? Besides the stocking and the gloves?'

'I didn't have a chance to see.' She looked puzzled. 'There was no time.' Then her expression changed a little. 'I think he may have been wearing a dark jacket.'

'Suit jacket or a topcoat of some kind?'

'Er . . . topcoat, I should think. But shortish. About knee length. It had a hard feel to it . . . like oilskin.'

'Oilskin? Or waxed, was it?'

'Yes. That's it. A waxed jacket,' she came back promptly. 'With a zip down the front.'

'Good. Did you notice his shoes?'

'No. I felt them all right. One of them. When he kicked me. That's all.'

'So after he hit you on the forehead?'

'I screamed. I . . . I felt then I was falling. That was when he slammed his knee into my ribs. Then I was on the floor. It was after that he kicked me.'

'So it was three single blows? To your head, your ribs, then the kick to your thigh?'

'Yes. It was enough too, I can tell you.'

'I'm sure.' Inwardly, though, he still wondered why the assailant had stopped when he had. 'And it all happened while you were still in the hall?'

'Yes. And then . . . then he just left. I remember he had to fumble to find the latch. I was praying he'd go. I'd expected . . .' She broke off in mid-sentence.

'What did you expect, Mrs Bodworski?' Jeckels pressed.

'I don't know. That . . . that he'd hurt me some more. That he'd burgle the flat. Or try to take me with him. It was terrible. Awful.' Suddenly her words were becoming hurried, her heightened pitch hinting that she was on the verge of an hysterical outburst.

'Take your time. You're doing fine,' Jeckels offered with a smile. 'So he left without doing anything else?'

She nodded, and reached for a paper tissue to dry the edges of her eyes. 'I was so relieved. He banged the door after him. I didn't try to follow. Well, I couldn't move. I was hurting so much.'

The Night Sister had just appeared from her office opposite the work station in the corridor outside. She was a big, middle-aged, motherly woman with apple-red cheeks and two wedding rings. 'All right, dear? Not wearing you out, is he?' she asked Mrs Bodworski brightly, and giving Jeckels a fairly disapproving glance in passing. When the patient responded with a smile the Sister turned her attention to another patient, the one Jeckels thought had probably passed away. 'That's all right, then,' she said, a moment later, more or less to herself after very gently feeling the woman's pulse. The inert figure hadn't reacted in any observable way—but the Sister's action and comment gave the watching Jeckels consolation.

'There's a panic button by your front door,' he said to Mrs Bodworski as the Sister moved to the other side of the ward.

'I know. But I couldn't reach it. It was too high up.'

'I see. And didn't he speak at all?'

'No. Not the whole time. Well, I suppose it didn't take very long. It just seemed like for ever when it was happening.' She caught her breath.

'You OK?' he asked. 'We can stop if you want, you know?'

'No. I'd rather get this bit over.'

He leaned forward towards her. 'Can you tell me, are you sure he didn't try to . . . to interfere with you? In any way?'

She smiled in genuine amusement at his embarrassment and his tact. 'You mean, did he try to rape me? No. Nor even grope me. Nothing like that. It was just . . . well, hit and run.'

'And you don't know yet, of course, whether he stole anything?'

'No, but I don't believe he could have. He never left the hall, and there's nothing much to steal there.'

'Did something frighten him off, do you think?'

She thought before answering. 'My hollering maybe?'

'Nothing else?' Mrs Bodworski shook her head. 'And could you judge his height and weight?' he continued.

'About the same height as my hus—About five feet nine or ten,' she corrected herself. 'But it's only a guess. I can't be sure. As for his weight, I've really no idea.'

'When he overpowered you at the start, did he do it by sheer strength, do you think, or more because he took you by surprise?'

'Both. But more by the surprise, probably. I've been thinking about that. About all the things I should have done. I was so scared. He may not have been all that strong. I don't know.'

'But you're sure it was a man?'

'Of course I'm . . .' She stopped in mid-sentence, her face clouding with doubt. 'No, come to think of it, I suppose I can't be absolutely sure. I'm just pretty certain it was a man.'

The Inspector nodded. 'It seems most likely it was.' He watched her expression carefully as he went on: 'So is there anyone you can think of who'd want to hurt you? Someone with a big grudge?'

'Not so far as I know,' she answered, but her eyes had dropped to study her clenched hands on top of the bedcover. 'You think it was someone who came intending to beat me up? Not a burglar.'

'Difficult to say, madam.' He glanced at his notebook. 'Well, thanks very much for your help. It must have been a very nasty experience. We're doing everything we can to find whoever it was. Forensic may turn up with something yet, and it's more than possible someone saw him.'

'Thank you.' She took a painful breath, then rearranged herself on the bed. 'So is that it?'

'Yes. On the assault, anyway.' He ran his tongue around his lips. 'I was just wondering, though, could you help us as well by answering just a few questions relating to Sir Ray Bims's death.' He took her silence to mean consent, and added: 'I believe you were good friends.'

'Oh? Who told you that?' she demanded, evidently on her guard.

'Quite a few people, as a matter of fact.'

'He was my boss. I'm Marketing Director of the Eels.'

'I know that, Mrs Bodworski, yes.' He turned back several pages of the notebook. 'I gather you were in Birmingham this morning. On business. Although you'd been expected back at Hugon Road later on.'

'That's right. I was at the trade fair. At the opening lunch. It went on a bit. I missed the return train I'd intended to catch. I'd meant to be in the office late afternoon but I didn't make it. And . . . and I didn't ring in to say so because I'd left my telephone behind. I got to the flat around five-thirty.'

'You originally planned to travel up yesterday evening. To spend the night?'

'Well, yes, but I—'

'But you stayed in London instead,' he interrupted again firmly.

'Yes.' She had hesitated before answering.

'And you spent the night in Room 529 at the Hans Tower Hotel, where you checked in around six last evening. A room was reserved by fax yesterday afternoon for EBR Enterprises, that's the Eel Bridge Rovers exploitation division, isn't it? Which you operate as the head of marketing?'

'That's right,' she answered quietly. 'We use the Hans Tower for business meetings, and for putting up visiting VIPs. Look, I was held up in London last evening. That's why—'

'Please understand it's not your movements we're interested in, Mrs Bodworski. Honestly it's not,' Jeckels broke in once again, anxious, as he had been throughout, not to give her the opportunity to lie to him, because her lying would be counter-productive for both of them, but more especially for him.

'But my husband will be interested, even if you're not,'

she answered stonily. 'He thinks I was in Birmingham.'

'Well, there's no reason why we should necessarily have to tell him where you were. It's Sir Ray's whereabouts we need to confirm.' He paused. 'He was supposed to be in Birmingham last evening too, for a dinner, also to do with the fair. Except he cancelled. We know he went to the Hans Tower directly from Hugon Road and that he was in Room 529 from approximately six-forty, although he wasn't registered as the occupant. You were.' When she didn't respond he went on: 'There are plenty of other likely witnesses to his movements we can call on, except some of them would be witnesses to the movements of both of you, if you follow me? I'd rather restrict it to you. That way we can keep the whole thing—'

'Confidential?' she broke in quickly.

'For the time being, madam. Perhaps permanently. I can't promise.'

There was a long pause before she replied. 'All right. We were there together. But if you knew that already why are you asking me?'

'You had dinner for two served in the room last night, but you didn't order breakfast this morning,' he said, ignoring her question. 'You signed the bill and checked out of the hotel just before eight, but you left your car in the hotel car park. You'd ordered a taxi to take you to Euston to catch the 8.40 Intercity. That got you to Birmingham International at 10.01. Just as the fair opened. Sir Ray entered the hotel restaurant alone at seven-thirty, and he was joined there by another man shortly after that. They had breakfast together.'

'The other man was his lawyer,' she said. 'Ray had to see him first thing this morning. It's why he cancelled going to Birmingham yesterday. Why . . . why we both did,' she ended, staring blankly into space.

'Thank you. What we need you to confirm is that Sir Ray was with you in the room from the time he arrived at the hotel last evening till he left you there at seven-thirty this morning.'

'Oh God.' She closed her hands over her face, then opened them again. 'Yes, he was. And his car was in the hotel garage.'

'We know that, madam, yes. But it's still possible he could have left the hotel and returned again without using the car.'

'Well, he didn't. We were together . . . the whole time.' There were tears welling in her eyes. 'You're not going to tell my husband any of this?'

'Not unless it becomes absolutely necessary, Mrs Bodworski, and I don't believe it should be.' He was embarrassed as she began to weep, but grateful at least that she did so silently—otherwise it might have alerted the Night Sister and got him into trouble. 'Speaking about your husband, were you aware that Sir Ray Bims had instructed he should be dropped from the Eels? Put on the transfer list?'

She stopped sobbing and her face was suffused by a look of shock and total disbelief. 'That's a lie,' she uttered. 'A dirty lie. Who told you that?'

CHAPTER 13

'So it's in Gloria's own interests to insist he couldn't have committed suicide? Her financial interests?' said Molly Treasure to her husband over the breakfast table. They were in the kitchen of their house in Cheyne Walk.

'Yes. If he carried life insurance, which he probably did,' Treasure replied, spreading Gentleman's Relish on his final piece of toast. 'And if his wife's the beneficiary under the policy. But she won't get anything if he did himself in.'

'I should have realized that. But if his death had been an accident, or from natural causes?'

'Or murder.'

'Murder?' Molly looked up sharply.

'Well, if he died of strychnine poisoning and it wasn't suicide, there's no chance it was natural causes and very little that it was an accident. Anyway, I'm sure it's just wishful thinking on his wife's part not to accept it was suicide.'

'Even though everyone was saying he was the most unlikely person to take his own life? More coffee?'

'Please.' He pushed his cup towards her. 'I think he was under enormous pressure.'

'Anyway, I can't believe Gloria was trying to condition me into believing he was . . . well, murdered, I suppose.' Molly smoothed the heavy gold chain she was wearing on top of her black polo-neck sweater.

It was just before eight, and scarcely light yet outside where the sky was deeply overcast after a night of rain. Both the Treasures were dressed ready to leave, he for the bank soon, and she later for a dress fitting in Knightsbridge. 'After all, I don't have any influence on insurance companies,' Molly continued. 'Oh, I suppose she might think because you are—'

'On the board of one I could get the rules on suicide waived?' he interrupted with a chuckle. He was the non-executive chairman of Regal Sun Assurance. 'No, I expect she was voicing a genuine if self-interested conviction.'

'Didn't you say Berty would be paying one and a half million to buy back the Eels? Gloria will get that, won't she?'

'Shouldn't think so. It'll become part of Bims's estate. The general opinion is that his liabilities will hugely exceed his assets. Mark you, that's supposition, not fact.'

Molly pulled a face. 'I'm pretty sure Gloria is counting on getting the Eels' money.'

'She mentioned it?'

'Yes. But not how much it would be.'

Treasure drank some coffee. 'You evidently revised your first opinion of the lady during your time together. Revised it upward.'

'Yes. And not just because she became a widow at the beginning of the evening either.'

'Which was something that didn't seem to affect her that much?' the banker questioned.

'No, it didn't. Nor did she pretend it did. Not to me, anyway. There's so much more to her than one could have guessed from first meeting.'

'And the clothes she was wearing?' he questioned wryly. 'Those colours?'

Molly shook her head. 'Purposely overstated, of course. For a good reason. You know her husband insisted she appear like that? For the party afterwards. To show she was rooting for the Eels as hard as he was supposed to be.'

'But she must have designed the outfit?'

'Sure. Only as fancy dress, though. She regarded it as a joke, rather.' Molly hesitated. 'I grant you she's not the greatest designer, but she's better than that.'

'And I suppose what she was wearing would have got the photographers at the party concentrating on Bims's Hugon Road interests. As opposed to those in the Cayman Islands. Of course, since there was no party and no photographs, simply the death of the chairman . . .' He completed his comments with a dismissive shrug.

'And all his own doing. It does seem inexplicable.' Molly was adding slices of banana to a small bowl of muesli. 'I still can't get over how marvellous Gloria was, coping with the Bodworski eruption,' she said.

'Seems to me you both did pretty well.'

'Oh, it was a lot easier for me. I wasn't being pinioned by a burly Polish footballer, and drunk with it. Mark you, it was tragedy reduced to farce in the end. The way he let Gloria go and rushed out as soon as I'd told him his wife was in hospital.'

'And then rushed back, you said, because you hadn't told him which hospital.'

'And for the second time when he found his car had a flat tyre.'

'Was he very drunk?'

'Fairly. He was quite maudlin while we were waiting for the taxi to take him to the Fulham Cross. That was over Bims's death. He kept telling Gloria he'd forgive her dead husband for dropping him from the team.'

'How did he come to think he'd been dropped when he hadn't been? Not according to Harden, the manager.'

Molly swallowed some food and touched her mouth with her napkin. 'It was something he'd heard on the radio after lunch,' she said. 'A rumour they reported. He'd tried to check it by phone with Mr Harden, who equivocated. Said he wasn't sure if Bodworski would be in the team.'

'Which made Bodworski mad?'

'Yes, so mad, he told us, he slammed the phone down on Mr Harden.'

'Other people reported hearing that broadcast. Someone suggested it was Bims who leaked the story,' said Treasure. 'Curious that Bims didn't tell Ian Crayborn he was having Bodworski dropped. Apparently he never referred to it on their way back from lunch with Berty. Come to that, he never mentioned it to Berty either.'

'It was a shame Joyce Bims had the announcement of her engagement fall so flat,' said Molly, changing the subject. 'In the circumstances, I mean. You know, she seemed more moved over her ex-husband's death than Gloria was?'

'She was probably more fond of him than Gloria was,' Treasure responded drily. 'I imagine it can sometimes turn out that way. She was certainly in a state of shock after finding him in that dressing-room. I'm glad it wasn't you went in first.'

'Me too.' She wrinkled her patrician nose. 'Is Ian Crayborn well off?'

Treasure looked doubtful. 'The opposite, Berty says. The partnership he was in was dissolved during the recession. He's been on his own for some time, and I don't believe he's got many clients. Or any big ones.'

'He's a director of the Eels?'

'That pays nothing. Being their accountant will be more important to him. Because of the fee. He's no financial catch for Joyce, if that's what you're getting at.'

'I wouldn't have thought that was the biggest consideration,' Molly replied a trifle loftily. 'I'd say they were drawn together by much higher motives.'

'You asked the question,' he responded, pushing his plate away and picking up *The Times*.

'They're so suited in every respect.'

'Both rather dull, you mean?'

'That's unfair. They don't scintillate perhaps, but they're both on their own, and both nice people. Genuine. They deserve each other.' She paused, then nodded an inward affirmation. 'Still, it's a pity Joyce doesn't have money either. Not from what she was telling me last night.'

'Well, she's probably better off than he is,' Treasure replied absently, studying a front page picture of Princess Margaret smiling stoically while reviewing a Scottish regiment in a snowstorm.

Molly hesitated, then got up and began to clear the breakfast things. 'It seems to have been a rather whirlwind romance,' she said.

He looked up from the paper. 'Are you sure? I thought they'd known each other for donkey's years. Berty says Crayborn was Bims's accountant when he had the do-it-yourself business.'

'Oh, they've known each for a long time. He's been her private accountant since . . . since her divorce. But love didn't walk in till the night before last. When it did so with a vengeance apparently.' She licked the honey spoon clean, waiting to see if he'd ask to know more. When he didn't,

she went on despite his irritating lack of interest: 'He was
staying the night after they'd been to the theatre together.
In Guildford. All quite proper, I expect, but that's when it
happened. She was quite starry-eyed when she told me.
Refreshingly romantic, don't you think?'

'Why was it quite proper? You mean she didn't say
they'd slept together?'

'No, and I certainly didn't ask.'

'Much as you wanted to,' he commented with a grin.

'Darling, you really do have a knack of reducing everything to its crudest level.'

Treasure looked mildly chastened but continued in a less
than penitent voice, 'All right, so it was a beautiful meeting
of two souls, if not bodies. So far as we know. I wonder
why it took so long? Did something important happen on
Tuesday to precipitate this chaste consummation?'

Molly was emptying the coffee percolator into the waste-
bin. 'Her first husband died the next day, of course,' she
said thoughtfully, then added quickly: 'No, I know that
couldn't have had anything to do with it.' This had been
to pre-empt Treasure saying the same thing. 'It might have
been a sort of augury, I suppose,' she ended.

'A pretty ghoulish one, if it was.' He turned a page of
the paper. 'Come to think of it, Bims's death just could
have a favourable impact on his first wife's fortunes.'

'Surely he's not likely to have left her much?'

'Or even anything. Except, if I've got the dates right, it
could be—' Whatever he intended to say was interrupted
by an insistent ringing on the front doorbell.

It was Molly who went to open the door. She returned
shortly afterwards shepherding a breathless Andras
Linkina in front of her.

The barrel-chested pianist was clad in a brown tweed
topcoat with a shoulder cape, and was carrying a narrow-
brimmed hat in the same material. He lifted a hand in
greeting to Treasure, then slumped down at the table where

Molly had been sitting. 'Oh dear,' he said, looking from the banker to Molly, then back again. 'Oh dear. It's a calamity,' he continued, in his deepest, guttural voice. He blew out a breath, then hit his chest twice with his fist in a *mea culpa* gesture.

'D'you want to take your overcoat off before or after you tell us about it, Andras?' said Treasure.

The other man looked down at his coat in surprise, as if he had been unaware that he was still in street clothes. 'My apologies,' he said, 'for breaking in on you. Unannounced. It is unforgivable.' He raised his arms in capitulation, an action that served to lift the edges of the cape so that he looked a little like a large bat about to take wing.

'You're forgiven. Would you like some coffee?' Molly asked.

'Coffee, no, thank you. I have come from the Fulham Police Station.' Linkina made the last pronouncement sound like a qualification of the first—as though attendance upon the Fulham police precluded the ingestion of coffee for an indefinite period afterwards.

'And you've walked all the way here?' said Molly in surprise.

'My flat is half way, you know? I was going back there. Then, it seemed to me I should come to you. Without delay. And here I am.' The speaker paused, lifting his snowy white head, but he still made no move to divest himself of his overcoat. 'You see, they have taken Stanislaus Bodworski,' he completed, in the same ringing tone that a Polish forebear might have used to announce the Mongol invasion of 1241.

'You mean they've arrested him?' said Molly. 'What for? Surely not for breaking into Bims's house last night? Gloria said she wouldn't bring charges.'

'It is for the murder of Sir Ray Bims. It is not an arrest. Not yet. They are questioning. Interrogating.' The Slavonic 'r's were being rolled with more than usual gusto to underline significant issues. 'But soon it will be an arrest. It's certain. Unless we act.' He looked sharply at Treasure.

'When did they pick him up?' asked the banker.

'Last night. At the hospital. At the bedside of his wife where he had arrived out of . . . solicitude.' Linkina slowly laboured each syllable in the final word, then gave a loud and disparaging tut before continuing. 'And because he was drunk, they said, they kept him overnight in a cell. They started to question him this morning.'

'But why do they say Bims was murdered?' Molly pressed.

'It is because they have proved he could not have taken the strychnine from Edingly's office. There was no opportunity, it seems. He was . . . under observation through all the relevant hours.' Linkina's hands rose skywards again despairingly. 'When they first find this out they interview Edingly himself. They are quick to do that.'

'Yes, I remember that Inspector was questioning him when we were both there, after the match,' said Treasure, 'but—'

'No, no. This was later,' the other man interrupted. 'At the police station. More serious.'

'You mean they suspected Edingly of being the murderer? Of . . . of staging the burglary himself?'

'They don't say. Not to me. Only to Bodworski who tells me. But they let Edingly go when his rifle is found in the boot of Bodworski's car. In Mulberry Grove. Where the car was left last night.'

'That's bad,' said Treasure quietly.

'But Bodworski did not steal the strychnine, nor does he know how the rifle got into the car,' protested the pianist. 'It's a frame-up.'

'Have they any other evidence against him?' questioned the banker.

'Circumstantial only. Like they say he killed Bims because Bims dropped him from the team.'

'That's hardly a reason for cold-blooded murder,' put in Molly hotly.

'But of course,' Linkina scoffed. 'Also they say that Bodworski knew his wife was having a love-affair with Bims. It was Edingly who discovered this.'

'Edingly?' Treasure questioned in disbelief.

'Yes. And the police say he told Bodworski. They both deny it, but Edingly couldn't deny he had told others the same thing. Like Trisall. Edingly was deeply shocked at what he called Bims's sinful conduct.' Linkina paused, breathing heavily, while lids with several folds of skin blinked over narrow eyes like the opening and closing of ruched curtains. 'He is known to be a very religious man. All . . . all fire and brimstone, as they say.' He shrugged to indicate his failure to understand why they said it, then he continued: 'At first the police thought he might have struck Bims down in retribution for the adultery.'

'But they wouldn't have thought it for very long,' said Treasure.

'That is true,' Linkina agreed. 'Not after they found the rifle. They say Bodworski knowing about the affair, whoever told him, is why he beat up his wife. After he poisoned Bims.'

'It's all nonsense, of course,' said Molly. 'If he'd killed Bims, why would he have been in the man's garden last night waiting for him to get home? And if Bodworski had assaulted his own wife, why did he rush off to see her when I told him she was in hospital? If the police are right, his actions were quite illogical.'

'Not, I suppose, if he was spreading a smoke screen. To suggest his innocence,' commented Treasure, but with doubt in his voice.

'That is exactly what the Fulham police are saying,' the pianist growled. 'That yesterday he was playacting. In the Bims's garden and also at the hospital.'

'Was Bims really having an affair with Mrs Bodworski?' asked Molly.

'The police say so, in front of me. That she's admitted it. Bodworski tells me, in Polish, it's true. That Bims seduced her. She was flattered by the attentions of a man she considered so important. It is how she got the Eels' marketing job. She met Bims first when she worked for another football club. The police were not intending to tell Bodworski about the affair, but he found out from his wife at the hospital.'

'She confessed to him?' asked Treasure.

'Yes. I do not know why.' True mystification showed on Linkina's face.

'I expect she thought he'd find out anyway,' said Molly, matter-of-factly. 'And preferred to tell him herself.'

'It's possible.' Linkina nodded a doleful agreement. 'Bodworski now thinks it was because of his wife that he too was bought by the Eels. It doesn't please him.'

'How come they let you in to see him, Andras? At the police station?' asked Treasure.

'He pretends his English is bad. That he needs a translator. They say there's no translator available so early. He says there's me. So they telephone. At six this morning. Felix Harden also comes to the police station. Later.'

'They sent for him too?'

'No, Mark. I did. We both protest at the injustice. Nobody takes any notice, of course.'

'Bodworski is entitled to a lawyer.'

'Yes. I get Charles Wigtree for that. At seven o'clock,' Linkina affirmed with some satisfaction.

'Is he a criminal lawyer?' asked Treasure, already knowing the answer.

'No, but he's a director of the Eels and he knows Bodworski. He's with him now. Me, they send away when some official Polish translator arrives at eight.' Linkina ran both hands through his hair in the familiar movement he made

before the start of every concert performance. 'Mark, you
are the man of affairs,' he said solemnly. 'Stanislaus Bodworski is innocent. That I can swear. You must find the
murderer who has framed my poor compatriot.' He took a
deep breath. 'We all help you, of course,' he added, magnanimously.

CHAPTER 14

'I never liked Lilian Bodworski. Tricia doesn't either,' said
Susie Harden with an adamant nod. Her friend Tricia was
the wife of Malcolm Dirn, the Eels' captain. 'They're
all the same, those high-powered business birds. Always on
the make. Always after something better. Including husbands,' the ex-nurse added firmly. 'Nigel, you eat the rest
of those cornflakes or you won't go to school. I mean that.'
She leaned over the white plastic-topped table, filled Nigel's
spoon with milk-sodden mush and pushed it into his mouth.

Nigel accepted the mush because he adored his nursery
school. He was in his first term there.

Two-year-old Kevin banged the tray of his high chair,
his yellow pusher in one hand and the spoon in the other:
he was demonstrating because his brother was getting all
the attention.

Felix Harden's hands moved to direct Kevin's eating
implements into his plate of apple purée. 'It's not Lilian
I'm worried about. It's Stan being accused of murder,' he
said.

'He didn't do it, did he? Even though he had provo-
cation.'

'For murder? You serious? You don't kill a person
because he drops you from a football team.'

'Even if he's sleeping with your wife as well?'

'Not murder?' But there was a lot more question than

shock in his voice. He'd had enough shocks for one morning
—and it was still only twenty past eight. He wished he'd
had his breakfast before he'd gone to the police station, in
a hurry, before the others had been up. Doing things on an
empty stomach never suited him, and now he seemed to
have lost his appetite.

'You wouldn't murder for that, but a Pole might.' Susie
poured herself more tea. 'Polish men are quick-tempered.
Easy to arouse. It's well known.' Her plump fingers pressed
her glasses further up the short bridge of her bob-ended
nose. 'You said he could have done the burglary for a start.'
She leaned across again to wipe Nigel's mouth with his
napkin.

'Anyone could. Anyone who knew the combination of
that lock.'

'And Stan did.'

He shrugged, toying with the rest of the sausage and
bacon she had cooked for him. 'Can't know for certain.
Malc Dirn knew it, and he could have told a few others.
Players go to the Supporters Club to autograph pictures
and that. Out of hours.'

'But if he didn't do the burglary, how did the rifle get in
his car?'

'Easy. He never locks the boot. He's known for it.'

'But not by the police? Did you tell them?'

'Of course I did. But I don't think they believed me.'

She made a dissatisfied noise with her moist Cupid's bow
lips. 'But they certainly believe Stan did the murder,' she
said. 'Except he wasn't even there at the right time.
Between three and four yesterday? That's what the police
are saying now, is it?'

'Yes. As near as they can estimate.' Harden looked disconsolate. 'He swears he left at one. We finished game
practice at twelve. For the evening match. Like always.
Some of the lads stayed around for a bit after that. For
therapy, or to use the exercise room.' He reached for the

tomato ketchup as he went on: 'Lilian was away. In Birmingham. Stan would have taken her out for lunch otherwise, he said. He sent for sandwiches instead. Ate them in the dressing-room, watching TV. Then he left. Did some shopping, then went home. To their flat. He didn't see anyone there.'

'But that's when he heard on the radio Sir Ray had told you to drop him. To put him on the transfer list?'

'That's what he told the police.'

'And did he ring you straight away to find out if it was true? To know if he was playing last night?'

'Yes. I had to say I wasn't certain.' He moved uneasily in his seat. 'I asked him to ring back at four.'

'And when he did, you still hadn't made up your mind about playing him?'

'I'd made up my mind,' he answered pointedly.

'To play him?'

'Yes. But . . . but I still couldn't tell Stan then. Not for sure. Not till I'd cleared it with Sir Ray.'

'So what did you tell Stan?'

'I said Malc and I were still not sure who was playing.' He paused, lips pressed together, the edges of his mouth downturned before he continued. 'That's when he put the phone down on me. I was just going to say I'd ring him back. Which I did do. Ten minutes later. Except there was no answer.'

'But Stan had taken what you'd said already to mean he was out of the team?'

'He's told the police that, yes.'

'So what did he do then?'

'Went out and got drunk. At some Polish club.'

'He didn't ask anyone else what they thought? Any of his mates?'

'Too proud, he says.'

'Too ashamed, more like. They said on the radio the whole thing was only a rumour. Maybe Stan thought he knew the truth already. Sir Ray told you Tuesday morning, didn't he? Plenty of time for something like that to have leaked out. People can't help passing on bad news.'

'Well, I didn't tell . . .' He stopped without completing the sentence.

'You told Mr Linkina.' She gave a reproving nod as she spoke, while leaning down to retrieve the plastic toy bus Kevin had thrown on the floor.

'Well, he wouldn't have told Stan,' said her husband.

'Perhaps not. All I meant was other people could have found out by yesterday. Someone must have told LBC Radio, for instance.' Susie scratched the fold of her neck, under her chin. 'Did anyone actually see Stan's car leave after lunch? Drink up, Kevin, there's a good boy.' She was holding the child's cup to his mouth when he swung away, spewing milk, thumping his hands on the highchair, and screaming heartily. 'Kevin, that's very naughty.' She put down the cup, screwed the child's head round to the front, wiped up the mess, picked up the cup, then, with her threatening face close to his, firmly put the cup to his lips again.

Harden watched the performance before he said: 'Someone might have seen his car. Nobody's said so yet. There's a lot of action at Hugon Road on a match day.'

'On the chairman's floor?'

'On the mezzanine, yes,' he answered, but less certainly than before. 'Well, after about four-thirty,' he half corrected. 'When the caterers come. If any of the private boxes are being used. Besides the chairman's suite, that is.'

'And were the boxes being used?'

'I'm not sure yet. Some must have been.'

'It's time for school, Mummy,' Nigel broke in urgently. His anxiety about getting an early education was close to making him precocious.

'No, it isn't time. And you haven't finished drinking your tea yet. And what about the rest of that bacon?' Susie shuffled plates about in front of him. Nigel made his vegetarian face while stabbing the fork into the bacon. His mother returned to making Kevin drink his milk while saying to her husband: 'But if anyone went up and down again alone in the lift from the car park, or by the stairs before half past four—'

'To the mezzanine floor?' he provided, frowning.

'Yes, and went to the chairman's suite, no one need have seen them?'

'Possible, I suppose.'

She thought for another moment. 'When Sir Ray came back from lunch at quarter to three, was there anyone with him?'

'One of the other directors. Mr Crayborn.'

'Did he go up to the suite?'

'No. His own car was in the basement and he left straight away. Mr Edingly saw them come back from his office window. In Sir Ray's car. But he didn't notice Mr Crayborn leave.'

'So Mr Crayborn could have gone up to the suite and left later?'

He hesitated. 'I suppose so. But no one's going to accuse him of lying. Or committing murder.'

'So who else was at Hugon Road after lunch?'

'Er . . . I saw Gareth Trisall. When I was on the way to my office. He was topping up his tan. On one of the sun-beds.'

'When?'

'About three. Jimmy Atler was doing the same. They say they left together later.'

'Could either of them have done the burglary?'

'I expect so. They didn't, though. I'm sure of that. And they didn't do the other, either.'

Susie gave a negative and vigorous shake of her head. 'Why? Wouldn't they have been the next players Sir Ray would have wanted put on the transfer list?'

'Because they'd fetch the most money? No. He wasn't

transferring Stan for the money. He said it was because
Stan wasn't . . . er . . . fulfilling expectations as a player.'

'So have Gareth and Jimmy fulfilled expectations? I know
you're doing your best, love, but the Eels have had a dia-
bolical season so far. In spite of getting three new players.
Expensive ones. I'd say those two would think they were
for the chop next, once Stan had gone.' She waited for her
husband to answer but he stayed silent, looking perplexed.
'Was Malc Dirn around after lunch yesterday?' she went
on, more thoughtfully.

'Yes. With me. We had lunch together, then we went
over who we'd play if Sir Ray came the heavy. If he really
insisted Stan had to come out of the squad. I mean, after
I told him I wanted Stan in.'

'And what did you really decide?'

His expression became more morose. 'I told you. That
Stan had to play. I knew Mr Linkina would back us.'

'So Malc knew you'd been told to put Stan on transfer?'

'No. Only that Sir Ray didn't want him in the squad last
night.'

'What did Malc do after that?'

'I dunno. Went home, I expect.'

'Had you told him what Sir Ray said to you about never
selling Hugon Road? About him being against moving to
Cherton?'

'I did sort of mention that, yes.'

'You know Malc and Tricia have definitely bought that
sports shop in Cherton?'

'Of course I do. He hardly talks about anything else.'

'She's the same. She'll run it alone till he retires from
playing professionally. They're putting everything they've
got into it. Malc's always believed the Eels would move
out to Cherton. It's just the boost he needs for trade now.
Along with him being captain and everything. So what did
he say when you told him Sir Ray was against moving?'

Harden pushed his plate away. He had finished all the

food on it to set an example to the boys. 'He didn't like it. No more than I did.'

'But did you *say* you didn't like it either?'

He hesitated before replying. 'Not exactly. I think Malc knows what I feel about Cherton. Deep down, like.'

'Except you promised to back Sir Ray. Because of what he was doing over your contract?'

'Sort of, yes,' he answered, avoiding her gaze.

Susie didn't say anything for a moment, then she asked: 'And when you went to see Sir Ray just before four? To tell him you were going to play Stan, he wasn't in the suite?'

'He didn't answer when I knocked, no. Of course, he could have been lying dead in that dressing-room by then. I just thought he was doing one of his tours round the stadium. I didn't get too bothered about not seeing him till later on.'

'About telling him you were playing Stan?'

'Yeah.'

'That was going to take a lot of guts, Felix.' In a way more guts than she believed he had, she thought to herself —more guts even than it might have taken to drop strychnine in a glass of brandy if someone had the chance. She studied her husband's face carefully.

'I wasn't looking forward to it,' he said, then glanced at the time. 'I just remembered, I promised Mr Linkina I'd ring Malc. Tell him what's been happening, like.'

'Nigel, wash your hands and face and get your coat,' said Susie, standing up and lifting Kevin out of his chair.

She had wanted to put more questions to her husband, but time was pressing. In any case she couldn't have asked the questions in front of the children, she told herself, before finally owning that there was something else more fundamental that had stopped her. She and Felix were pretty close, not as close as some couples they knew perhaps, but close enough in the normal way. Except she didn't believe she could bring herself to ask him the ultimate question

now, in case he had to lie to her. She usually knew when
he tried to do that, as surely as when either of her children
tried it. She already had a sick feeling in her stomach that
Felix had avoided telling her the whole truth a moment
ago.

The police could hardly know how much safer Felix was
going to feel now Sir Ray Bims was out of the picture.
Susie had felt all along that for the Eels' chairman to have
extended her husband's contract for a year, instead of
renewing it for three, had done little permanently to relieve
Felix's feeling of insecurity. In a few short months he would
have been just as worried as he had been up to the beginning of this week about the longer term future, just as he
would have become even more beholden to Sir Ray. His
claim that he would have stood up against the chairman
last night over playing Stan Bodworski could just have been
bravado. The confrontation had never actually taken place.
At least, according to Felix it had never taken place. Susie
just had to pray that this was the truth. If it wasn't the
truth, the possible consequences simply didn't bear thinking about. Except suddenly she could scarcely think about
anything else.

Nor did it assuage Susie's fears to know that if her husband had found Sir Ray in his suite between three and four
o'clock yesterday, then for Felix to have murdered his boss
at that point meant that he would need to have been in
possession of the strychnine. The worst interpretation of
this meant not only that her husband was a murderer, but
also that he was a premeditated murderer.

The simple fact was that there was no one Susie could
think of who could have had better reasons for wanting
Bims dead than her own husband. So far as she knew,
his reasons were far better than Gareth Trisall's or Jimmy
Atler's, for instance—or even, she admitted to herself, even
Stan Bodworski's.

CHAPTER 15

'Oh, come in, Mr Dirn. My husband's expecting you. Since
you telephoned. He's just finishing his breakfast.' Millie
Edingly opened the front door wider to admit the captain
of the Eels, then nodded him through. 'That's a nice car
you've got.' She was looking at the red Ford Sierra estate
he had parked outside the house in Flower Terrace.

'Three years old it is,' the Midlander replied, wiping
his feet on the mat. 'It'll have to do another three as
well before Tricia and me are done with it, and that's
a fact.' He wasn't here to give the impression he was
well off—quite the opposite.

'Fancy!' She closed the door. 'Your wife's all right, is
she?'

'Yes, thanks, Mrs Edingly.'

'That's good. See her in the shop sometimes. Not lately,
though.' The implication left hanging was either that the
Dirns might be cutting back on fruit and vegetables, or
else that Tricia Dirn had removed her custom to another
establishment—that is, until the speaker added the afterthought: 'Well, perhaps she shops in the mornings now. I
only work afternoons.'

'That's it I expect, yes.'

'Would you like to go in there? Arnold will be along in
a sec.' She motioned him towards the open door of the front
room. 'I've just switched on the fire, but it's not so cold as
it's been, is it? Not quite.'

'That's right, Mrs Edingly.' In fact the room felt close
to freezing, and smelled as musty as a cupboard full of
worn-out football boots. A fitted gas fire—fitted some
decades before—was popping fitfully inside an imitation
wood surround below the mantel. It might have made some

difference to the temperature, he thought, if it had been alight two hours before this, instead of two minutes.

'Would you like a cup of tea? It's no trouble.' Millie smoothed both hands energetically back and forward over her skirt and pinafore, as if her palms were engaged on a waist- and stomach-reducing exercise.

'No tea, thanks, Mrs Edingly.'

'Right you are, then. I'll . . . er . . . I'll leave you to it,' she said, without specifying to what. 'And sit down, won't you?' she completed as she returned to the hall, closing the door behind her at the crashing third attempt, since the door didn't fit its frame properly.

It was a small, nearly square room, the northern dimension extended by a bay window. The interior was veiled from the street by closed net curtains and heavier, half-closed blue damask ones with tasselled edges. There was an ornate and thronelike carved wooden chair in the bay, facing inwards, and in front of this a smallish, polished round table. On the table, resting on a purple satin runner, was an immense, gold-coloured metal lectern in the shape of a two-headed eagle—or waterfowl. An eagle was what might have been expected, but both the creature's beaks though hooked were also flat, and the feet were definitely webbed. Dirn noted all this without finding it exceptional once he had allowed that a bird with two heads was pretty daft anyway.

A fittingly large Bible stood open on the lectern at what must have been a page of one of the earlier books of the Old Testament. The Bible and lectern dominated the room, which otherwise accommodated a surprisingly large number of chairs. The chairs came in a variety of shapes, sizes and states of repair. They were arranged mostly around the walls, with some of the larger specimens crowded into the centre, which left room for very little else —including human movement. There was a glazed book-case on one side of the fireplace that housed rows of matching, small, leather-bound volumes of a distinctly devotional character, almost certainly prayer books.

Several embroidered texts hung on the walls. Above the mantel, the framed print of William Holman Hunt's illuminating *Light of the World* would have illumined better, practically and spiritually, if it had been in full colour instead of monochrome, and if it had been exhibited in a less dark part of the room, although the whole place was fairly gloomy.

'Well, Malcolm, sorry to keep you waiting.'

Dirn jumped and swung round at the sound of Edingly's voice. The footballer had been studying one of the texts when the other had entered—and with less noise than would have seemed possible allowing for the misfitting door. There was no doubt a knack with the door, Dirn thought. Then he figured that Edingly probably moved about stealthily through professional habit—that his work must involve taking pests by surprise. 'That's all right, Mr Edingly,' he said.

'Nice of you to come over straight off. I thought it was best if we could finish off our talk in private. Never know with telephone lines these days. This is our prayer-meeting room. Prayer-meeting room,' Edingly repeated pointedly, as though to emphasize that you could scarcely do better than that when it came to a confidential environment. 'The Second Pentecostal Evangelical Church worships in members' homes as well as in chapel.'

'Is that right?' Dirn wondered if being second accounted for the two-headed bird, then decided it probably didn't.

'You can feel the atmosphere, I expect. Do much praying yourself, do you, Malcolm?'

Dirn cleared his throat. 'Sometimes,' he lied, but only out of tact and respect.

'I couldn't last without prayer. I saw you reading that text. *To speak with other tongues.* From the New Testament, that is, of course. *Acts of the Apostles*, chapter two, verse four.

One of the Pentecostal miracles. Other tongues meaning
many. Sit down, Malcolm.'

Edingly himself took what seemed to be the first chair to
hand. His visitor then did the same, but the host's chair
proved to be measurably higher, suggesting the choice had
been contrived. The two finished sitting unduly close
together in front of the fire, but with Edingly looking down
on the other man, who when standing was much the taller.

'Other tongues are all right. It's forked ones are dangerous. And forked ones we're meeting, by the sound of it,'
Edingly continued. 'So what exactly did Felix Harden say
the police had told Mr Linkina about me?'

'Well, it was really what they'd said to Stan, and what
Stan passed on to Mr Linkina. In Polish.'

'Other tongues? Other tongues?' Edingly interposed
sagely.

'Sorry?'

'Go on, Malcolm.'

'Well, when they found out Sir Ray had been murdered,
because he couldn't have nicked your strychnine, they wondered if there'd really been a burglary. Whether you'd just
sort of staged one. It's why they brought you in for questioning last night.'

'That's interesting, Malcolm.' It was so interesting that
it was why he had stopped any more of it being blabbered
over the telephone, in case the conversation was being overheard by anyone at Dirn's end—by Mrs Dirn, or a neigh-
bour, or any busybody who might happen to have been
passing through. 'The police never said that to me,' Edingly
continued. 'Only asked if I'd kindly help them further with
their inquiries, that's all.'

'Well, Stan said they had you down as a suspect. Because
you knew Lilian and Sir Ray were sleeping together.'

'But why—'

'Because you'd caught Sir Ray with her in ... er ...
having relations, Felix said. Because of the adultery, like.

Because you're very religious.' Dirn shifted uncomfortably, then glanced at the picture of Christ over the mantel. It meant raising his eyes higher than when he was looking sideways at Edingly, but only just.

'And Stan knew about his wife and Sir Ray?'

'Stan says only since last night. She told him. In the hospital. When she knew Sir Ray was dead.'

'Ah.' Edingly sounded partially relieved.

'Of course, the police thought you could have beaten up Lilian too. For her sins as well,' the footballer added, anxious to get all his reporting responsibilities finished and out of the way.

'But now they've arrested Stan for that and the murder?'

'They're going to, Felix Harden says. It's because they found your rifle in his car. Only . . .' The Eels' captain hesitated.

'Only what, Malcolm?'

'Only Felix told them Stan was always forgetting to lock his boot.'

'Is that so?' Edingly ruminated for a moment, leaning forward, at first it seemed to warm his hands in front of the fire, until he reached out further and turned the gas down. Now the flame was scarcely evident at all, though the popping noise it made grew even more frenzied than before. 'Well, let's pray Stan is innocent. As we know I am,' said Edingly, with heavy solemnity. He moved back into his chair, then gazed down sternly at his companion, weighing the impact of the last words. 'No doubt Ray Bims will have punishment meted out to him. For his manifold transgressions. In the hereafter. The hereafter.' His eyebrows lifted. 'Being meted out to him already, I expect. But I didn't have any hand in . . . in prejudging the wrath of the Lord now descended upon him. Descended upon him,' he ended with sermonizing fervour and a continued study of his visitor to ensure the message had registered.

Dirn looked quizzical. 'And you had nothing to do with

his death?' he asked, being one for clear and simple understanding in important matters.

'Of course I didn't.' Edingly, outraged, had reverted to
secular terminology. 'And you'll kindly not repeat what
Felix Harden said to you. About the police suspecting me.
Nor to anyone else. Not ever.' He took out a handkerchief
and wiped his mouth.

'Right, Mr Edingly.'

'The police were wrong. Saw their mistake soon enough,
of course. But talk like that can leave a nasty taste. Spread
rumours. Evil rumours that can hurt the reputation of a
Godfearing man.'

'That's true enough,' Dirn agreed, a little too readily,
judging by the other's pained-faced response. 'Would you
like me to have a word with the Gaff, with Felix?' he added
quickly. 'About not repeating what Mr Linkina said he told
him?'

'No. I'll see to that. And Mr Linkina.' If there were coals
to be hauled in that quarter, Edingly would rather be doing
the job himself.

'Yes, Mr Edingly.' Though a commanding enough personality on the football field, the Eels' captain was often
subservient in private relations with his elders and betters:
there was a particular reason for his being so with Edingly.

'And you'll keep in mind we were together yesterday at
the time Mrs Bodworski was attacked? When we were in
my office? At six? When you were signing copies of last
night's programme. I remember looking at the time when
you came in.'

Dirn swallowed. 'I thought . . .'

'Six o'clock exactly. Gareth Trisall was over the same
time the night before. Signing photos. I wanted Jimmy
Atler then too, but he couldn't come. Anyway, it was six
on both nights I remember.'

'Yes . . . six it was.' Dirn nodded his confirmation while
avoiding Edingly's gaze. He knew the time must have been

nearer half past six, but he wasn't inclined to argue.

'Not that anyone's going to ask now. Not ask you or me,' said the other man. 'Still, it's good to know I got a witness, just in case. Independent witness. Means you got one as well. Stands to reason.' He shifted his body to the right, a fraction closer to his visitor. The move was really more symbolic than physical, but Dirn found the increased proximity vaguely uncomfortable and a bit threatening. 'Nobody knows about the money I've got in your Cherton shop, of course? That the shop's a partnership?' Edingly continued in a dramatic whisper into Dirn's ear, though there was no one to overhear.

'Nobody, Mr Edingly. Nobody except Tricia, that is, and she hasn't told a soul.'

'And you haven't let on either about Mr Linkina asking me last autumn about the move to Cherton? To know what the official supporters would feel about it?'

'Definitely not. Tricia and me kept that strictly to ourselves, like you told us.'

'That's just as well. Real march you stole on everyone else there, Malcolm. Working out that the move was certain as night following day. Buying the lease on the shop. After I told Mr Linkina the supporters would back the move.' He nodded approvingly at his companion.

Instead of showing pleasure over his alleged astuteness, Dirn looked puzzled. 'And you really didn't think Sir Ray meant what he told you last week? That he'd be against moving? Felix seemed to know his view about that, too. Well, he kind of hinted he did.'

It had been more than a week ago when Bims had volunteered to Edingly that he wouldn't approve the Eels moving from Hugon Road to Cherton. It had happened during one of the chairman's walks around the ground before a weekday match. He had extended the tour to take in Edingly's office. Because Edingly guessed Bims might be telling other people the same thing, he had felt there had been no purpose in keeping the comment secret—though now he regretted having shared the information with Dirn. At the time he had been concerned that Dirn might be told by someone else, and get himself, and that wife of his, in a panic.

'Sir Ray was just testing reactions, that's all,' he now insisted loftily. 'I did say that. Remember?'

'Well, yes. Except when I thought about it, it looked as though we could have been in trouble over the shop,' Dirn responded.

'Well, there're no problems now,' said Edingly. 'Mr Linkina's plan will go through. No doubt at all of that. Oh, and by the way, I'll be able to let you have that extra twenty thousand pounds you need. For the shop-fittings and stock. Same arrangements as before.' He paused to ensure that the last point had registered before finishing with: 'We want to be the best sports shop in the area, don't we, Malcolm? Best in the area.'

'Thanks, Mr Edingly. Thanks very much.' Dirn's genuine relief showed clearly enough in his face. Getting this decision was the reason he had taken the trouble to drive the mile from his home to Flower Terrace at Edingly's request, instead of completing their conversation on the telephone earlier. It also underlay why his relations with Edingly remained both obsequious and formal—apart from the fact that his patron preferred them to be both.

The Eels' captain wasn't flush with money, unlike the three newest members of the team. He had started as an apprentice player at Hugon Road fifteen years before this and had never moved clubs. His captaincy was a reward for loyalty. His adequate but still modest salary and bonus arrangements reflected his status as a dependable team leader—but not as a high flyer. Never having been transferred to another club, of course, he had never received a percentage of a transfer fee, the surest way players have of accruing capital. This was why now, when he was approaching retirement age as a player, he lacked the savings to set himself up in his own business. It was also why he was so dependent on Edingly's good will.

The President of the Eels Supporters Club, in turn, enjoyed receiving—indeed demanded—the outward respect of the people who owed him any, as much as he enjoyed making money. By his standards, he had made a nice little pile years before when he had bought—for a song —the freehold building now occupied by the Supporters Club, before selling it on, leasehold, to his own committee, and without the members ever knowing he was the owner.

More recently, Edingly had been the anonymous buyer of a disused cinema and adjacent shop close to the Cherton practice ground. He had also acquired those at a knockdown price. His agent would shortly be completing the sale of the cinema to the Supporters Club for converting into its new premises. The committee members had been persuaded, once again by their President, that it was an offer they couldn't resist since he was certain that the Eels would be moving to Cherton in the very near future. The shop had not been offered because the agent had already been in the process of selling it to Dirn. Edingly had magnanimously helped the younger man with the cost, in return for interest on the loan, plus a half share in the new business.

Edingly's final stroke of genius, not to say duplicity, had yet to generate the fortune he confidently expected of it. His agent was arranging to buy back for him the present Supporters Club premises at Hugon Road. The price was high—other members of the committee might not be as mentally spry or as avaricious as Edingly, but that wasn't to say they were cretins. They knew that the Hugon Road building, like the stadium beside it, would become part of a major property development once the Eels had moved. In consequence, the price the committee was to receive was substantial enough to pay for the cinema at Cherton and its refashioning into a club. But it was still nothing like the potential value of the old premises which Edingly looked forward to realizing for himself before long.

Of course, if Sir Ray Bims had succeeded in preventing the Eels from moving, the losses to Edingly, to the Supporters Club, and to Malcolm Dirn would have been disastrous—most particularly to Edingly. The losses might not have been so disastrous perhaps as to persuade the police that Edingly could have committed murder to prevent them. That, in any event, was Edingly's own opinion, but it didn't stop him from trying to keep his tortuous involvements a continuing secret.

CHAPTER 16

'Can we come in, Mark?' asked Lord Grenwood, allowing that he and the two men with him were already across the threshold of Treasure's office. This was on the fifth floor of the newly built Grenwood, Phipps House in Chiswell Street, close to Whitbread's Brewery and the Barbican Centre.

The chairman of the bank was the only person, other than possibly the reigning monarch, who Miss Gaunt, Treasure's estimable secretary, would not have barred from entering his office unannounced or, as in the present instance, an hour ahead of an appointment. If Andras Linkina, immediately behind Berty Grenwood, had been by himself he would not have got beyond the middle-aged Miss Gaunt's own office without challenge, even though the lady, a keen concertgoer, was one of his most abject admirers. The third visitor got through because Miss Gaunt could see no purpose in attempting to stop him. It was only incidental that he was much the most physically formidable of the three: Miss Gaunt relied on personality, not force, to maintain her protective rôle.

The bank had only recently moved its headquarters from Old Broad Street. The new building was made of sand-coloured stone. It had six storeys and a double basement, and was post-modernist in concept with a pleasing Italianate flavour. The interior was equally unbrutal: its climate control was estimable, its art collection enviable, its electronic data and communication systems incomparable, and its worker-friendly attractions admirable—the latter including a fitness club and squash courts in the upper basement, and a winter garden on the roof with open terraces for the summer. There was still a traditional banking hall on the ground floor, airier and loftier than the old one since it was set beneath a soaring central atrium. Here too was a cluster of glass elevators that moved silently about their business, their journeys from the topmost to the lowest floors in full view from anywhere within the atrium, their illuminated cages resembling giant moving valves in some massive steam organ at a travelling fun fair.

At first the lifts had given Berty Grenwood vertigo, but latterly he had taken fleeting, harmless, and, he imagined, secret pleasure in riding the glass cages as often as possible studying the legs of the younger female employees as they glided past him ensconced in neighbouring glass cages.

'Disastrous events demand grave remedies,' Berty commented next without waiting for Treasure's response to his opening question, but offering an oblique explanation for his presence, with entourage. He made heavy progress across the thick and still new carpet towards Treasure's desk, his short legs pedalling, his bent elbows working the air. It was clear that he was not in the benign frame of mind usually induced by his morning outing in the lift. 'You know Charles Wigtree? Lionel's son,' he went on, halting and waving a hand at the beefy young man wearing a dark pinstripe suit and an ingratiating smile who was still bringing up the rear behind Linkina.

'Don't think we've met before, have we? Know your

father, though,' said Treasure, assuming that this was not
the engineer of the disastrous event that was impelling
Berty. He got up to have his proffered hand enclosed in a
vice-like grip by the third generation Wigtree to serve as a
partner in Dottle, Ram and Wigtree, respected City solicitors. 'I understand you and Andras Linkina went to Bodworski's aid earlier this morning,' Treasure continued.

Wigtree's smile faded. 'Yes. But I've since turned the
matter over to the partner who handles our criminal work,'
he said.

'Stanislaus Bodworski is no criminal,' Linkina protested
flatly.

'I'm sure not, sir, I only meant—' Wigtree began.

'You can spare a minute,' Mark?' Berty cut in. It was
the nearest he had got so far to an apologetic afterthought.
He had now changed course and was moving in the direction of the small circular conference table in the centre of
the room. 'I know we weren't due till later, but something
new's come up. Something serious. Ian Crayborn won't be
here yet. Gone . . . somewhere else.' He frowned because
he couldn't immediately remember precisely where, then
sat himself down in the nearest chair. Linkina sat next to
him.

'My father retired last year,' said Wigtree loudly as he
and Treasure moved to join the others around the table.
The lawyer, who was average height with curly hair, had
the build and movements of a middle-weight boxer, and,
to go with this impression, a broken nose on a somewhat
flattened face. He looked to be in his early thirties. 'I was
Father's proxy on the Eels' board for years,' he continued
in a hearty Home Counties inflection. 'They made me a
director in my own right two years ago,' he added, without
quite the same confidence as before.

Treasure certainly sensed that the last statement came
over less as a boast than an admission, and speculated that
he might be about to hear why.

'Fact is, there's been a cock-up,' Berty offered on cue. 'Over the custody of the Hugon Road title deeds.' He bounced up and down in his chair.

'Been lost, have they?' asked Treasure in an unperturbed way that was intended to lower the octogenarian's concern as well as his blood pressure.

'No, found, I'm afraid.' This was Wigtree, who then failed to stifle an involuntary, high-pitched nervous chuckle that ended as a sort of strangled cough. 'At the Krasna Masira Bank in Lombard Street,' he completed, rubbing the end of the broken nose and making it appear even flatter than before.

Treasure's eyebrows had lifted a fraction even before the unquestionably pained silence that followed the last surprising intelligence. 'Perfectly respectable institution,' he said warily. 'If a somewhat exotic repository for the title deeds of a London football stadium. Unless . . . Oh Lord!' He had been watching the ever lowering expressions on the faces of the other three. 'You don't mean someone's been using the deeds as collateral? Illegally?'

'Precisely that,' Berty uttered with a sigh. 'How d'you guess?' he asked sorrowfully and without sounding as if he expected or required an answer.

'Sir Ray Bims arranged a two-year renewable loan of three million pounds with the Krasna Masira, using the deeds as security. That was eighteen months ago,' said Wigtree, pawing nervously at the tie of an expensive school whose pupils were more noted for sporting than academic prowess. 'Because of the timing, we think the money was used to fund his investment in the BNMR. In the Caymans.'

'But, Berty, you told me the ownership of the stadium was established in trust. In perpetuity?'

'It is, Mark.' The disconsolate Lord Grenwood grasped the arms of his chair, levering himself up as he did some strenuous crossing of his legs, first one way and then the other.

'So how could the deeds to the property be used as security?'

'They can't be in the ordinary way, Mr Treasure,' said Wigtree, then his face clouded. 'Only in very special circumstances. On a temporary basis. For the benefit of the club. At the direction of all the trustees.'

'From memory, the trustees being Lord Grenwood, the late Ray Bims, and . . . and yourself?'

'That's right.'

'And where do you usually keep the deeds? I assume not at the Krasna Masira Bank?'

Wigtree cleared his throat. 'Actually, they're lodged here. At Grenwood, Phipps.'

'Oh crikey,' the Grenwood, Phipps Chief Executive responded without troubling to cover his disquiet.

'For safe-keeping.' Wigtree unintentionally rubbed salt into the wound. 'In the Eel Bridge Rovers' strongbox. Except . . .' He hesitated while glancing towards Lord Grenwood.

'Except Bims took 'em away in July, the year before last,' Berty expostulated. 'Can you credit such a thing? Under our noses. He nicked them, the . . . the unmitigated bounder.' He cleared his throat loudly. 'Don't usually speak ill of the dead of course, but, but, but, but—'

'Quite,' said Treasure, stemming the string of buts that was beginning to resemble the idling emission of a two-stroke petrol engine. 'How many trustees have to be present to open the Eels' strongbox?' he continued quickly.

'Only one, I'm afraid,' said Wigtree. 'Any Eels trustee or director can ask to see the contents at any time. We've just found out from the records it's only been opened that one time in the last three years. By Sir Ray. So we know exactly when he acted.'

'And no one's ever missed the deeds?' asked Treasure.

'Because no one's ever needed them,' said Wigtree.

'He took a hell of a risk, of course,' the banker observed. 'And what sort of inquiries did the Krasna Masira Bank make before they advanced the loan?'

'Ian Crayborn's with them now, finding out,' Berty replied in a triumphant voice since he had just recalled where Crayborn had gone. 'They were said to be pretty flush with funds two years ago, I remember.'

The Krasna Masira was a Middle Eastern bank controlled by a wealthy merchant family.

'He went there first thing,' Wigtree enlarged. 'The head of their securities department had faxed him at his office overnight. Chap had heard about Bims's death. Wanted to know when we'd be appointing another trustee in his place. To manage the loan. Showed he was pretty much on the ball, I thought.'

In sharp contrast to the footwork exhibited by some others, Treasure concluded inwardly. Aloud he said: 'Hang on. Was the loan arranged in the name of all the trustees or just Bims's?'

'All of them. The wording of the deed would have stopped Bims doing it on his own,' Wigtree replied. 'But he handled all the negotiations himself.'

'Except other signatures were involved?'

'Yes. Of all three trustees,' said Wigtree. 'Two of them must have been forged, of course. Lord Grenwood's and mine. We've neither of us ever signed a loan agreement.'

Treasure leaned back in his chair. 'Well, that's the first good news,' he said. 'If we can prove forgery in court, the Krasna Masira will have to return the deeds and whistle for its money. Or sue Bims's executors for it, perhaps.'

'You're sure of that, Mark?' Linkina had spoken for the first time since sitting down. 'It's what we hoped you'd say.'

'I'm quite sure. One forged signature is sometimes difficult to prove beyond reasonable doubt, but we should be home and dry with two. You agree, don't you?' He had turned to the lawyer.

'Absolutely. I'd like to get counsel's opinion, all the same,' Wigtree replied with evident relief.

'Agreed,' said Treasure. 'And as quickly as possible. Incidentally, how were the loan funds made available?'

'They were put on deposit at the Krasna Masira. Most of the money was withdrawn fairly sharpish on letters of instruction, again purporting to be signed by all three trustees,' Wigtree supplied. 'But there was always enough in the account to cover the quarterly interest on the loan. It was arranged that any correspondence was addressed to Bims at his Mayfair office.'

'Hm. Very neat,' Treasure observed with a sigh.

'It does seem the Krasna Masira should have taken more precautions than it did to protect itself,' Wigtree added, a touch sanctimoniously in the circumstances.

And the same might have been said of the Eel Bridge Rovers trustees, Treasure considered privately. 'The precautions of honest men can usually be confounded by crooks, of course,' he observed aloud. 'And what seems to be established beyond reasonable doubt is that Bims was a crook.'

'And we know now why he wouldn't even discuss the club moving to Cherton. Not the possibility of it,' said Linkina sourly, shaking his head. 'He could not have anyone starting negotiations to sell Hugon Road. That would have meant producing the deeds. He could not risk that in any circumstances.'

'It might also have a bearing on why he was murdered,' said Treasure unexpectedly, and turning to Linkina. 'By someone desperately anxious for the move to take place, perhaps?' His glance had dropped to the plaster dressing on the pianist's injured finger, but the action had been involuntary.

*

Two attractive teenage girls emerged from a taxi outside the new red brick police station in Fulham's Heckfield Place, bringing glamour and colour to a sombre area. At least, that is what the duty constable behind the front desk thought as he watched them come in and then dealt with their request.

'Two charming young ladies wanting to speak to DI Jeckels himself,' he explained to whoever was answering his call to the CID office upstairs. There was a hint of sarcasm in his voice, particularly in the heavy emphasis he put on the word 'himself'. Most people in the station knew that Jeckels was shy in the presence of pretty women. 'It's to do with the Bims death. They say it's important, and they're not willing to speak to anyone else,' the constable added, waited a moment, chewing the end of his pencil, nodded, and then put the phone down. 'If you'd like to follow me, ladies, Detective-Inspector Jeckels is available now, but he hasn't got long. He's coming down to see you.' He pressed the door release for the girls to come through into the station proper, and studied their bottoms as they did so.

Some minutes later, slim brunette Mademoiselle Claire Demoins, and buxom blonde Fräulein Ruth Scheimer, both just sixteen, were seated side by side at a table in one of the interview rooms on the ground floor. Jeckels was alone on the other side of the table.

'So you're both students at the Grantock Finishing School in South Kensington? And that's just across the street from Leinster Court—'

'Where Mr Stan Bodworski is living, yes,' cut in Ruth Scheimer, sharply pushing aside the long golden hair off her face with an energetic movement of one arm. She did this quite frequently, with the effect, each time, of making her well-developed breasts wobble in an uncontrolled manner under her red jumper. It was an action that had Jeckels in thrall, that is until slim Claire Demoins stood up, and allowed her calf-length leather topcoat to part at the front. Beneath, she had on a tight skirt, also leather, which she then busily employed both hands to ease around her slender buttocks before she sat down again primly with a demure smile. She had done this twice already, making Jeckels gulp both times.

'Quite so,' the policeman observed, writing Leather Court instead of Leinster Court in his notebook. He corrected the mistake and then initialled it in case the notes were ever used in evidence. There was extra reason for his punctiliousness. He had just been admonished by his detective-superintendent, unfairly in Jeckels's own opinion. It was why he was playing everything by the book, especially anything to do with the Bims case, of which he was still the officer in charge—but only just. This was the reason Jeckels had decided to see the girls himself instead of sending down an underling. So far, no one else had come forward volunteering anything on the case, despite the publicity. The girls might be offering a breakthrough.

When Jeckels had been sent to the scene of Bims's death the evening before—because he had been at the stadium already—there had been nothing at the time to suggest it was anything other than a case of suicide. All those present, including the team doctor and the police surgeon, had accepted that Bims must have taken a lethal dose of strychnine, self-administered, in a glass of brandy. The body had duly been removed to the mortuary for examination, and Jeckels had done everything required of a responsible, senior police officer in the circumstances, including arranging for the poison container and the brandy glass to be turned over to the coroner's officer.

Most pertinently, it was Jeckels himself who had later deduced, after questioning Lilian Bodworski and interviewing, then re-interviewing Arnold Edingly, that Bims could not possibly have stolen the strychnine himself. Thus, it was on his own initiative that the case had been converted into a possible murder inquiry.

It had been on Jeckels's instigation also that Bodworski

had been picked up promptly and detained as a likely suspect.

Unfortunately, by the time all this had happened, the chairman's suite at Hugon Road had not just been tidied but also cleaned and burnished throughout by the diligent outside firm of cleaners and caterers who regularly performed these duties immediately after matches. They had not asked special permission to proceed on this occasion, but if they had done, no one would have refused it because Jeckels had placed no embargo on entry to any part of the suite once the body had been taken away. For this reason, the possibility of forensic experts now picking up any useful clues at the scene of the crime was so remote as to be virtually non-existent—though they were there now, trying.

Jeckels was also trying—to retrieve the goodwill of his superiors.

'And we are watching always for Stan. In the afternoons. When he is returning sometimes. Like yesterday,' Ruth had just finished telling him, her tongue protruding delicately to wet her half-open, naturally pouting lips.

'We watch from our window. By our desks. Because he is so beautiful, and we love him deeply,' said Claire with intense feeling in her voice, and an expression of pure innocence illuminating the long thin face and the huge pleading eyes.

'And we go to watch him play also,' said Ruth.

'You've been to Hugon Road stadium? To a match?' Jeckels was unfamiliar with the less than demanding and sometimes eccentric curricula of London finishing schools maintained mainly for the academically ungifted daughters of wealthy Continental families.

'*Yah*, twice we have been there. You are understanding, always with the class?' Ruth explained heavily. 'This is so we . . . assimilate, is right? With English society, yes? But in a glass box. So we don't assimilate so much.' Her robust chuckle made her breasts jump about with complete and, for Jeckels, delicious abandon.

'But that is how we fall in love with Stan Bodworski,' Claire enlarged.

'You do mean Bodworski?' the policeman inquired carefully. 'Not one of the other Eels? Not er . . . not Gareth Trisall, for instance?'

Both girls hooted their disdain over what to them was evidently an inane suggestion, even falling into each other's arms before their slightly overplayed derision was stemmed.

'This Trisall? He is only pretty. So the Italian girls in our class, they like him. But he is not a hero. Not like Stan,' the French girl insisted. 'Stan is such a player with the ball. *Formidable*. So fast. When he puts it in, he makes us crazy. You understood what I am meaning?' Her eyes bored into Jeckels's while her whole body shuddered.

Jeckels thought he understood what she was meaning.

'Only last night, is not possible we see him play,' said Ruth next. 'We are at the theatre. Is not very good. Not like football. Then we are telling . . . sorry, we are told today, much worse than this. It's that Stan don't play.'

'Also, they are making an explanation on breakfast television,' Claire took up their story again. 'He is arrested. By the police. By you. Detective-Inspector Jackals.'

'Jeckels,' he corrected with an apologetic cough.

'*Oui*. For murder. Yesterday. In the afternoon. *Mais c'est impossible*. We are knowing. *Bien sûr*.' She got up to pull at her skirt again in an agitated manner.

Jeckels closed his eyes for a moment. 'He hasn't been arrested. Are you saying you were with him in the afternoon?'

Both girls gave yearning sighs, spontaneously.

'For a little only.' This was Ruth, with regret. 'But we are knowing where he was. Because he comes to his apartment at . . . at five minutes to three.' She looked at the other girl, who nodded agreement. 'We see him park his car and go inside. Then lights come on in the apartment. He comes to the window. The day, it is dark. With clouds? He is closing the curtains.' She shrugged brusquely, an action that affected her bosoms and the Inspector to roughly the same disturbing degree. 'Then we watch. While we have the class. So boring.' She leaned forward as she spoke, extending the consonants. 'It's English etiquette we are learning. You are learning English etiquette at school? No? That's what we are thinking.'

'Then at four, when etiquette class is over, we go across to wait for Stan to come out,' said Claire. 'So we can speak to him. Touch him.'

'You stood outside the flats?'

'*Yah*. By the front door,' said Ruth. 'Then he comes. After the lights in the apartment go out.'

'At what time was this?' Jeckels asked.

'Ten minutes after four,' Claire provided promptly. 'But he is so angry. He is not seeing us even. Not stopping.'

'But you spoke to him?'

'No. At first we are so scared because of his crazy look. It's terrible. Then it was too late for us. He's gone.' She threw both arms up over her head. 'Like zoom. In his car.'

He regarded the two for a moment. 'But you'd swear you saw him go in to the flats at two fifty-five, and come out again at four-ten?'

'Sure,' said Ruth.

'Sure,' chorused her partner. 'So now you are letting him go, no?'

There was a back entrance to the flats, into a yard. Jeckels had checked on that yesterday. But it worked on bolts and a deadlock. You had to call the caretaker from the basement flat before you could get out or in that way. It was a security precaution. A good one. He'd need to check that the Pole hadn't used it—couldn't have used it. Of course, if Bodworski hadn't killed Bims it was still possible he could have assaulted Mrs Bodworski—but the

Inspector was beginning to doubt that possibility as well.

'Mr Bodworski is only here to help us with our inquiries. When he's done that he should be free to go,' Jeckels told the girls, despond in his mind if not in his voice. 'Thank you for coming in.'

CHAPTER 17

'Sorry to have kept you waiting, Inspector,' said Treasure, hurrying forward to shake hands with Jeckels, and nodding at the uniformed commissionaire who was holding the door open for him as he came in from Pall Mall.

'Not at all, sir. I've just arrived. It's a nice building,' Jeckels replied.

They were in the vaulted and marbled entrance hall of the Institute of Directors, a monumental edifice in the classical style at the Trafalgar Square end of one of London's widest and most dignified thoroughfares. It was a minute after midday.

'Impressive pile, yes. By John Nash, if you're interested. 1827 or thereabouts, with titivations later by Decimus Burton. Used to be the Unites Services Club. Also known in those days as the Senior.'

Treasure's usual club was only walking distance away from here in St James's. It was architecturally more interesting and its membership somewhat more rarefied than that of the IOD. He had eschewed arranging this meeting there because, as with most London gentlemen's clubs, the rules forbade members to produce business papers on the premises. The papers in the slim leather document case under his arm, brought especially to show Jeckels, were evidence of too much rule-breaking for their bearer to risk their being the subject of any more.

Treasure led the policeman past the busy reception desk

and down the short corridor on the left into the cavernous, high-ceilinged room at the end. Here, the dark red-papered walls were hung with heavily framed paintings of uniformed, stony-faced generals and admirals mostly from another age, on long loan from the previous occupiers of the premises who might otherwise have had some difficulty, not to say possible embarrassment, over providing accommodation for them anywhere else.

'My dad was in the regular army. Regimental Sergeant Major,' Jeckels volunteered unexpectedly. He beamed at the full-length portrait of the First Earl Kitchener of Khartoum as he passed it, and as if greeting a respected familiar. Kitchener's severe return stare, fixed in oils since around 1915, seemed scarcely deserving of such civil acknowledgement.

'Well done your father,' said Treasure whose mind's eye impression of an RSM allowed for a person altogether more robust than Jeckels. Perhaps the policeman had taken after a weedy mother. 'This used to be the dining-room,' the banker offered. 'They've kept the tables and chairs. Handy for meeting like this. Under-used too.' He motioned Jeckels towards one of several small, empty oblong tables standing between an Ionic column and one of the massive sash windows overlooking the street. 'Take a seat,' he said. 'Ian Crayborn should be here shortly, with Charles Wigtree. I gather you met Wigtree earlier this morning? Like a drink or anything?'

'No, thank you, sir.' The policeman pulled out one of the four chairs. Treasure took the one opposite.

Of the fifty or more similar tables in the room, only about half were occupied, mostly by small groups of business-suited men, and some women, engaged in close discussion. White-bloused waitresses were taking orders or bringing refreshments.

Since his encounter with Berty and the others, Treasure had been to another hastily convened meeting—with a lawyer whose office was off Piccadilly. He was due for lunch in Westminster an hour from now. 'Right, Inspector,' he said briskly, checking the time and looking about him to be sure they could not be overheard. 'In the first place, please accept that Grenwood, Phipps will do everything in its power to help the police find Bims's killer.

'Was he a customer then, sir?' the policeman asked ingenuously.

'No, he wasn't.' Treasure frowned, mildly affronted at the suggestion that the bank's sense of public service might be governed entirely by self-interested considerations. Then he concluded more charitably that the supposition might well be a reasonable one for a policeman to take. 'But as you're aware,' he went on, 'Bims was chairman and . . . and temporary owner of the Eels, a club too closely associ- ated with the Grenwood family for the present Lord Gren- wood not to feel personally and deeply responsible for its reputation. And its fortunes.' He took a long breath after this somewhat pompous declaration. 'Of course, it follows he's also embarrassed by its misfortunes.' He folded his arms tightly as he spoke. 'And it's a misfortune I'm going to tell you about. Anyway, rely on us, Inspector, for any help we can give you. The sooner the murder can be cleared up, the sooner we can sort out the problems of the club. Incidentally, Lord Grenwood is going to buy back the Eels from Bims's executors.'

'I see, sir,' said the policeman. 'Well, we certainly don't turn away expert assistance when its offered. For the right reasons,' he completed carefully.

'Fine. Well, as I said on the phone, we've unearthed some pretty damning information on Bims. Eighteen months ago he stole the title deeds of the Hugon Road stadium. Used them as collateral to raise a loan of three million pounds from the Krasna Masira Bank. To do that he needed to forge the signatures of the two other Eels' trustees.'

Jeckels seemed to accept this grave report on the rank

duplicity of a titled member of the British business establishment without undue surprise. 'And he used the loan for his own purposes, sir?' he asked.

'Without any question. Mostly to invest in the BNMR. Some of the remainder was possibly used later to pay transfer fees. For the three new Eels players.'

'There's proof of this loan, sir?'

Treasure nodded and produced the stapled sheets from his document case. 'That's a copy of the loan agreement. We got it from the Krasna Masira Bank today. The situation hasn't been reported to the Fraud Office yet. We're getting counsel's opinion on the legal status of the loan and the property deeds first. It's what Crayborn and Wigtree have been doing since mid-morning.'

Jeckels thumbed through the four tightly printed pages without much attempt at reading what was on them until he came to the end page. This contained a number of signatures. He studied the names, then looked up with a nod. 'You think this'll have a bearing on the murder, sir?'

'Well, let's say if it had been suicide, not murder,' Treasure replied thoughtfully, 'I think I'd have assumed the chap had done it to avoid facing criminal proceedings. You should know that he was about to be deposed as chairman of the Eels, and he was aware of that since lunch-time yesterday.'

'He had lunch with Lord Grenwood, Mr Linkina and Mr Crayborn, didn't he, sir?'

'That's right.'

'Did they tell him then he had to go, sir?'

'No. They asked him politely to resign. When he refused he must have guessed the consequences. He would also have twigged then that the Hugon Road stadium would be put up for sale. Despite his opposition. When that happened, of course, it would have come out immediately that the deeds were missing.'

'And if he'd resigned, like he was asked to do?'

'I'm afraid the same thing would have happened. He knew that too. So he was cornered.'

Jeckels blinked. 'But it wasn't suicide, sir. Though we know now he did die of strychnine poisoning. The autopsy's confirmed that this morning.'

'Which means he could possibly have been murdered by someone else involved with the BNMR. Someone who knew how he'd raised the three million, and that the source of the money was about to be disclosed.'

'With Bims arrested for fraud?' The policeman paused, sucking his lips. 'I don't see—'

'The drug barons who set up that bank have been counting on anonymity,' Treasure interrupted. 'Bims was one of their apparently respectable front men. Possibly their remaining slender hope of still making the bank look honest. For him to be arrested on a criminal charge would have cancelled out his value in one stroke. It would also have meant he could be pressured by the authorities to disclose how the bank worked.'

'To name names, you mean, sir? Hoping to earn clemency for himself?' Jeckels made a clicking noise with his tongue. 'Of course, he was telling people earlier he planned on going to Miami. To go before a Grand Jury.'

Treasure nodded. 'That was most likely at the instigation of his partners in the bank. While they still considered him capable of whitewashing the operation for public viewing. Anyway, I've just left his lawyer. Name's Martlone. Partner in a reputable law firm in Albemarle Street. I think you'll want to see him. He and Bims met for breakfast yesterday to discuss whether Bims should go to the States. When they parted, Bims said he'd definitely decided to go, insisting he was innocent of the pending charges. He even insisted the bank was straight.'

'Did Martlone believe that, sir?'

'He believed Bims was being honest about his own innocence, but he had reservations over the bank. In fact, Bims might really have believed the bank was straight, though on the face of it that still seems hard to swallow.'

'Or did he just think he could persuade a Grand Jury to believe it, sir?'

Treasure smiled. 'He was cocky enough. But I have my own theory about his motivation. I think his instructions to Martlone were a ploy. You see, he'd arranged for Martlone to tell the media about his firm decision to go to Miami, but not till later in the day.

'Why not straight away, sir?'

'Martlone didn't know. But he had to wait for final clearance from Bims before making any announcement.'

'Did Martlone know about the loan, sir?'

'Definitely not. But he knew Bims had at least two and a half million staked in the bank, and that the investment had grown enormously in value in the last year. He said Bims had been trying desperately to get some of the money out just before the bank's assets were frozen all round the world. Martlone understood the stake money had come originally from Bims's cash reserves.' Treasure paused. 'Then suddenly after lunch yesterday, Bims phoned Martlone to say he wouldn't be going to the States after all.'

'Has Martlone told anyone else that, sir?'

'No one other than me. It seems clear enough that Bims had decided to call off the American trip either because he thought the loan details were about to be disclosed, or because he'd found a way of stopping that happening.'

'By getting the drug barons to stake him in repaying the loan?' suggested Jeckels. 'That could be the reason Martlone was to hold up on the announcement. Bims was using it as a threat to get the money.'

'I've been wondering about that. It's possible. But one has to bear in mind that the BNMR assets are not only frozen but likely to end up confiscated. In those circumstances, instead of staking Bims with another three million, I think his criminal associates might have found it cheaper to have him shut up for good. That way they could possibly use him as a scapegoat. And that's maybe what's happened. In which case, Bims's threat to those associates was a more than sad miscalculation on his part.'

The policeman nodded slowly. 'So we have to find out who's been acting for the drug barons here. Besides Bims, I mean.'

'Something the banking industry and the police have been signally failing to do for some weeks past.' Treasure leaned back in his seat. 'Well, at least all this takes the heat off Bodworski, your . . . your current suspect,' he offered speculatively. Despite his saying he was activated by Berty Grenwood's concern in this whole matter, there was no disguising, from himself at least, that a large part of his purpose throughout the morning had been to fulfil his promise to Linkina to get Bodworski released.

'Might have done that, yes, sir.' Jeckels sounded uneasy. 'Sorry, I should have told you we're not holding Mr Bodworski any more. We sent him on his way half an hour ago,' he added with an embarrassed grin.

'I hadn't heard. So he's in the clear?'

'Two witnesses have come forward from Merlin Court, opposite his flat. They say he was there at the right time yesterday. Couple of underaged foreign students. Girls.' Jeckels made it sound as if he'd have preferred elderly British graduates, and preferably of the male gender.

'Well, that sounds fairly conclusive,' said Treasure.

From his expression, the policeman didn't seem quite so convinced. 'On the face of it, he may not have been directly involved in Sir Ray's death. But he could still have beaten up his own wife.'

'That was a much lesser crime, surely?'

If Jeckels paused to decide whether the last remark was intentionally sexist, and therefore deserving of censure by an officer of the law, he must have concluded that it wasn't. 'A lesser crime that we still think could be connected with the other, sir,' he said. 'She was badly hurt. They're keeping her in hospital till the end of the week.'

'Well, her husband's release will still please Andras Linkina.'

The Inspector's eyes narrowed, then his nose twitched as if he might have detected escaping gas. 'Mr Linkina's been beside himself to get Mr Bodworski cleared, sir.'

'They're both Polish, of course. And friends. Perhaps Linkina had a hand in Bodworski joining the Eels? I've been meaning to ask him.'

'Not according to Mr Harden he didn't, sir. Seems it was Bims himself who wanted to hire Mr Bodworski in the first place. Though he'd conveniently forgotten that when he saw Mr Harden on Tuesday.'

'When he told him to suspend Bodworski?'

'That's according to Mr Harden, yes.'

'I suppose Bims might have taken advice from Linkina. About hiring Bodworski.'

Jeckels leaned forward across the table. 'Mr Linkina's a widower, sir?'

'That's right. Wife died three or four years ago. Very sad. She was also a gifted musician. Solo violinist. Not up to his standard as a performer. But then, few people are.'

The policeman blinked. 'She was Colombian, sir?'

'Yes. I believe they met when he was doing a concert tour of South America.'

'Still makes appearances down there, does he, sir?'

Treasure was suddenly aware of what might be prompting the inquiries. 'Yes, I believe he does,' he answered carefully. 'And in North America, and Australia, and pretty well everywhere else where good music has a following. You know he's an international pianist of enormous repute?'

'Of course, sir. Do you happen to know if Mr Linkina knew Bims before Bims bought the Eels?'

'At a guess I'd say not. Linkina has been on the Eels

board for a lot longer than Bims. Maybe you'd better ask
Linkina that yourself, Inspector.' A hint of stiffness had
crept into the banker's tone.

'I will, sir. But it seems they'd have known each other
at least three years,' Jeckels still persisted. 'That's before
Bims was connected with the BNMR. But the South American connection—'

Whatever it was the Inspector had intended to add was
left unsaid because it was at that moment that Ian
Crayborn and Charles Wigtree appeared, after hurrying
across the room. They took the spare seats at the table.

'Sorry we were so long,' said Crayborn, who looked pale
and hot. 'Traffic's ground to a halt in the Strand. There's
a demo going on. Had to abandon our taxi the other side
of Trafalgar Square,' he offered breathlessly, while searching for his glasses.

'Worth the effort, anyway. Seeing counsel, I mean,'
Wigtree put in, red-faced but not exhausted like his companion. 'After counsel had looked at the loan agreement
and the letters of instruction, he said the court is certain to
declare them invalid. Bims's imitation of my signature
wasn't even close. Lord Grenwood's was better, but it was
clearly a forgery when you look at an example of the real
thing. So you were dead right, Mr Treasure. The Krasna
Masira Bank will almost certainly have to give back the
deeds to Hugon Road. They can sue the BNMR for most
of the loan, or alternatively they could go for Bims's estate,
but I shouldn't think they'll have much luck there, would
you?'

'They just might,' said Treasure unexpectedly, recalling
something he had twice intended to check before this.
'What do you think, Ian?'

Crayborn's pallor seemed to increase at the question
while the beads of sweat on his forehead multiplied. It was
as though he had been accused of something, not asked a
simple question. 'I . . . I can't believe Bims's estate will

have a positive value,' he replied haltingly, removing the glasses he had just put on. 'There's probably some life insurance, but that'll go directly to his wife. Otherwise . . .' He shrugged his shoulders.

'To his second wife, of course,' Treasure said thoughtfully.

'Yes,' the accountant answered, mopping his face with his handkerchief.

'Can't help feeling Bims's murder was all to do with the loan, Inspector,' said Wigtree. 'Doesn't seem Mr Bodworski—'

'Bodworski has been released,' Treasure interrupted, grinning at Jeckels. He was aware that the young lawyer would still be as anxious over the Pole's fate as he had been himself—and as beholden to Linkina about it, despite Wigtree having passed the responsibility for Bodworski's legal representation to a colleague more familiar with criminal law.

'That's right, sir,' Jeckels affirmed, and making to rise. 'Well, if you'd excuse me, gentlemen?'

'Sure. Let me see you out,' said Treasure, looking at the time. 'My car should be outside. My wife and I are going to a charity lunch at the House of Lords. Can we drop you anywhere?'

CHAPTER 18

'I had to come to Chelsea. To see my dentist. He's just round the corner from here,' Joyce Bims uttered nervously. Molly Treasure had just opened the front door to her in Cheyne Walk. This was roughly at the time that Treasure had been greeting Jeckels in Pall Mall. 'I've never changed dentists, you see. Not since I used to live here,' Joyce went on in a garrulous manner. 'And I didn't want to cancel this

visit, in spite of . . . well, you know. Usually it takes so
long to get another appointment. So kind of you to let me
drop in like this.' She took a quavering deep breath, fiddled
with the strap of her large leather handbag, stepped over
the threshold warily, then looked about her as though she
wasn't quite sure where she was.

Molly had waited to embrace her visitor. 'I'm glad you
rang,' she said, kissing her on the cheek. 'And I'm delighted
to see you. Was the dentist painful?' she asked.

Joyce seemed nonplussed by the question. 'Oh . . . oh
no. It was just a check-up.'

'Well, let me take your coat. I wish I could offer you
lunch. But Mark and I are on parade. A charity do. He's
sending the car for me.'

'Then I'll be delaying you?' She turned as if to leave.

'No, you won't. I shan't be going for ages yet.'

The other woman divested herself of the quite stylish,
dark blue woollen topcoat. Then, turning to the hall mirror,
she made an adjustment to the rakish little hat she had on.
'I don't usually wear furs in London any more,' she said,
making this almost reflex assertion sound even more rueful
than usual. 'Oh, did I say that to you last night? I keep
repeating myself.' She sighed heavily, and too intensely to
mark a simple lapse of memory, or the mere abandoning
of furs, or, as she had just admitted, to signal any lingering
discomfort from the dental visit.

'Still getting over the shock of Ray, I expect,' said Molly
perceptively. She took Joyce's arm and led her through the
hall and up the wide staircase to the next floor. 'I think
you're being very stalwart. Coming out of it so quickly, like
this,' she added, while being far from certain yet that the
compliment was justified—nor would she have been surprised if it was not.

'It isn't that. Really it isn't. Of course it was a shock.
His dying. And finding him like that.' As they reached the
drawing-room, Joyce bent low to her handbag to take out

a handkerchief which she then dabbed at the sides of her mouth. 'You'd think it wouldn't matter so much. After he'd left me. Three years ago nearly. But . . . but it's not the years apart that count, is it? It's the ones you spend together.' Her eyes were becoming decidedly waterlogged now as she continued: 'I know what people are saying about him, but really he had many good qualities. Many.'

'I'm sure,' said Molly, while wondering uncharitably about their likely nature. She seated her guest in a comfortable armchair in the Regency bay window at the back of the room, overlooking the garden.

'My daughter Liza offered to come down. From Liverpool. But I've said not to,' Joyce went on. 'She has so much work to do always.' She paused briefly, to no purpose opening and shutting the handbag which she was now nursing on her lap. 'Liza and her father weren't close, I'm afraid. Not ever. She'll come for the funeral later. To . . . er . . . to represent both of us, I suppose you'd say. I can't very well be there, can I?' she finished, in a seriously questioning tone.

'I should do what you feel is best. There are no rules. I'm sure everyone would understand if you decided you wanted to be there,' Molly replied, uncertain if this was the main reason why Joyce had come to see her, but somehow doubting that it was. 'What about a glass of sherry?'

'Oh, a sherry would be lovely. Thank you. You're so understanding.' Joyce was fiddling with the bag again. 'It's as though we were close friends, and we're not really.' She breathed in so deeply that it caused a grating noise in her throat. 'It's just I feel I can talk to you. It was the same when we first met. I don't have any really close friends, you see. Not any more. You lose them when a marriage breaks up. And . . . oh dear, I'm so worried . . . I'm . . . I'm distracted.' Her voice broke on the last word, and quite suddenly, all pretences abandoned, she was weeping piteously.

Molly hurried over, setting down the sherry glasses on the side table beside Joyce's chair. She knelt beside the stricken woman, putting a comforting arm around her, and making consoling noises. For some time she let the sobbing go on, confident it would cease eventually, which it did. 'I'm sure that's eased things a bit, even if it hasn't solved the problem,' she said encouragingly afterwards. 'Want to tell me what's bothering you? If I can help? Only if you want to, mind.' She pulled over a smaller chair and sat in it, still keeping a hand on the other's arm. 'Would you like to go and tidy up first?'

Joyce looked up shamefacedly, shook her head and wiped her eyes and cheeks. 'No, I'll be all right. I'm so sorry.' She shook her head again, reached for the sherry almost greedily, and took a sizeable sip. 'It . . . it was this phone call I got this morning. From someone in financial services. That's what he said he was.'

'From a firm selling insurance, you mean?'

'That's what I thought at first. Except he said his company were advisers, independent advisers, on investments. On investing large sums of money. Money that people inherit. Unexpectedly. He did say how sorry they were to hear of Ray's death.'

'How absolutely appalling,' said Molly, in genuine outrage. 'There really ought to be a law against telephone-selling to the bereaved.' She gave the Cartier triple string of pearls around her wrist a disdainful rattle. 'And I suppose he thought you were Ray's current wife?'

'No.' Joyce blinked. 'He was quite clear that I was his . . . his ex-wife. I said I wouldn't be inheriting any money.'

'Which was none of his business anyway,' Molly protested.

'I know. But I wanted to get rid of him.' Joyce stopped to blow her nose, quite noisily. 'Sorry. Then he explained. About the money I could get back. From the tax Ray paid three years ago. The capital gains tax. After he'd sold the company. Bims DIY.'

'I'm afraid I don't understand.'

'Well, neither did I. Not at first. And he said not many other people would either. It was only because he was an expert, and knows the law. The intricacies. So I let him explain. It's quite simple, really.' But her expression of strained concentration belied the last comment as she went on. 'Ray got thirty-four million pounds for the company when he sold it. It was in the papers at the time,' she added, with a hint of pride. 'But he had to pay out quite a lot of it, of course. In tax. About twelve million, I remember. That's what Mr Fifield said too.'

'Mr Fifield?' Molly questioned gently.

'Oh, he's the man who phoned. He knew all about it.' She leaned forward in the chair. 'He said I could claim it back. All of it. The capital gains tax. Because Ray made big capital losses on other companies later, the new ones he invested in. That was last year, and the year before. Mr Fifield was involved with Ray in two of them, and he'd kept track of the others. His company sometimes advised Ray, he said.'

'So why didn't Ray claim the twelve million himself? Against the losses?'

'Because . . . because he was still alive.'

For a moment Molly thought her visitor was going to burst into tears again, but another quite noisome noseblow seemed to eliminate that risk for the moment, although Joyce's still woeful expression and lacklustre delivery hardly seemed appropriate in someone who had just come into a huge fortune, even in melancholy circumstances. 'How interesting,' said the actress, waiting for further elucidation.

'It is, I suppose. Mr Fifield says a person can't claim back the tax paid on gains in one year . . . not against the losses he makes in later years. Not himself, that is. But if

he dies, his widow can claim. For up to three years after.'
She swallowed. 'I think I've got that right.'

Molly cleared her throat unnecessarily while she considered the phrasing of her next question. 'But . . . er . . .
but are you Ray's widow in the sense—'

'Oh yes,' Joyce cut in. 'It's only the wife at the time who
can make the claim. I mean the wife at the time the tax
was paid. Ray's second wife wouldn't qualify. And . . . and
I have to claim soon. Before the beginning of April. Before
the end of this tax year.'

'Because that'll be the end of the third year since Ray
paid the capital gains?'

'Yes.' Joyce's voice had broken over the word as she had
tried to stifle an unmistakable sob.

'Now really, Joyce, there's nothing for you to be upset
about in this,' said Molly, again extending a sympathetic
hand. 'Of course you're distressed over Ray's death still,
but if this Mr Fifield is right—'

'He sounded quite certain,' Joyce interrupted again, tearfully this time and with ominous, not hopeful, conviction
in her voice.

'Then it's a case of an ill wind that's blowing somebody
a bit of good. You,' the actress insisted. 'And you deserve
it too. The money will make a very nice wedding present
for the two of you. For you and Ian.'

Although Molly had not expected whoops of joy to greet
the presentation of what to her had seemed a simple and
welcome truth, neither had she anticipated a response that
would have been a touch more celebratory if she had just
announced that the *Queen Elizabeth* had sunk with all hands.
Compared to her earlier tears, the weeping that Joyce now
embarked on was even more heart-rending, and it took
comparably longer to stem as well, despite the mystified
Molly's deep and sympathetic attentions.

When Joyce was eventually quietened, her head bowed,
her eyes fixed on the now soggy handkerchief that her hands

were kneading on top of her handbag, the next words she whispered were: 'You don't understand.' She paused, seeming to rally a little, then continued doggedly as though what followed was something she had rehearsed in her mind before this. 'Ian is an accountant. He would have known the law. About a widow and the tax.' She sniffed, her breasts heaving. 'In all the years he's known me, he's never . . . never looked at me as a woman before the other night. Never said he cared for me in . . . in that way at all. Then suddenly he . . . he made passionate love to me. And asked me to marry him. Just when they say his practice is failing. So it wasn't because he wanted me, you see? It's so obvious, it was for the money. The taxes I'd claim back when Ray was dead. That's all it was, except I was stupid enough not to see it. Not even when it was explained to me. Not straight away.' There was a pathetic drop in her voice at the end.

'Oh come, my dear, surely you've got it all wrong?' Molly exclaimed with a confidence she wasn't feeling one bit. 'You told me yourself, Ian asked you to marry him when Ray was very much alive. On Tuesday evening, wasn't it? At your home?'

Joyce looked up slowly, her eyes reflecting the self-imposed misery she was going through. 'And after I said yes, when he was certain of my money, then, don't you understand what happened? That's when he left me and . . . and went off and . . . and murdered Ray.'

'And that's what she honestly believes?' asked Treasure nearly an hour later, as he drove the Rolls-Royce west along Pall Mall. His wife was beside him in the front passenger seat. After bringing Molly to the Institute of Directors, Henry Pink had been excused further duties for the afternoon so that he could attend the funeral of an aunt in Penge.

'She has no doubt of it at all,' Molly answered, tight-lipped.

'That Ian Crayborn is a cold-blooded murderer?'

Molly shook her head. 'Except the murder seemed to be incidental. I mean, that isn't what's bothering her the most.'

'Oh, come. If it isn't—'

'I'm quite serious,' Molly broke it. 'It's the prospect that Ian Crayborn isn't madly in love with her after all. That's what's hurting her so deeply. As a woman. You wouldn't understand,' she completed primly.

'Of course I understand. But the whole thing's still a bizarre supposition on her part,' he insisted as he swung the car left at St James's Palace, heading it down towards The Mall. 'Naturally she hasn't confronted her fiancé with any of this?' he added. 'With his being her first husband's killer?'

'Of course she hasn't. How could she? In any case, as I've said, for Joyce the murder really isn't the point,' Molly continued insistently.

'Well, it'll be very much the point to everyone else involved, especially the police. Has she told other people, d'you suppose? Her dentist, perhaps?' he inquired with a caustic smile.

'I'm sure she hasn't told anyone but me. And she won't either. Not till we've talked again. I told her I'd ring her this afternoon. At home.' Molly paused before adding, 'After I'd spoken to you. After you've decided what we should do.'

'I see.' Treasure didn't at all welcome the responsibility that was thus being thrust upon him. 'Well, I can tell you now, I find it very hard to credit that Ian Crayborn is a murderer,' he said flatly. 'And my guess is he does care for Joyce a great deal. More than enough to want to marry her.'

'But he never—'

'And he'd not asked her to marry him earlier, probably

. . . probably out of shyness,' he interrupted. 'I mean, he hasn't been a widower all that long.'

'So you've no doubt she's got it wrong? That it's coincidence she accepted Ian hours before Ray died, and that his murder made her a millionairess ten times over?'

Treasure hesitated before replying, and only partly because the traffic was heavy as he crossed the car over into Horse Guards Parade. 'I've very little doubt that Bims's death—' he began.

'His murder,' Molly corrected.

'All right,' he conceded, 'that his murder just after Joyce's engagement was coincidence. Granted a possibly awkward coincidence in the circumstances. The tax rebate is simply a bonus for Joyce, and . . . and only very indirectly so for Ian.'

'But why hasn't he told her about it too? He's her accountant, for heaven's sake? Would you imagine he doesn't know about it?'

'It's possible. Quite possible,' Treasure offered, but this time his tone was a touch less certain.

'But it's his job. Surely he couldn't be that ignorant? Not about something as important as this?'

'Don't you believe it. Even the best accountants have blank spots in their knowledge, just like everyone else. Tax law is terribly complicated. This could be something he's never come across before. Bims only died last night, after all. There's hardly been time for Ian to go into all the formal consequences for Joyce. Not in detail.'

'Not if he wasn't planning on Bims's dying before it happened.'

'Darling, that's a really preposterous implication,' he protested.

But Molly had been watching the doubt growing in his expression during his earlier comments. 'I'll bet you knew Joyce could be affected financially by Ray's death, didn't you?' she insisted.

'That she might be, yes. But only vaguely. The regulation involved isn't one most accountants would be referring to very often. But I'd come across it somewhere, certainly.'

'Because Grenwood, Phipps has more rich widows as customers than Ian?'

He shrugged. 'That might have something to do with it. As a matter of fact it *was* something I'd intended to check on. Wigtree, the lawyer who was at the meeting just now, he said there'd be nothing in the Bims estate to pay back a bank loan. Something did make me wonder if he was right.'

'But wasn't Ian at the meeting too?'

'Yes.'

'And he didn't say there'd be lots of money in the Bims estate?'

'No.' The banker shifted slightly in his seat as they passed the bottom of Downing Street. 'Although he could have been thinking the same thing as me,' he said. 'Not wanting to volunteer anything till he'd checked the facts.' There was a pause before he added: 'Except, come to think of it, I believe I did give him the chance to comment. But . . . but only indirectly.'

'You mean you didn't ask him if he thought Joyce would be getting tax repayments? Was that because you didn't want him to look suspicious? Because Inspector Jeckels was there?'

The banker gave a diffident sniff. 'I thought it might be more appropriate to ask Ian when he was by himself, yes. But there was another reason. I'm not sure whether anything Joyce may get back in taxes would be part of her ex-husband's estate. It could be the money will be legally hers alone. If it is, Bims's creditors would have no claim on her.'

'Meaning it may be nobody's business except her own? Hers and her future husband's?'

'That's right, yes.'

'So it'd be nothing her future husband would feel he had to raise in front of others? Especially not in front of a policeman? Not during an inquiry into her former husband's murder?' Molly completed with deliberation.

'If you mean Ian could innocently justify professional reticence in the matter, while incidentally avoiding putting himself forward as a murder suspect, I suppose you'd be right. Uncharitably so, but right all the same.'

'And it could be for the same reason that he's avoided telling Joyce about her entitlement?' she persisted, ignoring his last stricture.

'For the moment, yes. But he'll need to put her claim before the Revenue soon.'

'But not quite yet? Not while Ray Bims's murder is still in the front of everyone's mind?'

Treasure didn't reply to his wife's questions but his face indicated that he was deep in thought. He was still beating a regular rhythm on the steering-wheel with the fingers of one hand, waiting for the traffic lights to change in Parliament Square, when suddenly he asked, 'So Joyce said Ian was late getting to the theatre to meet her on Tuesday. Did she say how late?'

'Late enough for him to have had time to burgle the office at Hugon Road after Mr Edingly had left. She'd worked that out.'

'And we know he went back to the stadium with Bims yesterday, after their lunch with Berty.' Before driving the car off around the Square, the banker was waiting for a mounted policeman who had reined up beside them to get his frisky horse moving.

'Yes,' said Molly, also keenly watching the horse whose rear end was doing a rumba step dangerously close to her window. 'He said he left straight away afterwards in his own car. Without going up to Ray's suite with him. But if he did go up, no one need have seen him.' The police horse now controlled, the car had moved off. She reached down for her handbag. 'Is Ian's practice in as much trouble as Joyce thinks?' she asked.

Treasure pulled a face. 'According to Berty and Andras Linkina, it's ground to a halt. He's been pressing both of them to help him find new clients. At least, he was up to last weekend,' he completed grimly.

CHAPTER 19

'CADS must have made a packet out of this lot,' said the wiry Scottish golf professional, a member of the European Ryder Cup team, who was queuing alongside Treasure. The two, who were friends, had returned to the buffet to refill their coffee cups after a modest, stand-up meal consisting mostly of cold meat cuts and fresh fruit.

'Yes. Best attendance I can remember,' the banker agreed, turning to survey the packed room. 'Food was adequate too. All things considered,' he added with a grin.

'Considering the price of a ticket, you mean? Enough to pay for a slap-up dinner at the Ritz probably.' The other chuckled. 'Oh, don't get me wrong, I know the money's needed. And it's a grand cause. I'm glad to ante up for it any time. My wife's just shared a sprig of grapes with the Prime Minister and a Hollywood Oscar winner. That's heady stuff, don't you think?'

The Celebrities Against Drugs Society, CADS for short, usually held its early spring invitation luncheon here at the House of Lords—in the long, prettily papered Cholmondeley Room (pronounced Chumley) next to the terrace overlooking the Thames. As always, the event this time was high on prominent attenders and low on pomp. The other three CADS' quarterly lunches were held at the MCC Cricket Ground in May, at Wentworth Golf Club at the

start of a tournament in September, and at Covent Garden
Opera House in November.

At the foundation of the CADS, members had been
recruited almost exclusively from among sportsmen and
women, but, in the ensuing nine years, leading figures from
politics, religion, the arts and industry had been drawn in.
Individually and collectively, members engaged to give
their time, talents and money in the fight against drug
abuse, and, as rôle models, to promote the same objective
by setting a personal example, especially to the young.
Molly Treasure, who her husband had last seen sharing a
joke with the Bishop of Chichester and a bespectacled pop
singer, had been one of the first actresses to join. She had
been recruited by Berty Grenwood, a featherweight boxing
Blue in his Oxford days, and one of the organization's first
sponsors, as well as the titular host at today's function.
Mark Treasure had never formally become a member
because he refused to be rated as a celebrity. He just contributed to the funds and came to some of the lunches in
support of Molly and Berty.

'I think your delicious wife is signalling you,' said the
golfer as he and Treasure moved away from the serving
table.

'Time to leave, I expect,' said the banker, looking at his
watch. CADS lunches were usually arranged to be over by
two-fifteen. There were no formal speeches, only some brief
words of welcome and thanks from the annually elected
Chief Cad—on this occasion a recently knighted novelist.

'Darling, you haven't said hello to our favourite dancer,'
Molly exclaimed after her husband had elbowed his way
back to her. He had stopped to exchange greetings with
Andras Linkina, whose recent dour mood seemed to have
been temporarily lifted by the vivacious female German
violinist he had brought as his guest.

'Good to see you, Stephen,' said the banker, shaking
hands with one of the Royal Ballet's most admired soloists.

'We're coming to watch you in the new production of *Façade* next month,' he volunteered, fairly but not totally certain that he had the details right. Ballet came some way after opera in his list of favourite diversions.

'Thank you, Mark, and for turning up today,' replied the dancer, who was a member of the CADS committee. His voice was breathy, and deep-throated.

'Actually it's a revival of *Checkmate* they're doing, darling, not *Façade*,' Molly corrected her husband.

'Good try, though,' said Treasure, unabashed.

'Absolutely. Same period, but music by Arthur Bliss not William Walton. Easy mistake to make, love,' Stephen put in quickly, with a sympathizing smile, and leaving it uncertain as to which of his two listeners he had been addressing with the last endearment.

The dancer was well built, fair-haired and ruggedly handsome, with laughing eyes, a lantern jaw, and as mannered in his movements off the stage as he was on it. 'And now I want you both to meet a really very dear friend of mine. Very dear indeed,' he went on, with an over-played preamble, as he moved gracefully to one side revealing a drab young woman who had been standing behind him. Whether the woman had been waiting there for some time or had been engaged with someone else wasn't clear, though it seemed that the former was the likelier case judging from her forsaken appearance. Stephen now presented her to the others with rising fervour, his right arm pressed into the small of her back, his left hand taking hers, and deftly lifting it chest high across his own body. It was altogether as though she was a dancing partner he was bringing forward for a curtain call—except that the shapeless, shabbily clad figure and the object of these special attentions made them seem comical and, for her, evidently embarrassing.

'This is Nora Hawker,' said Stephen. 'Nora's the committee's most indispensable honorary secretary whom I love to distraction,' he completed, this time drawing her closer to him and planting a kiss on her pallid cheek in a somewhat less than distracted fashion.

'I've heard a great deal about you, Nora,' said Molly, taking her hand warmly. 'I believe Stephen told me you once worked for one of my husband's companies. Was it the bank? Grenwood, Phipps?'

Nora Hawker gulped. 'No . . . not the bank . . . it was . . . I worked for Regal Sun Assurance. In Holborn . . . but only as a secretary,' she replied in a dry, halting voice, twice having to clear her throat as she spoke, and leaning forward, shoulders hunched, chest hollowed, hands now clasped together tightly below her waist.

'Sounds as though we were careless in letting you leave,' said Treasure, hoping she wasn't someone he should have remembered—although as non-executive chairman of the insurance company there was an excusable limit to the numbers of employees he could be expected to know, even at head office.

'My mother was taken ill. I had to give up regular work to look after her.' In addressing Treasure the speaker seemed a trifle less nervous than she had been before.

'Our gain, though,' Stephen enthused. 'Nora keeps the membership list up to date from home. And the annual subscriptions. So complicated, and such a labour.' He ran one hand up across his curly hair, then down the back of his head bringing it to rest finally under his uplifted chin, the fingers posed like an open plinth.

'It's . . . it's a privilege to be of service,' the woman put in seriously, and boldly for her.

'Bless you,' cried the dancer, then, turning to Molly, he said: 'And you must remember Nora's twin brother Bobby, the dancer? He was such a promising boy.'

The actress's right hand went to her mouth in a sharp reflex reaction. 'My dear, you were Bobby Hawker's sister? I should have realized. I can see the likeness now.' She reached out to touch the other woman's arm. 'He had such talent. I was . . . I was so sorry at the time. You must miss him still.'

'Yes.'

Molly turned to her husband. 'You remember Bobby Hawker? He died very young. So tragically. It was . . .' She hesitated.

'They made him a drug addict. They killed him,' said Nora with stark firmness, and to Treasure again.

'Bobby and Jimmy Atler were . . . were very close,' Stephen supplied, filling the ensuing conversational gap, and darting a glance at Molly.

'Atler the footballer? Who plays for the Eels now?' asked Treasure.

'That's right,' said the dancer. 'Great CADS supporter. Absolutely dedicated to the cause. Especially since Bobby's death. Jimmy and Nora don't really . . . What I mean is, Jimmy never makes the spring and winter lunches, but he always buys tickets.'

'That's why I'm here,' Nora said with firmness, as though she were under an obligation to admit as much. 'Jimmy's always offering to bring me. Or give me his ticket like now. I've never wanted to come with him before, though. Except today I . . . I'm glad I'm here.' She took a deep breath. 'I'm sorry Jimmy couldn't be here too.'

'That's right, love,' said Stephen putting his arm around her again and giving her a squeeze as though she had said something especially commendable.

'It's certainly an impressive gathering,' said Molly.

'Yes,' the younger woman answered, but hesitantly as though that might not have been the reason for her presence.

'D'you follow football, Miss Hawker?' Treasure asked.

'Not really.'

'Although if Jimmy Atler's a friend, of course—'

'He was my mother's friend, not mine,' she put in, pulling

at the corners of the orange silk scarf knotted around her neck.

'I see.'

Stephen again broke the awkward silence that followed. 'The papers say you're going to be chairman of the Eels, Mark. Was Ray Bims going anyway? Because of the scandal? And was he really murdered? By Stan Bodworski? They're saying the police are keeping—'

'The police interviewed Stan Bodworski and haven't . . . detained him,' the banker interrupted.

'Is there anyone else in the frame, as they say?'

'I've no idea,' Treasure replied untruthfully, since he had several candidates in mind for that unenviable position.

'Poison is too kind a death for a millionaire drug dealer,' Nora Hawker uttered suddenly in a penetrating voice, loud enough to turn the head of the attractive Olympic swimmer being charmed by Berty Grenwood several paces away.

'Why does Merlin Court mean something to me? The police inspector mentioned it, and it's been bugging me ever since. Do we know someone there?' Treasure asked Miss Gaunt as he was leaving her office for his own after arriving back at the bank. They had checked his appointments for the afternoon.

'I believe Mrs Grantock has premises there,' Miss Gaunt replied, looking up again from her keyboard.

When Treasure's meticulous secretary volunteered to him that she 'believed' something, he had long understood it meant that the something was indisputable fact. Otherwise she'd have gone to look it up.

'Whoever Mrs Grantock may be,' he replied, still hovering in front of her desk, his eyebrows raised while he waited for further enlightenment.

Miss Gaunt pushed back her chair and removed her glasses. 'She and her husband run a finishing school for foreign nationals. She wrote last year asking if you'd recommend it. You said you would, if . . . if opportunity arose.' She made a face indicating that he hadn't thought opportunity ever would. 'Oh, and Mrs Grantock is Linda Linkina that was. Andras Linkina's oldest daughter. He sometimes gives talks to the students.'

The last valuable intelligence gave Treasure a sudden empty feeling in the pit of his stomach, despite the adequate lunch. He called Linkina immediately, but the only reply came from an answering machine, which is why he had Miss Gaunt telephone the Grantock Finishing School.

'Mrs Grantock wasn't available. But you were right about Mr Linkina being there recently,' Miss Gaunt related, coming into Treasure's office between meetings later, and with her notebook and a folder. 'He was there this morning. Gave a talk to the girls with illustrations on the piano. It's the most popular session in the term. Well, that's not surprising, is it?' Being one of Andras Linkina's keenest admirers, for once she was unable to suppress a personal opinion. 'He stayed for coffee with some of the girls afterwards.' She paused, opening her notebook. 'D'you want to write to him?'

Treasure shook his head.

'Here are the papers for your meeting at the Stock Exchange at four-thirty.' She handed him the folder. 'And Mr Harden, the manager of Eel Bridge Rovers, rang, asked if you'd ring him back.'

'Sure.' He glanced at the time. 'Would you get him for me?'

After his secretary had returned to her office, Treasure contemplated the worst interpretation of what he had just learned. Linkina, obsessed with the need to clear Bodworski of murder, could well have suborned students from his daughter's finishing school into clearing his compatriot with false testimony. If this was what had happened, not only would the two girls be liable to prosecution, but Linkina himself could be risking arrest as an accessory to murder—or even, perish the thought, as an actual sus-pected murderer.

Naturally, Treasure was never going to accept that Linkina had poisoned Bims, or beaten up Lilian Bodwor-ski. The fact remained that the Polish pianist had motive enough for both crimes and could have made the opportu-nity for committing them. At least, that was the way the police might see things, starting with the fact that Linkina could certainly have burgled the Supporters Club since he was one of the people officially in possession of a key to the place.

In the case of Bodworski the banker did not have misgiv-ings born either of friendship or dogged partiality. He had done his best to prove the man innocent at Linkina's urgent request. In cold reason, if Bodworski didn't have a real alibi for the afternoon of Bims's murder after all, in Treasure's estimation he was still someone with a massive motive for the crime—until, of course, one considered the new compet-ing claim of Ian Crayborn.

If Bodworski had killed Bims, in the last analysis, his reasons could even be defended. If Crayborn had done it, the reasons were despicable, which was why Treasure could not yet bring himself to believe what Joyce Bims must have been equally reluctant to accept. Circumstantially there was a case against the accountant, but only that. Treasure had firmly told Molly to dissuade the first Lady Bims from doing anything irrevocable in the matter for the time being. He had also promised to confront Crayborn and asked Miss Gaunt to find him.

In the course of the busy afternoon, something else perti-nent was temporarily driven out of Treasure's mind. It had stemmed from his parting conversation with Stephen at lunch. They had been alone at the time, and the dancer had enlarged on what he had said earlier about the personal relationship between Nora Hawker and Jimmy Atler. On reflection, this had suggested a possible new relevance to

Treasure. He had intended to get back to Stephen about it, but missed doing so.

'Hello, is that you, Felix?' he said into the telephone when Miss Gaunt transferred the call to Harden. 'What can I do for you?'

''Afternoon, Mr Treasure. Thanks for ringing back. Very good of you. Very good indeed.' The voice was noticeably hesitant, the gratitude overdone. 'This is probably out of order, but me and three of the players . . . we'd like to see you. It's pretty urgent. To talk about the future, like. Off the record.'

'I see. You know I've no official status at Hugon Road yet?'

'You're chairman elect. That's good enough for us.'

'Which three players?'

'The important ones. Malc Dirn, the captain, and the two strikers, Gareth Trisall and Jimmy Atler.'

'Not Bodworski? Isn't he important enough?' But he was testing more than Harden's opinion of the Pole as a footballer.

There was a pause at the other end. 'No insult to Stan, Mr Treasure, but he's too cut up to think straight at the moment.'

It was a stand-off reply. 'I think I understand. But perhaps some of the other directors should be involved too?'

'Just you, Mr Treasure,' Harden replied with more spirit than before. It was evidently the point he was determined to stand on—he and the others, probably.

'All right. I'll see you. But off the record as you say.' He leaned forward to eye his diary. 'What about this evening?'

'This evening?'

'Yes. You said it was urgent.'

'Oh . . . oh, great.' The response was one of pleasure, tinged still with surprise.

'My house at eight. I'll arrange a bite of supper.'

CHAPTER 20

'Thank you, Mrs Pink. More coffee, anyone? Another drink?' Treasure asked. He was seated with his four guests at the round Chippendale table in his study in Cheyne Walk. Plump Mrs Pink, Henry's wife and the Treasures' cook/housekeeper, had just cleared the table and the remains of the meal which she had prepared and served. She left now with a contented smile.

The two-windowed ground-floor room was on the entrance front. Book-lined, it was a bit cluttered, with unimportant personal debris of the unforsakeable sort, and furnished in an unfussy, eclectic way. The burgundy-coloured curtains were heavy silk, the chairs comfortable, their covers mellowed with use. The desk was modern but in sympathy with the slim table, if more so with the small computer and the fax machine on the desktop. There were some photographs, and pictures—mostly etchings—but nothing that detracted from the sensitive, arresting John Ward portrait of Molly Treasure that was hanging opposite the desk.

The room lighting was fairly subdued but not over the area where the shirtsleeved men were seated in amiable proximity. They might have just finished a poker game—or been about to start one, since the protective green baize cover on the table had only just been exposed by the removal of a linen dining cloth. But the footballers had been involved in more than card play. The discussion over supper had been about their professional futures, and the outcome had been satisfactory judging from the expressions on their faces.

For his part the Eels' chairman elect had given the impression that he was glad of the opportunity to table some of his own ideas for the club. In truth he had been hopeful that the occasion would provide answers to some of the questions left begging over Bims's death—it was why he had arranged for the encounter to take place so soon, and privately at his own home. Anything the Eels did currently in public he felt was bound to suffer from overexposure in the media.

He wished his exchange with Ian Crayborn earlier could also have been face to face. It had been after six o'clock when the accountant had finally responded to the messages Miss Gaunt had left for him in various places. Even then he had explained to Treasure on the telephone that he was just finishing a meeting in Camberley, some thirty miles from Town.

Because the banker had other plans for the evening, it hadn't been possible to arrange a meeting with Crayborn before the next day. So he'd had to ask the man bluntly on the phone what he was doing about Joyce Bims's right to a substantial tax clawback as a result of her ex-husband's death. Crayborn had responded with the unexpected but totally disarming claim that he had only just heard about the entitlement—from Fifield, the same financial adviser who had been in touch with Joyce earlier.

Crayborn had added that of course he should have got on to Joyce's windfall, as he called it, without prompting from a relative outsider, but, he had pleaded, tax regulations were so complicated these days, and always changing. No doubt, he added, he would have come upon the pertinent regulation in time—time enough to put in his client's hefty claim to the Revenue. What he had left unsaid was something that, in the circumstances of his own creating, had not needed spelling out. Simply, he could not have proposed marriage to Joyce *because* of her bounty since he had been ignorant of its existence at the time.

So Crayborn had been either incredibly ingenuous or devilishly cunning. His had been the innocent explanation

of a woefully ill-informed accountant, or else the diaboli-
cally contrived defence of a premeditated murderer: there
had seemed to be nothing in between.

Treasure had been considering Crayborn's explanation
again during Mrs Pink's busyings, as well as quietly
assessing the possible involvement of each of his guests in
Bims's demise. None of them seemed to have the inven-
tiveness necessary to have carried off a devious crime—not
if you compared their qualifications with Crayborn's. That
any of them might be capable of cold-blooded murder and
assault was different. Certainly if Bims had been done in
by a member of the Eels team, then in logic, and not just
by coincidence, that member was most likely to be present
here now. With the single exception of Bodworski, each of
the four in his way had a great deal more to lose by Bims's
survival than any of the other Eels—something Treasure
had confirmed in the call he had at last succeeded in making
to Linkina just before his guests had arrived.

'Nothing more to drink for me, thanks, Mr Treasure.
Better we all stick to that Malvern Water from now
onwards. Earn a good opinion from the new chairman,'
Trisall broke in appropriately on the banker's glum rumi-
nations. 'That's not to say we'd be so abstemious if the Gaff
wasn't here as well, mind,' the Welshman added, aiming a
grin at Felix Harden, 'but he is here, see? And it pays to
advertise. Isn't that right, Jimmy?'

Atler, who had just returned from the hall cloakroom,
nodded and moved back to his chair without attempting to
share the other's humour. 'Nothing for me, either, thanks,'
he said. He had contributed less to the exchanges than his
companions all evening and had drunk nothing alcoholic.

'Yes, we've all got training in the morning, and Jimmy
and me are driving,' said Malcolm Dirn, the captain,
unusually ebullient because he felt the money he had
invested in the sports shop was safe after what Treasure
had said about the move to Cherton. 'We'd better all be

going anyway,' he added. 'Won't your wife be home from the theatre soon, Mr Treasure?'

'Quite shortly, yes.' Treasure looked at the time while debating whether this man would have contemplated murder to protect a shop—except, of course, it was rather more than just a shop. Thanks to Linkina, he knew all about Dirn's future plans and what the move to Cherton meant to him—how Bims's categoric commitment to block that move might have ruined the footballer and his family. To the banker, Dirn seemed an uncomplicated person, dour not jolly, but with a solid judgement as befitted a team captain. Only Treasure was uncomfortably aware that the same attributes had been noted in the make-up of calculating murderers. 'Curtain time is about now,' he continued. 'Anyway, Molly will be delighted to see you all.' He helped himself to more coffee. 'She was sorry to miss the game on Wednesday. Doesn't get that many nights off.'

Trisall rubbed his chin. 'Life must be hard with your wife on the stage most evenings,' he said, seriously this time, and with a touch of awe in his voice.

The banker looked up over his cup. 'It might be a lot harder for us if she weren't,' he joked. 'In any event, I'm glad we did this. Seems it was worth the effort for all of us. Myself included.' The others murmured agreement.

At the start of the evening, the footballers had wanted to know whether Treasure believed the club had a future, whether he would advise Lord Grenwood to put fresh cash into the operation, whether in his view the move to Cherton was on, and whether their own positions were secure for the next season. There had been other questions, but these had been key. The answers Treasure had given had all been affirmative, if weighted by reasonable caveats.

The banker's initial diffidence about the danger in admitting a self-elected, privileged group of Eels to his confidence had quickly dissolved. As manager, Harden would inevitably have had to be consulted about the club's future, assuming he was to be kept on, and Treasure had already decided he ought to be. Nothing would be gained, he reasoned, if an already demoralized team had a new manager thrust upon it by a new chairman.

Harden was evidently liked and respected by the players, to whom he represented the most stabilizing factor in the club's parlous set-up. If it was a questionable tactic on the manager's own part to have involved not only the Eels' captain but also two other players in tonight's exercise, Treasure was ready to accept that the man worked best through consensus, and knew it. Linkina had said that Harden would have been right for the team in the recent past if it hadn't been for the interference of the overbearing Bims. Treasure was anxious for the point to be proved in a future without Bims—always assuming that Harden hadn't been responsible for Bims's abrupt removal. If Harden had murdered Bims, of course, it was unlikely that he would have revealed to Linkina that Bims had blackmailed him over extending his contract—unless he had seen Linkina's sympathy as something likely to have forestalled his suspicion.

'Pity Stan Bodworski couldn't have been here,' said Trisall.

Treasure nodded. This was the first time the Polish player had been mentioned all evening. It was as though the name had been avoided by agreement, at least up to this point when the controversial issues had been more or less covered. 'Felix, you'd like to have invited him, I know,' the banker suggested.

'Sure,' the manager responded quickly, while seeming slightly uneasy. 'But he wouldn't have come. I didn't want to embarrass him by asking.'

Trisall frowned which might have meant he disagreed. 'Of course he's pretty cut up over Lilian and Sir Ray,' he said. 'And what happened with the police. Him being a suspect and all that.'

'I think he'll want out at the end of the season. If not sooner,' Dirn offered, but speculatively.

'Meaning that bastard Bims will have beaten him in the end,' Trisall put in quickly. 'Sorry, Mr Treasure, but he was a bastard, wasn't he? Don't you think? Doing what he did to Stan? Seducing his wife? Aiming to sack him for no reason? No professional reason?'

'I think that sums him up pretty well,' Treasure agreed, marking the vehemence and the other fiery attributes.

'Any hope he and Lilian will stay together, I wonder?' asked Harden of no one in particular.

'Really it'll be hard for either of them to stay with the Eels, anyway,' said Dirn.

'Not for Stan to stay by himself, it wouldn't. Without her. It'd only be justice,' Trisall insisted.

'So you're assuming they won't stay together,' said Harden.

'No, I'm not, Gaff,' Trisall retorted but with less intensity than before.

'There's no possibility it was Stan Bodworski who beat up his wife?' asked Treasure. 'For what he considered justifiable reasons,' he added tactfully. In the context of his question, he wished he felt as much sympathy for the reportedly talented and alluring Mrs Bodworski as he did for the unprepossessing Nora Hawker whom he had met at lunch. There was no reason why he should be comparing the two women, or recalling Nora Hawker at all—except he had done so now unconsciously. He had meant to ask Atler about her, but there hadn't been an opportunity.

'There's not a chance Stan would hurt Lilian,' said Trisall, again in solid defence of his friend. 'Anyone who says he would deserves going over.' He glanced from side to side without moving his head, a sinister method of emphasis.

The banker wondered too how much 'going over' Trisall would be ready to do himself—and more than that if required. Linkina had been fairly sure that the arrogant

Trisall would have been the next player Bims would have fired, and that the late chairman would probably not have been making any secret of that fact.

Would Trisall have killed Bims on his own account, Treasure debated, and judged probably not. But Trisall might have done in Bims after persuading himself it was to protect Bodworski. Wasn't it a Celtic characteristic to effect self-help while righteously pretending to be working for the good of others? A Welsh maternal great-aunt of Treasure's in Llandovery had consistently opposed Sunday pub openings to ensure, she had insisted, that publicans would be free to attend chapel, but really because her husband had been an irredeemable alcoholic. Trisall, like the great-aunt, was endowed with many of the better Welsh traits; humbug might be included as one of the opposite sort.

'The police believe Stan could have attacked his wife.' Atler had spoken after keeping silence for a longish period.

'The police believe and don't believe a lot of things. And they're wrong most of the time,' Trisall answered hotly.

'But, Gareth, I can tell you they were sure he'd beaten up Lilian. When they had him for questioning this morning. I know. I was there,' Harden insisted.

'Yes, well, they've let him go since then, haven't they?' the Welshman snapped, pushing his turned-back shirt-sleeves further above his straining upper arm muscles.

'They let him go over the murder, not so much over what happened to Lilian.' This was Harden again. 'Of course, they are often wrong,' he agreed with Trisall.

'Like they were certain Bims was going to Florida. I wonder if he ever was? Whether it was just show? To pretend he was innocent? Clean?' said the Welshman.

'Bims himself said he was going, of course. Has anyone said he wasn't?' asked Treasure carefully, leaning forward a little in his chair.

Dirn drew in his breath as if he was about to answer the

question but he changed his mind, it seemed, after a glance from Harden.

'It was you said, wasn't it, Jimmy?' Trisall questioned with no doubt at all in his tone.

Atler looked puzzled. 'Did I? I forget. Oh yes, perhaps I did.'

'Did Bims tell you that himself?' asked Harden, interested.

'Of course not. It . . . it was Lilian,' Atler replied, but still uncertainly. He looked down to study his hands that were clasped in his lap.

'Would that have been before she was attacked?' asked Treasure.

Atler shook his bowed head. 'No . . . today. I . . . er . . . I went to see her in the hospital. Took her some flowers.'

'That was charitable of you,' Trisall offered in a genuinely complimentary tone tinged with unmistakable surprise. 'As a matter of fact, I tried to do the same.' He looked around at the others in a belligerent way. 'Well, she's a friend in trouble like Stan, isn't she? Whatever she's . . .' He broke off in mid-sentence, sniffed, then ended with: 'I called at the hospital this afternoon, but they said she was too tired for visitors.'

'She was pretty knocked out. Didn't want to talk. I didn't stay long,' said Atler.

'Tricia and me dropped by as well,' put in Dirn in the same nearly apologetic tone as Trisall. 'Went up to the ward. Only to ask how she was. Anything else seemed sort of disloyal. To Stan. Know what I mean? After what she'd done. Anyway, someone was with her already. One of the Eels directors. That's what the Ward Sister said.'

'Was it Mr Linkina or Mr Crayborn?' Treasure inquired. He assumed it hadn't been Berty Grenwood.

'The Sister wasn't sure of the name,' the team captain answered.

It seemed that most of the Eels present had felt embar-

rassed by their conflicting, separate loyalties to the Bod-
worskis, husband and wife—too embarrassed to have
admitted to each other until now that they had called on
the unfaithful wife in hospital.

'When did Bims tell Mrs Bodworski he'd changed his
mind about Florida, I wonder?' asked Treasure. 'Perhaps
when they were together on Tuesday night.'

Atler looked up to be sure it was he who was being
addressed. 'No,' he said, paused as if he needed to make a
decision, then went on, 'He rang her after lunch yesterday.'

'You know he was still telling people at lunch he'd probably be going?' Treasure questioned.

'I'd heard that, yes.'

'I see.' The banker nodded. Atler's information seemed
more or less to confirm what Bims's lawyer had said.

'If he wasn't going to America, to go before this special
jury, it's pretty obvious he was guilty as charged, isn't it?'
said Trisall pointedly.

Atler straightened in his chair. 'He was guilty all right,'
he said.

'How can a man who sells filthy drugs to kids—'

Before Harden could finish what he had started to say,
the study door opened and Molly Treasure was revealed
standing on the threshold. All the men stood up.

'Sorry, I didn't mean to disturb you,' said Molly, moving
into the room with enough allure and vitality to disturb a
whole regiment. 'I just wanted to see you've got everything
you need.'

'Yes, now we've got your wonderful, shining presence,
Mrs Treasure. To make a marvellous evening complete,'
said Trisall lyrically—the ladies' man performing to standard.

After that there were no further exchanges touching on
Bims's death. The visitors spent another contented hour at
Cheyne Walk, most of it chorusing around the grand piano
in the drawing-room upstairs where their glamorous hostess

and Gareth Trisall led them in musical comedy hits to Molly's own accompaniment.

'That Gareth, he's a real dreamboat, isn't he?' said Molly later as she and her husband were preparing for bed.

'So one . . . understands,' Treasure replied, under pressure. He was completing a prescribed number of energetic movements from the seat of the exercise machine just inside his dressing-room.

'Curious they none of them knew the tunes in that football bumper song book I unearthed.' Molly was at her dressing-table, methodically applying cream to her face and neck.

'No, it wasn't. It's a Rugby bumper song book. Soccer players sing different songs . . . when they sing at all. I've told you before they—'

'Gareth has a beautiful baritone voice, too,' Molly interrupted unchastened. 'Was it trained, d'you think?'

'You know, I've never thought to ask him,' the banker answered acerbically, between movements. 'He's just . . . just Welsh, I expect. They're all the same. Natural singers,' he added.

'No, I think he's had voice production lessons. I mean, you're half Welsh, darling, and your voice is good too.' She paused, putting a blob of cream on the end of her nose. 'But not that good.'

'Thank you.' Exhausted, he had stopped exercising and was taking deep breaths, head bowed, shoulders bent, arms limp by his sides.

'So did you get any closer to finding out who killed Ray Bims?' asked Molly.

'I might have been about to when you arrived.'

'Oh no, did I spoil it?'

He chuckled. 'Don't think so. Not really.'

'Good. They were nice boys, all of them.' Molly reached for another tissue. 'So what did you think of Nora Hawker? The woman we were talking to after lunch today.' Since there was no immediate response she repeated: 'After lunch. You remember surely? Bobby Hawker's sister ... Oh, you're all of a glow, as they say in the Wrens,' she completed approvingly after suddenly catching sight of her husband's reflection.

Treasure had emerged naked from the dressing-room, pulling on a white towelling robe as he went. He hurried across the room to the bedside telephone, looking wholly preoccupied. 'That's it, of course,' he said, half to himself, then adding something which Molly missed altogether.

'That's what, darling?' she asked, then, since his immediate needs didn't appear to involve her, she returned to examining one eyebrow closely in a hand mirror.

'She couldn't have,' he said, dialling a number. 'Not after lunch, she couldn't.'

CHAPTER 21

The man waiting in the shadows outside the hospital was stockily built and moved like an athlete—except he hadn't moved at all for some minutes. Standing in the courtyard opposite the casualty entrance, he was wearing a tweed hat pulled well down, a knee-length blue overcoat, dark trousers and shoes, and soft leather gloves. If anyone noticed him, and nobody seemed to have done so, he looked respectable enough and preoccupied enough to be here on legitimate business. He could have been a doctor, or the relative of a casualty, or even a policeman in plain clothes involved in one of the accident cases. Only a sharp-eyed observer might have questioned why he was wearing trainers, not conventional shoes.

Just after 12.30 a.m. an ambulance drew in, warning lights still flashing. It backed up to the centre pair of the three double doors, ten yards across from where the man had

stationed himself. It was the opportunity he had been waiting for since moving here from the front of the hospital.

The main entrance to the Fulham Cross Hospital was
around the corner on the next side of the building. The
door there was locked from eleven o'clock. This hadn't prevented the man from satisfying himself about the degree of
activity—or lack of it—in the big ground-floor concourse.
He had been watching the whole place through the clear
glass frontal. It had been a lot different from the way it
had looked on his previous visit. That had been in daylight,
at the busiest time.

The shining floor area was now almost deserted. The
marshalled rows of plastic seats on one side, arranged in
sections for waiting patients and visitors, were all empty.
The self-service general store was locked behind its glass
partitions, like the flanking newspaper shop and snack bar.
Close to the main door, a lone male uniformed porter had
been sitting behind the long reception counter. It was his
official duty to unlock the door to let people in and out—
something he had done only once in the period while the
man had been observing him. The watcher had noted that
the four lifts at the rear of the concourse rarely stopped at
the ground floor at this time of night. And even when they
did stop, people seldom got in or out.

The closed-in stairs had been more difficult to watch.
They lay to the left of the lifts and some feet beyond them.
But so far as the man could see, simply nobody used them
at all at night: he had been counting on that.

He had known that the front entrance to the hospital
would be locked. It was a security measure to beat the
plague of prowlers who put upon patients and staff. It was
a countrywide problem that the man deplored as much as
anyone. By his own definition he was certainly no criminal
prowler. He believed he was here to administer a just sentence. It was likely to be riskier than Bims's elimination
had been, but this did nothing to deflect him. If there had

been doubts about the need for this second execution they had been dispelled. What had been said had made it an unavoidable as well as an urgent necessity.

Of course, Lilian Bodworski was only an accessory to Bims's vileness—but a conscious beneficiary from his crimes all the same. At first it had been intended to let her off with the beating. But this way everything fitted better. This way the responsibility could be seen to lie again where the police had believed it belonged from the start—where it had been directed so expertly until those two stupid foreign bints had stuck in their prying noses.

He had no regrets about what he had done, nor about what he had to do next. The just revenge he was taking would be blamed on someone whom the law would treat lightly. Bodworski was alone at home in South Kensington. That had been confirmed by the phone call to his flat ten minutes ago. There would be no schoolgirls to provide an alibi at this time of night.

He waited until the ambulance crew and hospital staff were clustered around the rear doors of the vehicle, busy bringing out the injured victim of a road accident. While they were engrossed in their delicate task, the man came out of the darkness and walked to the nearer pair of doors into the hospital. They opened automatically to his deter-mined, brisk but unhurried approach.

With the same outward coolness, he followed his planned route along the well lit, green-painted corridor to another set of doors. Beyond these he headed away from the casualty area, around a bend and towards the rear of the ground-floor concourse. He had met no one so far. Only the silence threatened him now when the smallest, careless sound would be amplified.

He moved forward stealthily to the space behind the islanded lift shafts. From there he could see the uniformed porter was still at the desk at the other end of the concourse, and still engrossed in a newspaper.

Delaying only to listen for footsteps on the stairs to his right, he broke cover and sprinted across to the shelter of the steps.

The closed staircase was the one Jeckels had used on the previous night. The man mounted the steps between floors with the same easy alacrity as the policeman, but soundlessly and pausing to listen before each turn. When he reached the third floor, with extra caution, he slipped through the door on to the landing.

The wide ward corridor lay open immediately ahead of him. He moved to the first doorway on the right. It led to a storeroom. The door opened as silently as it had done when he had tried it on his last visit.

The nurses' station was thirty feet along from his present refuge. it had been only dimly illuminated. A single uniformed female figure had been seated there writing, her back towards him. He hadn't been able to see into the sister's office to the left of the station, but no light had been reflecting through the glazing of its upper half. The door to the side ward he would move to next was the second along on the side he was on. He stuffed his hat into his pocket and pulled the nylon stocking over his head and face.

In another two minutes it would all be over. By then he would be down the stairs again and out of the building, clean away by the same route that he had used to get here, despite any alarm they might raise. From here on surprise and speed would be everything, and surprise and speed were on his side.

He re-emerged slowly into the corridor. The nurse was where she had been before. He crept towards the next doorway, body pressed hard against the wall, face inwards. Then without warning the nurse leaned back, stretched her arms, and yawned audibly. He froze against the door, scarcely daring to breathe. The girl massaged her neck with her hands, moved her head from side to side, sighed, scratched her right leg above the knee, checked the time and returned to her writing. He had willed her not to look around, and she hadn't.

A moment later he was gently depressing the door handle to the side ward. It gave to his touch, silently and easily. He sidled round the door, closing it even more gently from the other side.

The room was in total darkness. His heart thumping in his chest, he steeled himself to stay calm, keeping his back against the door as he closed his eyes and counted five. When he opened his eyes again his vision had adjusted to what dim light was coming from the windows. He could see the shape of the furniture now, the beds and the side tables, the medical paraphernalia hung on the walls—and the outline of Lilian Bodworski in the centre bed. Her figure was turned towards him, the head buried beneath the sheet.

He took the knife from his pocket, flicked out the blade, and began moving carefully across the room.

It was then that the patient in the bed nearest the door began to snore, very loudly. The intruder stopped, freezing in his tracks.

Suddenly the door flew open and the place was ablaze with light. Men in blue battledress rose up in the far corners of the room levelling guns. The figure in the centre bed— also male—jerked upright and was pointing a revolver, two-handed, straight at the man's head. Uniformed 'patients' in two of the other beds were doing the same. A voice immediately behind him shouted: 'Armed police. Stand still. Drop the knife.' He heard the click of a safety-catch being released close to his right ear.

He let go the knife and heard it clatter on the floor.

'Lie down. Flat on your face. Now!' the same voice ordered brusquely.

He did as he was told.

*

'So what time did you get back this morning, darling? You were quiet coming to bed. Didn't wake me,' said Molly Treasure, taking her husband's boiled egg from the saucepan with a long, wooden-handled spoon.

'It must have been nearly three. Jeckels kept producing more cups of tea. Free tea seems to be his ultimate intimation of gratitude. It was difficult to refuse or to leave,' Treasure answered, sipping his second cup of coffee with evident pleasure, and coming more awake with every sip.

It was nearly nine now. The Treasures were breakfasting late, both of them in dressing-gowns, although Molly had been up for an hour. Henry Pink had been told not to bring the car around until ten.

'I'm just so relieved Ian Crayborn had nothing to do with Ray Bims's death,' Molly exclaimed.

'Not nearly as relieved as Joyce Bims will be,' her husband replied, digging a spoon into a half-grapefruit.

'And thank God you stopped Joyce making a fool of herself. Confronting Ian with what she'd said to me.' Molly's gaze had literally lifted heavenwards as she spoke.

'Mmm. If you remember, I effectively had to do that for her. On the telephone last evening.'

'You didn't actually accuse him—'

'Only in the most indirect way,' Treasure broke in. 'So indirect, I'm glad to say he didn't at all appreciate what I was getting at.' He paused. 'Well, of course he didn't because he was innocent. And not all that bright about it, even so. Anyway, he needn't know how Joyce's faith in him evaporated when the chips were down. Not ever.'

'It was understandable. Her attitude,' said Molly firmly, bringing the egg over from the cooker. 'Except you obviously don't think so. I wonder if she'll still want to go ahead with the marriage?'

'Why ever not? Those two seem to balance each other nicely. I remember your saying so yourself. And it isn't his shortcomings as a husband she should be worried about in future.'

'What, then?'

'I'd say his indifferent performance as an accountant.'

Molly looked surprised. 'But you said yesterday how complicated tax law was. How he could easily have missed the important bit. Important for Joyce.'

'Mm. Well, that's when I thought he might be a murderer. Missing a legal technicality seemed an excusable misdemeanour by comparison.' He gave a low chuckle and sliced the top off the egg. 'Thankfully, her new-found fortune should buy them better financial advice than she's had from Ian in the past. Perhaps they'll retain this Fifield chap. The one who alerted both of them to her rights. He sounds as if he's on the ball.'

'Will you go on using Ian as accountant to the Eels?'

Treasure's nose wrinkled as if he might be testing the freshness of the egg on his spoon. 'Probably not, now you mention it,' he said, eating the egg. 'He can stay as a director if he wants. That's unpaid, of course.'

Molly sat down at the table too, bringing a bowl of muesli with her. 'You hadn't told the Inspector that Andras's daughter owned that finishing school?'

'No. At first I was leaving him to find it out for himself. Hoping he wouldn't.' He shook his head and frowned. 'He shouldn't need to trouble with that now. Otherwise he'd have come up with it eventually, you know. And twigged that Andras had put those girls up to giving Bodworski an alibi.'

'You don't know that for certain.'

'Yes, I do. Because I know Andras.' He drank some more coffee. 'He took a terrible risk interfering like that. Serve him right if he'd got himself arrested as a result.'

'But he was only trying to protect Bodworski.'

'A lot of people seem to have been doing that, including your friend Gareth Trisall. As a matter of fact, I had the feeling he was protesting too much in Bodworski's cause.

Getting him in deeper rather than extricating him, while doing a whitewash job on himself.'

'Shame on you,' said Molly righteously, and consuming her muesli as though she were enjoying it.

Her husband ignored the reproach. 'While Edingly without any doubt was setting Bodworski up to protect Edingly.'

'Did the Inspector truly suspect Edingly?'

'Yes, when he found the chap was arranging an alibi.'

'For the murder?'

'For the time Mrs Bodworski was assaulted. Edingly wanted Malcolm Dirn to say they were together at six on Wednesday.' Treasure broke a piece of toast in two as he continued: 'Trouble was, Dirn had already accounted to the police for his movements. But he didn't dare tell Edingly that, for fear of upsetting him. He did go back to the police, though. Tried to correct his own statement.'

'To help Edingly?'

'Partly, yes. But he'd also realized that saying he'd been with the saintly Edingly at six provided an alibi for himself. Earlier he'd said he was just driving alone to Hugon Road.'

'Did he need an alibi?'

The banker paused for a moment, pouting. 'Really, as things transpired, I suppose all four Eels who were here last night needed them,' he said. 'Once it was clear they each had good reason for doing in Bims. But in Dirn's case the police realized he'd been put up by Edingly to change the account of his movements. So they determined to find out why. That's what Jeckels told me.'

'Why was Dirn afraid to upset Edingly?'

'Because Dirn's dependent on him for money. For his shop. He had to admit as much. That set the police inquiring deeper into Edingly's financial situation. They discovered he secretly owns property in Cherton next to the Eels' practice ground there. Some freeholds that have become a lot more valuable since the word got out the club is moving there.'

'The move Ray Bims was opposing?'

'Right. All of which put Edingly in a very vulnerable position. In the end, though, it seems he's been nothing more than avaricious.'

'So why did he need an alibi? If he'd done nothing actually criminal?'

Treasure licked the end of his finger. 'He's been engaged in sharp practices but not indictable ones. Although as an elder of the Second Pentecostal Evangelicals perhaps he should be searching his conscience. He needed the alibi to keep his name out of the inquiry. To stop people delving into his business affairs. Disclosing details of his property arrangements. His dealings have cost others a great deal of money. And they've been mostly his friends too. The members of the Supporters Club for a start.'

Molly shook her head slowly. 'Curious that Jimmy Atler seems actually to have had higher moral motives than the others.'

'Even though he was the murderer?' Treasure gave a doubting smile. 'He's totally unrepentant, of course. For him, killing Bims was like Edingly exterminating a rat. In fact, that's the simile he used himself.'

'He hates drug traffickers?'

'Yes. Except with him the hatred in pathological.'

'And dates from the death of his friend Bobby Hawker?'

'For which he blames himself. For not stopping Hawker becoming a drug addict. For . . . for not getting to the people who were supplying him.'

'But that's unreasonable, isn't it?'

'One would think so. But not Atler. He's convinced he could have prevented Hawker's death. And it seems Nora Hawker has been stoking the guilt.'

'You mean she blames him too?'

'Yes, but it's a bit more complicated than that. Both men were gay, but she says Bobby wasn't until he met Atler. That his drug-taking came in as part of the gay scene. Atler says that's not true, but Nora's attitude got to him deeply, even so.'

Molly crossed her arms over her breasts. 'And killing Ray Bims has . . . has atoned?' she questioned, her hands rising to smooth her shoulders.

'So it seems. Do you remember yesterday Nora said she'd often been asked to the CADS lunches as Atler's guest, but had never accepted before? To him her acceptance was the sign of atonement.'

'Meaning she knew he'd murdered Ray? But surely—'

'Guessed, Atler insists,' Treasure interrupted.

'So she wasn't involved herself?'

'Certainly not. But it seems to me she would have been if he'd asked her. Liquidating a drug baron is the highest achievement imaginable for him, and for her too. Or so he implies.'

'It's a point of view,' said Molly quietly.

'It might be, provided you're sure you've got the right man.'

'Is there any question about Ray Bims's guilt?'

Treasure frowned. 'In my book none, but I'd still rather he'd been convicted in law.'

'Except he wouldn't have been. And didn't he convict himself by deciding not to go to Florida? By not being ready to go before a Grand Jury?'

'That's precisely what Atler says. It's the decision that sealed Bims's fate for him.'

'A decision reported to Atler by Lilian Bodworski? Isn't that what Atler told you here last night?'

'Except he was lying. She didn't tell him because she couldn't have known Bims wasn't going. On the contrary, she thought he *was* going. Or that's how I understood it. Dirn only pretended she'd told him the opposite when he went to see her in the hospital yesterday afternoon. He said she claimed Bims had called her after lunch.'

'Which was what got you so jumpy when you were going

to bed last night. The first time. Before you rang that lawyer and Inspector Jeckels, and got dressed again in such a hurry.'

'Because it dawned on me Bims couldn't have called her. Not between the time he called Martlone his lawyer with his decision and the time he was killed. The call to Martlone was critical. We don't know what finally sparked Bims's decision not to go to America. But he'd have needed to tell Martlone before anyone else. Martlone himself is sure of it.' Treasure reached for more toast as he went on: 'But Bims didn't call Martlone till ten to three. By that time Mrs Bodworski was on a train from Birmingham to London, and she had no telephone with her. She told Jeckels she'd left it at the office. And she wasn't available by phone again till after five when she got back to her flat. Bims was dead by then.'

'Couldn't *she* have rung *him* earlier?'

'Possibly, but Dirn had told me the opposite. He could have said she rang Bims, but he didn't.' Treasure shrugged. 'All right, I might have been wrong, but I thought he was lying about the whole thing.'

'Lying in the sense that it wasn't Lilian who'd told him Bims wasn't going to America but—'

'But Bims himself? Well, it *was* Bims. We know that now. Atler's admitted it.' Treasure stared for a moment at the butter knife he was holding in his hand. 'He went to see Bims around three on Wednesday afternoon,' he went on slowly. 'He'd decided that if Bims wasn't going to the States he was guilty of everything the reports were saying about him.'

'And he intended to kill him for that?'

'Yes. Unfortunately for Bims, he not only admitted to Atler that he'd just decided against going to Florida, he as good as admitted the Cayman bank had been financing drug trafficking.'

Molly's eyes narrowed. 'That's what Atler says? Sounds like mitigation, doesn't it? For killing Bims?'

Treasure made a debating noise in his throat. 'That's perfectly true. And of course we'll never know what was really said. Whether Atler took the law into his own hands because Bims admitted guilt or because of supposition.' He paused, looking up. 'Either way, he'd gone to see Bims unannounced, ostensibly to talk about his own future.'

'But didn't you say he was supposed to have left Hugon Road with Gareth Trisall?'

'Atler had said so to Ribarts, he's the assistant team manager, to prove that Trisall hadn't been drinking. In fact Trisall had left by himself, but he'd been grateful to Atler for volunteering what he did. Of course, Atler had simply been providing himself with an alibi for the time of Bims's death.'

'And given Trisall an alibi as well?'

'Yes, I suppose so. But I doubt that had been part of Atler's prime intention. Anyway, as soon as he entered the chairman's suite, Bims, who was at the desk, suggested drinks. Atler accepted and offered to get them from the bar —Coke for himself and a brandy for Bims which Atler doctored. He waited till the strychnine began to take effect and actually helped Bims to the bedroom when the spasms started.'

'And then left him to die? That was pretty cool,' said Molly with a shudder, and closing up the collar of her dressing-gown.

'The dying wouldn't have taken long.'

'Ugh.' The actress made a face. 'And he set things up to make it look like suicide? And it was he who beat up Lilian Bodworski? Was that because he knew she was Bims's mistress? In on the drug business with him? Deserving punishment too?'

'That's an appealing explanation, but the right one is

subtler, at least in terms of what happened at that stage. Atler was leaving nothing to chance. In case the police didn't buy suicide as the cause of Bims's death, and went for murder as the only possible alternative, he wanted to set up the cuckolded Bodworski as the obvious suspect. It was his fall back position.'

'To make it all look like a crime of passion?'

'Yes. It nearly worked too. After all, Bims was stealing Bodworski's wife *and* firing him from his job.'

'To get him off the scene,' said Molly. 'Gloria thinks he probably intended to divorce her and marry Lilian Bodworski. It seems Ray Bims was very much the marrying kind.'

'Mrs Bodworski didn't know he was having her husband dropped from the Eels. He hadn't told her.'

'Do you believe that?'

'I think so.'

'Hm,' Molly debated. 'So as well as beating up Mrs Bodworski, Atler planted the rifle in her husband's car? He doesn't like Bodworski?'

'No, it wasn't that. He says if Bodworski had been convicted he'd have got off lightly. Probably without a prison sentence.'

'That was hopeful.'

'Perhaps. Atler certainly seems to have a romantic view of how British courts treat *crime passionnel*.'

'And if Bodworski had been sent to gaol, would Atler have owned up, d'you suppose?'

'He said so, yes.'

'I don't believe him. Do you?'

'It's academic now, isn't it,' said the banker, who disliked offering hypothetical judgements on serious issues.

'So why did he lie to you last evening over what Lilian Bodworski had said to him? He must have known she'd have denied saying she'd talked to Bims after lunch?'

Treasure finished his toast and pushed his plate away. 'It was a slip on Atler's part. He'd told Trisall earlier that Bims wouldn't have gone to Florida, meaning, I suppose, it was something he'd guessed Bims wouldn't do. But Trisall had taken it as fact. He questioned Atler about it in front of us all. Atler didn't deny it outright because he probably couldn't remember what he'd told Trisall in the first place. Harden asked if Bims had told him himself. Well, of course he had, but Atler knew he couldn't say so without risking having to say when.'

'And he knew Bims hadn't made up his own mind until after lunch?' said Molly.

'Exactly. Rather than get in any deeper with complicated denials he said—'

'The first thing that came into his head?' Molly interrupted. 'That it was Lilian Bodworski who'd told him? So at the time did he hope to work something out with her later?'

Her husband shook his head. 'Not as soon as he realized the seriousness of the lie. I'm not even sure he regretted the mistake once he'd made it. You see, subconsciously he'd forced his own hand. Made it imperative he did away with Lilian Bodworski.'

'Because he'd had that in mind already?'

'Very much so, especially if it meant he could leave her husband to take the rap. For both murders. The knife he intended to kill her with belonged to Bodworski. It's a Polish army knife he used for cleaning mud off his boots. Atler pinched it from his locker. He'd even made sure Bodworski was alone at home last night. Called him on his way to the hospital. Invited him to drive over to his flat for a nightcap. To hear about what had happened here at the meeting. Bodworski accepted too.'

'So at the time of the murder Bodworski would have been driving alone with no witness. No alibi?'

'That's what Atler had planned.'

Molly emptied the remains in the coffeepot into her cup. 'But how were you so sure he'd try to murder Mrs Bodworski? And so soon after leaving here?'

Treasure pushed his chair away from the table. 'It was what you mentioned about Nora Hawker. Something about after lunch yesterday. It sparked the thought that if Atler was lying he'd have to do something about it pretty damn quickly.'

'On the telephone to the Inspector, you said you were certain Bims's murderer would try to murder Mrs Bodworski too, during the night. You told him he had to have her moved, and send armed police to the hospital.'

'Because if I was right it was going to save her life. It also promised to be the surest way of proving Atler was the killer.'

'And he was under observation from the moment he arrived at the hospital?'

'For the whole time, yes. Because they didn't want him alerted too soon, they actually stood down the normal hospital security patrol. A special police task force took over.'

'But even if it hadn't, he'd still have been spotted?'

'Almost certainly. Hospitals are pretty good on security these days. But if he'd been nabbed at the entrance, for instance, he might still have got away with saying he was there for some innocent reason.' Treasure stood up and re-tied the sash of his dressing-gown. 'As for Jeckels, being over-insistent with him in the first place was the best way to handle him.' He straightened his shoulders. 'You see he was strictly brought up.'

'How d'you mean?'

'His father was a Regimental Sergeant Major,' Treasure replied flatly as though that explained everything.

'So what?' Molly demanded.

Her husband smiled. 'So at an early age the Inspector was taught the vital importance of obeying orders first and asking questions afterwards—or taking the unpredictable consequences.'

Molly pondered for a moment. 'Like merchant bankers obeying instinct and making fortunes?'

'Sound enough comparison, yes. Good bankers and good policemen have much in common,' was Treasure's parting comment as he went upstairs to dress.